MW00467354

FIRE AND LOVE

A FIREFIGHTERS OF LONG VALLEY ROMANCE
NOVEL - BOOK 3

ERIN WRIGHT

WRIGHT'S READS

To Mom:

I know my books aren't your cup of tea, but it means the world to me that you support me anyway. Thank you for everything. I couldn't have asked for a better momma.

To Dad:

Thanks for bequeathing me with your ability to write and plot. I know that making a living by writing seemed like a far-fetched dream, but I've finally been able to make it happen, and every bit of my talent comes from you. Thank you.

Love you both.

CHAPTER 1

LEVI

LATE MAY, 2018

"Yeah, I know it's our tradition," Moose Garrett said, his disgruntlement coming through loud and clear, "but..." He groaned in frustration. "I just don't want to be away from Georgia for the entire weekend. C'mon, we've brought people along with us before."

"*Men,*" Levi Scranton retorted pointedly, perusing his fridge as they talked, shoving his cell phone between his ear and shoulder so he could use both hands to pull out empty takeout containers and nearly empty jugs of milk. "Not *people*. It's a *guys'* weekend to go camping and fishing and sit around the campfire and drink beers, not listen to girls squeal about how gross it is to hook a worm and toss it into the water."

"You really think Georgia is going to be squeamish about hooking a worm?" Moose asked, laughing. Levi ground his back teeth together. That was *not* the point, and Moose knew it.

Levi wanted a weekend where he could wander around in his boxers and scratch his nuts and spit into the bushes. You know, things you just couldn't do around a female of any kind, not even the Georgia kind.

"Oh hey, you should invite someone to come along with!" Moose said excitedly, clearly thrilled by the genius of his own idea. "Then you won't feel like such a third wheel."

Even as Levi was rolling his eyes at his best friend's obtuseness, he could hear Moose and Levi's former girlfriend mumbling to each other, the microphone apparently covered up by someone's hand, and felt a bolt of jealousy shoot through him. Georgia was there with him, just hanging out. Of *course* she was there with him. They'd just kissed and made up – quite literally – a few days ago.

And Levi was happy for them. Obviously.

It was just hard to hear them coo nonsense at each other, was all. He wouldn't want to listen to anyone coo nonsense. The fact that it was his best friend and his former girlfriend? That didn't enter into the equation.

Finally, Georgia's voice came on the line. "I think you should invite Tennessee," she announced without preamble. Shocked, Levi straightened up so fast from his inspection of his mostly empty fridge that he whacked his head on the freezer door.

"Shit!" he mumbled, rubbing the back of his head while shutting the fridge and leaning up against it.

"What? What's wrong?"

"Nothing," he grumbled. He touched the tender spot carefully. Dammit, he was gonna get a goose egg from that one. "But c'mon, Tennessee?! I can't ask her to go on a camping and fishing trip with me. With us. Even if you're her cousin. I mean, have you *looked* at your cousin lately? She'd freak the hell out as soon as she figured out that the tent didn't come equipped with electrical outlets for her curling iron."

Tennessee Rowland was Georgia's cousin, but God had never created two people more different than those two. While Georgia was a real fitness buff, ran the local credit union as the youngest branch manager in history, and wouldn't wear nail polish if her life depended on it, Tennessee…well, Levi wasn't quite sure what she did all day. Get her hair highlighted? Practice the piano? Go clothes shopping for shoes that cost more than Levi made in a month?

Yeah, Tennessee's manicured, perfect body didn't belong anywhere *near* a fishing pole.

"She'd kill me if she knew I was saying this," Georgia said quietly, "but honestly, Tennessee is struggling right now. She may not have loved Moose the way that I do, but their relationship had been a huge part of her life practically since she was born. Now, all of that's gone, and she really doesn't know what to do with herself. She'd love to go camping, I promise. But, if *I* ask her, then it'll seem like I'm trying to set you two up on a date or something. If *you* ask her as just friends, then it won't be weird."

Levi groaned.

Sometimes, he hated talking to Georgia. She made so much damn sense and honestly, it was a little annoying. Did she always have to be so rational? Somehow, Georgia had twisted it around so that asking Tennessee – one of the most gorgeous women Levi had ever clapped eyes on – to go camping with them had become something that a good guy would do, instead of being something that a creeper would do because he couldn't keep his tongue in his head while he was around her.

Not that Levi had any experience with that, of course. He knew better than that. Sure, Tennessee and he had flirted a little at the firefighter fundraiser a couple of months ago, but c'mon. There was no way she actually liked him. She should be dating Justin Bieber or some superstar, for hell's sake.

Levi Scranton, local hick and son of the town drunk? He didn't even register on her radar.

And that was how it should be.

"Just ask her and let's go have some fun," Georgia said firmly, obviously not budging. "Here's Moose back," and with that, Levi's conversation with Georgia was over. She'd decided, so it should be done.

"You there?" Moose asked, his voice coming back on the line.

"Your girlfriend is real stubborn, you know that?" Levi asked dryly.

"You dated her for three years and you're just now starting to figure that out?" Moose asked, laughing again. Levi ground his back teeth together. Again. When, exactly, had Moose started laughing every other sentence? Was he always this cheerful? Between that and the cooing of nonsense to Georgia, he sure was stretching Levi's patience. "But the problem is," Moose continued dryly, "she's almost always right. Sucks, that."

Levi heard Georgia whisper something to Moose and he may not have understood the words but he sure as hell understood the meaning. Sure enough, the sounds of spit swapping commenced. Levi gripped his phone harder. Were they trying to torture him?

All right, fine, even Levi thought that Georgia and Moose made a better couple than he and Georgia had, but that didn't mean that he *enjoyed* that fact.

"I'll think about it," he said loudly, and then hung up before he could be forced to listen to any more spit-swapping sounds.

For years, it had been he and Moose against the world. Now, it was him, Moose, and Georgia against the world. It was starting to feel a little crowded.

With a sigh, he turned around and reopened the fridge door, hoping that the food leprechauns had somehow delivered food while he wasn't looking. Alas, it was just as empty as it ever was: A moldy loaf of bread that he'd somehow missed during his first round of cleaning, a half-empty bottle of ketchup, and some generic soy sauce were the only food-like items to be found.

Levi wasn't half bad in the kitchen, but even he couldn't create something edible out of *that*. He grabbed the loaf of bread, chucked it into the trash can along with the rest of the empty and moldy containers, and headed for the front door.

He didn't much cotton to the idea of going to Boise that evening, not when he had to be at work bright and early the next morning, so he decided to feel rich for the day and shop at the local grocery store – the Shop 'N Go – instead. Some people called it the Shop 'N Blow, because shopping there meant blowing through your whole paycheck, but hell, beggars couldn't be choosers.

He pulled into the grocery store parking lot and swung out of his truck, focused on his mission. He'd get the essentials, plus pick up some stuff for the camping trip this weekend, and hopefully be able to escape with most of his bank account intact.

"I gotta go! Bye!"

He heard the whispered farewell as he walked through the sliding front doors and into the cool of the air-conditioned store. Suspicious, he looked up to find Tennessee hurriedly shoving her cell phone into her jewel-encrusted purse as she sent him a brilliant smile. "Hi, Levi," she called out, pushing her cart over to him. "How's it going?"

He couldn't shake the feeling that she'd just gotten off the phone with Georgia for two reasons:

a) It was just like Georgia to meddle so much that she wouldn't believe simply telling Levi what to do would be enough. No, she'd want to tell Tennessee what to do, too.

b) Tenny's smile was weirdly bright and her hands were fluttering everywhere, like butterflies unsure of where to land. In other words, she looked guilty as hell.

He couldn't help it. His eyes dropped and he studied her from head to toe.

He started with her brightly painted toenails in strappy sandals that probably cost more than he spent on food in a month, up her gloriously long and gloriously tanned legs, to her short shorts that were just barely cupping her ass, to her pink t-shirt that said *Princesses need love too* in sparkly letters over a sparkly crown, all the way up to her face – her gloriously perfect face. She had these blue-green eyes that changed depending on the light and her mood and the clothes she was wearing, all framed by the longest eyelashes God had ever graced a human with.

Oh yeah, and don't forget her long, blonde hair or perfectly straight, white teeth.

Tennessee Rowland, daughter and heir to one of the richest farmers in western Idaho, was so far out of Levi's league, he couldn't even see the baseball field she was playing in.

But dammit all, despite what Georgia thought, the truth was…Levi didn't want Tenny to come along as "just a friend" on this camping trip. Looking at her, he wanted so much more than that. Any man with two working eyeballs would want more than that.

Well, okay, other than Moose, who'd thrown it all away, but as best as Levi could figure, Moose was just a blithering idiot. Levi was Moose's best friend, so he could totally say that about him. Georgia was amazing, and Levi had spent his fair share of his life in love with the woman, but clearly, she wasn't Tennessee.

No one was Tennessee.

He propped his shoulder up against the cinder-block wall right inside of the front doors, and crossed one booted foot over the other. "Good," he finally grunted in response to her question.

Yeah, Tennessee would be at home around a campfire like she'd be at home running a chainsaw. Just this once, Georgia was flat-out wrong.

CHAPTER 2

TENNESSEE

"*I*T'D BE FUN," Georgia had said firmly, her mind clearly already made up. "It's just for the weekend, and it's just so Levi doesn't feel like he's a third wheel. It's hard for him, this whole change up. I used to date Levi, you used to date Moose, and now of course it's Moose and I who are together and... Levi was left flapping in the wind, you know? It'd just be as fri—"

"I gotta go! Bye!" Tennessee had whispered urgently and then had hung up, shoving her iPhone into her purse hurriedly.

Levi was walking into the store – of *course* he was walking into the store just then – and she wasn't about to let him overhear her conversation with Georgia. It was embarrassing enough that her cousin was hellbent on setting Tenny up on a date (or a pseudo-date, more accurately) – it didn't need to happen in front of said pseudo-date.

She flashed Levi a nervous smile, trying to pretend that she totally hadn't just been caught, and failing miserably. She was normally good at hiding her thoughts and feelings from the world – 26 years of training by parents who didn't give a damn about her feelings taught her to be real good at that, actually – but there had always been something about Levi that made it hard for her to keep up that façade.

"Hi, Levi," she called out cheerfully, pushing her cart over to him. "How's it going?" If she'd whistled innocently, she couldn't have been more obvious. She stifled a groan.

Awkward in social situations but only around Levi Scranton? Check.

Awesome.

His eyes perused her slowly, languidly, moving up her body, making her feel like he was stripping her naked as he went. Despite the fact that it was the beginning of June and thus the summer heat was only just starting to pound down on Sawyer, Tenny couldn't help but wish she'd worn a trench coat to the grocery store. Maybe a long-sleeved turtleneck and a pair of wool mittens, too.

Anything to cover her body from his gaze.

"Good," he finally grunted, leaning casually up against the grocery store wall.

They stared at each other for endless moments, Tennessee waiting for Levi to say something else, and him apparently doing the same thing. Finally, they both started to talk.

"I—" Tennessee said.

"You—" Levi said.

They stopped.

Awkwardddddd...

Tennessee, like most people who'd spent more than seven seconds in Georgia's company, tended to believe that she was always right. But as she and Levi stared at each other, the silence between them as empty and intimidating as the Grand Canyon, she was starting to think that in this particular case, her cousin was wrong.

So very, very wrong.

Sure, Tennessee wanted to go camping. Kinda. Well, it'd be something new and different, anyway, although the fact that there tended to be lots of insects in the great outdoors was not exactly enticing. Sleeping on the ground didn't add to the allure, either.

But what she was real sure of, was that Levi didn't want her there, too.

"Whatcha doin'?" Levi finally drawled, breaking the deafening silence between them.

"Shopping," she said, holding up a bottle of Russian dressing as proof. "The cook sent me down here to buy it; she'd forgotten it when she'd gone shopping in Boise a couple of days ago." She stumbled to a stop. Levi did *not* want to hear about the trials and tribulations of the family cook forgetting ingredients for the evening meal.

She put the bottle back down into the basket of

the cart and gripped the red handle tightly. Looking down at her nearly empty cart, she realized that grabbing one had been rather dumb – she didn't exactly need an entire cart to push a bottle of dressing around the store. But on the other hand, she was glad for its buffering effect between her and Levi. Being around him made it hard for her to breathe.

If he'd been able to stand even closer? She'd probably faint from lack of oxygen.

Before they could go back to their awkward staring contest, Tenny asked hurriedly, "What are you doing?"

"Shopping," he answered dryly.

Right.

Scintillating conversation we're having here.

As they continued to stare at each other, Tenny worried her bottom lip. She wanted to go camping with Moose and Georgia and Levi, even if it did involve a three-day stint with hordes of mosquitoes, and she wanted to be able to breathe while around Levi.

Somehow, though, it kinda looked like neither of those two things were going to end up happening.

She tried to think of a casual way to bring it up – *So, been doing much camping lately with Moose?* – but her mind was blank.

Well, not *blank*. It was whirling right along, focused on the Superman curl across Levi's forehead, and how his thick eyebrows and strong jaw gave off the all-too-true impression that he knew what he wanted and how he wanted it, and how his bulging muscles created dips and valleys everywhere she looked, tempting her to run her teeth over them...

Yeah, her mind wasn't blank. It just wasn't producing anything useful, or at least, anything she could say out loud.

"Well, I'll let you get to it, then," she said finally, when the silence was unbearable and she couldn't handle one more moment of it. "Cook will have my head if I don't hurry—"

"Do you have any plans for this weekend?" Levi broke in, his deep voice rumbling through her, starting with her turquoise-painted toes and working its way up her body.

"Ummm...no. Not yet," she said truthfully. *Not unless you ask me to go camping, that is.* She decided to keep her mouth shut and just see what he said. If weekend plans included being forced to practice yet another Beethoven piece on the piano, listen to her mother prattle on about how disloyal Georgia was for stealing Tennessee's fiancé away from her (everyone seemed to have forgotten that Moose had never actually proposed to Tennessee, let alone her having said yes to the idea), and listen to her father rant and rave about how you can't trust anyone these days, not even Rocky's children...

Well then sure, she had *plenty* of weekend plans.

Just none that she actually wanted.

"Moose, Georgia, and I were going to go camping

this weekend, up in the Goldfork Mountains," Levi continued.

"Oh, how fun!" Tenny said, an overly bright smile blossoming on her face.

"Fun?" Levi echoed, cocking one of his thick, dark eyebrows at her.

"Well, I mean, I think it's fun. I've never been camping before. But a tent, a sleeping bag, the great outdoors…that could be fun, right?" She stumbled to a stop, her cheeks flushing pink under his steady gaze. She was practically yelling, "TAKE ME, TAKE ME!" and wasn't *that* just embarrassing as hell. She wasn't used to begging people to include her in their plans. She was usually the center of people's plans, *or* the one doing the planning. Just one of the side benefits of being one of the most popular girls in town.

No, she definitely wasn't used to having to beg people to include her.

Silence.

Then fiinnnnaallly…

"Did you want to come along with? Give me someone to hang out with, since Moose and Georgia will spend all of their time either swapping spit or declaring their love to each other." He grimaced at the thought.

She mirrored that grimace. She was happy for her cousin, of course, and thrilled to pieces that she wasn't the one in a relationship with Moose, but really, their love for each other *was* a bit puke inducing.

"Well, if *you're* okay with that," she said hesitantly.

"I'm sure it would be fun, but I don't want to be in the way." Because yeah, she really wanted to go, but only if Levi wanted her there. Being an unwanted third wheel wasn't exactly her idea of a great way to spend the weekend, especially if she was going to have to do it without a single coffee shop in sight.

"Good," he grunted, ignoring her not-so-subtle plea for reassurance. "Usually we like to leave on Friday evenings but since Georgia has some things to do at work, we'll be leaving Saturday morning instead. Can you be ready by then?"

"Sure! Yeah! Of course!" she exclaimed brightly, and then mentally kicked herself. She really needed to tone down the enthusiasm. "Uh, well, see you Saturday morning. Bright and early." She flashed a smile at Levi and then pushed her cart towards the checkout line, her heart going a million miles an hour.

She was going to go camping with Levi.

Now *there* were some weekend plans she could get excited about.

CHAPTER 3

LEVI

*L*EVI MADE HIS WAY up the creaking, broken boards of his father's rickety front steps, trying to find the most stable planks to step on. He really didn't think that putting his foot through old, rotten wood could be classified as a good time, and as bonus points, his dad would just chew him out for "ruining" his porch. Levi rolled his eyes at the thought; as if this piece-of-shit conglomeration of rotten boards and rusty nails could actually be ruined. As he figured it, lighting it all on fire could only improve the look of the place.

He rapped three times on the broken screen door and then eased it open, stepping into the dank, dark interior of his childhood home. "You home, Dad?" he called out, shuffling through the maze of refuse and garbage that covered the grimy floors. He held the bag of burgers up next to his head, not wanting to accidentally drop them into a pile of garbage and never be able to get them back out again. This also had the side benefit of helping to drown out the smells of the slowly disintegrating house, by putting the cheeseburgers right next to his nose.

He heard a disgruntled grunt emanating from the living room, only barely perceptible over the blaring of the TV. *Judge Judy* was on, one of his dad's favorite shows. Yelling at people for a living was right up his alley; listening to someone else do it was almost as enjoyable.

Levi stepped to the doorway of the living room, his eyes still adjusting to the semi-darkness of the ramshackle house. His father kept the blinds drawn and a couple of lamps on 24/7, keeping his world in a constant state of twilight. He had no idea how his father knew what time it was.

Actually, his father probably didn't care what time it was. If his entire day consisted of drinking and watching TV, did it really matter if it was three in the afternoon or seven in the morning?

"You have some good stuff in there, boy?" his father demanded, peering suspiciously at the bag of burgers in Levi's hands.

Good stuff, of course, meant alcohol. Pabst beer if he could get it; anything else if he couldn't.

"I already told you – I'm only bringing you food from now on," Levi said firmly. "If you want alcohol, you're gonna have to get it fro—"

"Dammit, you worthless piece of shit!" his dad hollered, cutting him off. "If I wanted some damn food, I'd walk into the kitchen and get some. Worthless, just like your mother."

And so it began – the same rant his father always slipped into when Levi was doing anything other than supplying him with alcohol.

"When she ran off, leaving a crying baby in my lap, I should've known better than to take care of you," his dad snarled. "I should've dropped you off on the courthouse steps and gotten the hell out of Dodge. You've been nothin' but a disappointment." His watery blue eyes were like fiery orbs in the dim lighting, dancing with anger and hatred and disgust. "Why, if I could have back all the money I ever spent on you, feedin' you and clothin' you and makin' sure you stayed warm, I wouldn't have to ask you to bring your old man a little somethin' to tide him over. I'd be rich! You can't even—"

The screen door banged shut behind Levi as he walked out of the dark, dingy house, his hands shaking, the bag of burgers left sitting on the cluttered mantle over the non-working fireplace.

"I didn't say you could leave!" he heard his father shout, the words drifting out of the house on the summer breeze, but Levi ignored it all, hurrying towards his truck and freedom.

His dad, surprisingly short considering that he was his father, was also too lazy and too drunk to chase after him, not to mention that Levi had muscle and agility on his side. His dad had whooped his ass more times than Levi could possibly count growing up, but the beatings had stopped once he could stare his father in the eye. Bullies tended to do that – they only liked to beat on people who couldn't defend themselves. Thank God his mom had apparently been some sort of Amazonian, considering how tall Levi grew up to be. If he'd been on the shorter side, the beatings could've continued until high school graduation.

Not, of course, that Levi would ever know for sure how tall his biological mother was. His dad refused to discuss her at all, except to say she was a worthless whore who'd dumped a crying baby on his lap. The few times Levi had tried to pry information out of his dad, even the most basic of information like what was his mother's name, where was she born, and what did she look like, his father had simply told him that he didn't talk about bitches because they weren't worth the waste of oxygen.

Levi started driving the streets of Sawyer aimlessly, trying to get his hands to stop shaking and his heart to stop pounding. Despite the fact that he'd long ago told himself that he'd become immune to his father's screaming fests, they still weren't what he'd call enjoyable. Moose must've told him a hundred times to stop even trying, but Levi couldn't help it. Watching his dad practically mold himself into his recliner; his hairline receding in tandem with his beer belly growing; eyes getting so watery, walking through his trash-strewn house was probably a death-defying stunt for him…

It was hard to just turn his back on him, even if his father was a class-A douchebag.

Levi finally made himself go home, to the empty rooms that made up his house. Being at home by himself every evening was soul-sucking. There was a reason why Levi was willing to go on this camping trip with Moose, despite the fact that it had been polluted by the presence of the female gender.

Anything was better than yet another weekend by himself.

And okay, yeah, so he'd added to the problem by asking Tennessee to come along too, but hell, he knew Moose wasn't gonna agree to have a guys-only weekend, so if they were gonna be stuck with Georgia being there, Levi might as well have some eye candy to drool over. It was nothing more than that – it could *never* be more than that – but considering how stunningly, stupidly gorgeous she was, having Tennessee Rowland around wasn't exactly gonna be a trial.

Well, other than the whole no-scratching-his-nuts and no-wearing-just-his-boxers part.

The shit he was willing to put up with for his best friend.

He kicked off his boots and settled himself down onto his lumpy couch, flicking on the TV. Although it had been fun to have Moose sleep at his house for a couple of nights after he finally left his parent's home behind, Levi was glad to have his couch back when Moose had moved up to Franklin. He hadn't told

Moose this, of course, but Levi hated his bed. It was supremely comfortable, supremely large, and... supremely lonely.

Just him on a king-sized Tempur-Pedic mattress, all alone, just didn't work, whereas he could actually sleep on his couch, lumpy or not. Its narrow confines kept him from tossing and turning all night long, reaching for someone who wasn't there.

He turned on a documentary about bats, and, stuffing his pillow underneath his head, shut his eyes, trying to drift off to sleep. Red-rimmed, bleary eyes haunted him, floating in the darkness.

Worthless piece of shit...
Worthless piece of shit...
Shit...shit...shit...

CHAPTER 4

TENNESSEE

ENNY STOOD ON THE CURB in front of her parent's home, the smallest suitcase she owned propped up against her leg as she waited for Moose to come pick her up. She'd managed to fit everything that she needed for two nights out in the wilderness into only this tiny bag, which she considered to be nothing short of a miracle. She'd spent the day before packing and unpacking and repacking the suitcase, trying to shove and cram every last item into place.

It was stupidly early in the morning – who was honestly up at 7:30 in the morning on *purpose*?! – but on the bright side, it also meant that she didn't have to listen to her mother harangue her about "poor life choices" yet again while she was trying to get out the door. Her mother didn't get up before noon any more often than Tennessee did.

Tenny had needed the time this morning to get

her hair just right and stuff yet more last-minute items into her bag, but two and a half hours after her alarm had gone off, she was beginning to lose steam. Georgia had told her that their campsite was hours away, up in the mountains; maybe she could catch a nap in the backseat on the way.

She was hiding a yawn behind her hand when Moose's headlights caught her eye. They pierced the early morning darkness as he drove up Mansion Way towards her parent's house.

It wasn't actually named that, of course – that was too ostentatious even for the richest farmers and business owners in the area – but it's what everyone in town called it. Tenny was quite sure no one even knew the true name for the road (Golden Creek Way, which was only slightly less ostentatious, honestly) other than the post office employees.

They even occasionally got mail made out to "425 Mansion Way" instead of "425 Golden Creek Way" but their delivery person made sure it got to the Rowland home anyway.

Just one of the many benefits of living in a tiny town.

Moose pulled to a stop in front of her in his piece-of-shit truck and jumped out, shooting her a quick hello as he grabbed her Louis Vuitton suitcase and hucked it into the bed of the truck. Tennessee let out a little squeak of terror at the sight of a $3000 suitcase being thrown around like a sack of potatoes, and Moose looked back at her, surprised. "You okay?"

he asked, his eyes going up and down her, checking for injuries or an insect crawling up her leg.

"Yeah, fine," she said faintly. She looked through the cab over to Georgia in the passenger seat who was waving excitedly, obviously missing the fact that Moose was doing his best to destroy Tennessee's possessions. Tenny gave her a wane smile as she got up into the backseat of the truck.

"So glad you're coming with us!" Georgia said excitedly as soon as Tenny got inside. "What did Aunt Roberta say about it?"

Moose got back in and threw the truck in gear, pulling away from the curb to head for Levi's house.

"Oh, you know," Tennessee said dryly. "Only hobos sleep outside; that I shouldn't go on a camping trip without a chaperone; that I'm probably going to come back with Lyme disease…the uzh."

Georgia grimaced at her in sympathy, even as her hand wrapped up together with Moose's. It was like they couldn't stand not touching each other for more than three seconds at a time.

Puke inducing, indeed.

"I'll do my best to guard you from ticks and hobos," Georgia said solemnly. "Snakes are on you, though."

"There's snakes up in the mountains?" Tennessee half-shrieked, her eyes popping wide open with surprise. "Like, honest-to-God, going-to-kill-me snakes?"

Georgia and Moose both laughed at the terror in

her voice as they wound their way through the city streets to Levi's house. "Yes, there are snakes up in the mountains," Moose said, the laughter still plainly in his voice as he responded. Tennessee's spine stiffened. She did *not* like getting laughed at. "But they won't bother you for the most part, unless you bother them."

For the most part…

Those were not exactly reassuring words in Tenny's eyes.

They pulled up in front of Levi's house before Tenny could interrogate them further, and she sank back into the worn seat with a flustered sigh, not wanting to ask questions in front of Levi and have him laughing at her, too. Two people laughing at her per day – that was her limit.

A girl had to have standards, you know.

Levi carelessly tossed his duffel bag into the bed of the truck and then swung up into the backseat, greeting Moose and then Georgia in turn. Moose, who hadn't bothered to get out to help Levi load his bag, pulled away from the curb as Levi finally turned his dark eyes towards Tennessee. "Good morning," he said softly. "Sleep well?"

Why was Tennessee suddenly getting the impression that Levi was imagining her in her PJs? Despite what a lot of people thought, she did not sleep in silk negligees edged with lace. When she pulled out her flannel PJs that night, Levi was going to be sorely disappointed, she was sure of it.

"Yeah, okay," she said. "Just another night in the Rowland household." She laughed dryly. "And you?" His eyes flicked down her body and back up again so quickly that if she hadn't been watching, she might've missed it.

"Yeah, I slept great," Levi said softly.

Tenny couldn't breathe, which was, as she saw it, *completely* ridiculous. They were having a boring-as-white-paint conversation about sleeping well the night before but there was a part of her brain that couldn't shake the feeling that they were discussing so much more.

The conversation turned back towards their weekend plans and how Moose and Levi did this every year the weekend *after* Memorial Day ("Only an idiot goes out camping on Memorial Day weekend," Moose said firmly) as Levi settled back into the seat, his legs spreading apart as he tried to fit his long body into the small space. Their knees ended up pressed against each other, and somehow, this must've pushed blood up her body and into her cheeks, because Tennessee couldn't seem to keep her cheeks from flaming a brilliant red.

It was their *knees*, for hell's sakes. She'd rounded this base and blew right past it when she was in fourth grade, back when Moose still held an allure to her.

But despite her best self-recriminating speeches, she couldn't seem to get her cheeks to turn any other color than tomato red.

And anyway, she was being an idiot because no

matter what it was that Levi did to her, she was 99.34% sure she didn't do anything for him. He was in love with Georgia – he had been his whole life, an apparently very common affliction in their world – and likely just saw Tennessee as an annoying tagalong. She was a third wheel to a third wheel, which...did that make her a fourth wheel?

Her head hurt.

The air grew cooler as they climbed in altitude, everyone chatting and laughing as they went. Listening to Levi rumble, his voice about two octaves lower than every other guy on planet Earth, was an oddly erotic thing to do, despite the fact that he was currently discussing the best way to hook a worm while fishing.

Tennessee looked down at her manicured fingernails discretely, trying to decide what to do if Levi or Moose guilted her into fishing over the weekend. Would she do it? *Could* she do it? Could she push a hook through a wiggling, alive being and then drown it in water just so a fish could eat it whole?

She gulped.

Maybe she'd get lucky and could be in charge of something else. Like laying out the blankets or something. She could totally do that. She was fairly sure laying out a blanket didn't also involve hooking a worm *or* shooting a squirrel beforehand.

"What are you thinking about?" Levi asked, right in her ear, his deep voice setting her insides on fire.

"Shooting squirrels," she answered honestly, and

then gulped. She normally – read: Absolutely never – told people what she was really thinking. Doing so meant opening herself up to ridicule, or even worse, being told that what she thought just didn't matter.

Honestly, she wasn't sure which was worse.

Blurting out things without thinking them through first, but only with Levi? Check.

Levi straightened up a little and stared at her incredulously. "You were thinking about shooting squirrels?" he repeated.

She shrugged, doing her best to pretend nonchalance. "More like how I don't want to shoot them," she clarified.

"Ummm…good?" he said hesitantly. "That wasn't on the agenda for the weekend, but I'll make sure not to include it now."

"Good," she echoed him, and then lapsed back into silence again.

If she didn't stop making an absolute ass out of herself, and pronto, she was going to have to learn how to live like a hermit because leaving the house seemed awfully dangerous at the moment. It was a good thing her feet were so small; otherwise, she'd be choking on them.

They finally pulled into a woodland clearing and Moose stopped under the shade of some tall pine trees, cutting the engine, the instant silence allowing the bird calls and squirrel chatters to be heard. It was…peaceful. And naturey. And calm. And remote.

In other words, it was *not* Sawyer or Boise or Salt Lake City or Denver or New York City.

Tennessee's hands fluttered, not sure where to land or what to do. Why had she agreed to this? She couldn't remember in that moment. There probably wasn't a single mall within 200 miles of this campsite.

No, she wasn't used to this at all.

Levi and Moose both swung out of the truck and hurried over to the other side to help Tennessee and Georgia out. Levi easily swung her down from the truck's backseat, handling her weight as if she were nothing more than toddler-sized, and set her gently down on the ground. Their eyes locked for a moment, his hands on her waist, and then he moved away to help Moose unload the bed of the truck.

But the promise that had been there in his eyes when he'd been staring down at her…

Had she been imagining it? Maybe she had. Maybe she just wanted something so badly that she was starting to imagine it into existence.

So she could add delusional to her list of qualities that she only had while around Levi Scranton.

Awesome.

"You and Tennessee can set this up," Moose said to Levi, jerking her out of her thoughts. Moose had tossed a long nylon bag to Levi that clinked as he swung it effortlessly over his shoulder. Levi looked over at her.

"Well, are you coming or what?" he asked her, startling her into action. She hurried over to his side, happy to be put to work on a project that did not appear to include killing animals. Levi walked over to the shade of some pine trees, the ground a bed of fallen pine needles, and grunted, "This looks good."

Tennessee looked around and shrugged. *Sure. Why not.* She wasn't entirely sure what they were doing quite yet, but she refused to admit her ignorance. She'd figure it out soon enough. She was a smart, capable woman. She could absolutely do this... whatever "this" was.

Levi opened the bag and dumped out a mass of metal rods and nylon fabric, with mesh and zippers going every which way. Tennessee looked at the pile wide-eyed. This was going to make something? She gnawed on her bottom lip hesitantly. She really didn't know where to start or what to do, so rather than make a fool of herself, she decided to just wait for Levi to give her instructions.

He started rolling the fabric out, mumbling about facing the door the right way, and it finally occurred to Tenny that they were setting up the tent. *Ohhhh*...well, that made sense. Although, where was the other tent at? Were there two tangled up together?

"Are you gonna help?" Levi asked impatiently, arching an eyebrow at her.

"Of course, yes!" she said brightly. She waited for him to tell her what to do. He waited for her to... what? He was just staring at her. She stared back.

"Have you ever set up a tent before?" Levi finally growled, frustrated.

"No?" she said, but it came out as a question instead.

"Have you ever *seen* a tent before?"

"No?" This time, her voice was even higher.

With a grumble about worthless women and some other commentary that Tennessee pretended she couldn't hear, Levi started pointing out the parts to a tent. The tarpy stuff went on the ground, the nylon stuff went up in the air, and the metal poles held it all up.

Riiggghhhtttt…

Her mother's comment about how only hobos lived in tents flashed through Tennessee's mind. She'd made it her life's mission not to agree with her mother on almost anything, but in this case, she was starting to believe that she might've had a point.

Levi showed her how the poles slid inside of each other, eventually creating a long bouncy arc that reminded Tennessee of a pole-vaulting stick thingy, and then together, they wrestled the pole into the long strips of fabric connected to the side of the tent. Once they'd finally gotten it into place, Tennessee stood back, sweaty but proud. She'd actually gotten the pole in where it was supposed to go.

Levi stopped and looked at her. "Well," he prodded, "let's do the next one." He nodded to the folded-up stack of metal that happened to be lying next to her feet on the ground. She looked down at it, surprised.

"You mean we have to put more than one pole into the tent?"

"Yes, we have to put more than one pole into the tent," Levi repeated dryly. He began mumbling more comments about having someone put her shoes on her feet in the morning, and Tennessee's cheeks flamed a bright red. She didn't have servants put her shoes on for her in the morning! Just because she didn't know how tents worked didn't mean she was *completely* worthless.

She struggled with the poles and the fabric and the metal thingies apparently called "stakes" and did her best to avoid Levi's gaze as they worked together. She was in so far over her head, she was going to drown in ignorance at any moment.

And worst of all, she was about ready to wholeheartedly agree with Roberta Rowland on a topic, which as far as she could figure, would be a first.

Saying yes to going camping was absolutely a poor life choice.

CHAPTER 5

LEVI

*L*EVI KNELT DOWN and began pounding the metal stake into the ground to hold the guy-wire in place when he looked up into Tenny's face and saw...absolute devastation. She had apparently heard his not-so-quiet comment about servants dressing her in the morning.

He groaned inwardly. He shouldn't have said that. He just couldn't...how was it possible that Tennessee had been born and raised in Sawyer, Idaho and had never even seen a tent in her life, let alone helped erect one?! Had her parents really sequestered her away from life *that much*? She hadn't gone on any camping trips previously with him and Moose, but then again, she was a girl and up until this weekend, girls hadn't gone on their camping trips. They had been blessedly free of the female persuasion. But surely she would've gone with someone else. Not camping at all...Levi's brain didn't comprehend that.

Tennessee snuffled, turning away from him and wiping her arm across her face, staring up into the trees as if suddenly obsessed with how the Western white pine grew straight and tall.

Levi wasn't fooled one bit.

He pushed himself up into a standing position and wrapped his arm around her shoulders. "I'm… I'm sorry," he said awkwardly. "I've been going camping ever since my dad would let me," which since his father didn't give a rat's ass about him, meant he'd been going camping ever since he could walk, "and so all of it seems natural to me."

She gulped and continued staring up into the branches of the tree, studiously avoiding his gaze. He hurried on. "You were a fast learner, though," *liar, liar, pants on fire*, "and pretty soon, all of this will seem like an old hat to you."

She quickly and discretely wiped the tears from her cheeks, nodding as she did so. "My parents aren't, uhh, big campers. My mother thinks that she's being put upon if she has to stay at a four-star hotel instead of a five-star one." She shrugged, still looking off into the trees. "My father's mentioned buying a 5th wheel at some point but my mother said she couldn't handle having a toilet that wasn't hooked to an honest-to-God sewer system, so that's never gonna happen. I think she'd rather off herself than sleep in a *tent*." She said the word the same way a person would say *pile of shit*, and Levi grimaced.

What had he told Georgia? Despite his ex-girlfriend's certainty and usual correctness, in this one particular case, Levi was right. He forced himself to not march over and say "I told you so!" to her, no matter how strong the temptation was.

And then, Tennessee's next question caught Levi so off-guard, he completely forgot about his plans to rub Georgia's nose in it.

"So where's the other tent at?" she asked, finally turning to look at him.

"The other tent?" he repeated, confused.

"Yeah, the girls' tent. Or, the boys' tent. You didn't say which one this one was, so whatever the other tent is."

Levi struggled to follow her convoluted statement. "There's a girls' tent and a boys' tent?" he finally asked, hoping that he was guessing wrong.

"Ummm…yes?" she said hesitantly, her huge green eyes – they were green at the moment, not blue – practically swallowing her face. "I mean, I'm not sleeping with you and Moose tonight, right?"

"Not *with* us," Levi said. Her face brightened. "Not in our sleeping bags," he clarified. "You'll be in your own sleeping bag, but in the same tent." Her face dropped.

Levi felt simultaneously like an asshat for disappointing her, and completely confused by the line of questions. "Are you not allowed to sleep in the same tent as men?" he asked, trying to figure it out. She was 26 years old. She wasn't Amish, born-again Christian, or a Mormon, at least as far as he'd ever been told. Surely she and Moose had been banging all along, so…why the hesitancy?

She shrugged. "It's not a *rule*," she said, her cheeks glowing a little brighter under his questioning gaze. "I don't think my mother ever thought to specifically mention tents before, actually."

"Are you allowed to sleep in a hotel room with a guy?" he pressed. He kinda felt like he'd been dropped down a rabbit hole. Or dropped on his head. Or maybe just whacked upside the head with a 2x4. Tennessee Rowland, the cause of wet dreams for every guy under the age of 98 in all of Long Valley County…she couldn't actually be a virgin.

Could she?

"Oh no," she said, shaking her head firmly. "My parents would kill me for that."

"Do your parents think that you and Georgia are sleeping in a tent separate from Moose and me?" he asked, feeling faintly ill. Tennessee's father was best friends with Moose's father, and Moose's father was Levi's boss. Pissing off Robert Rowland seemed like a shitastically awful idea; a virtually guaranteed way for Levi to lose his job.

Tennessee shrugged. "Maybe," she said, her gaze darting past him, her hands fluttering everywhere, smoothing down her shirt, running over her shorts, playing with a long lock of hair.

Tennessee Rowland, the implacable ice queen that no one can read, has a tell.

He had an almost overwhelming desire to go ask

Moose if he'd ever noticed this before, but forced himself to stay on track.

"If your parents found out that you were sleeping in the same tent as Moose and me, would you get into trouble?" he pressed. It wasn't too late to call the whole thing off. They could pack everything up and head back to town and try this another weekend. One where Moose was able to disconnect himself from Georgia's side long enough to leave her at home.

"Oh. Well. Umm…maybe? I mean, probably, but I won't tell them."

"You're going to lie to your parents?" Levi was surprised. Shocked, honestly. Tenny had the face of an angel; the one that said she'd never tell a fib, not even if her life depended upon it.

"I wouldn't say *lie*. Just, not mention. They won't ask, and I won't tell." A shadow flicked across her eyes at that, piquing Levi's interest.

"How are you sure they won't ask?"

"They'd have to be interested in me to ask," Tenny replied, the pain in her voice painfully obvious. She straightened up and shot him a bright smile. "We should go see what Moose and Georgia are doing," and headed towards the lovey-dovey couple, her perfect ass swinging with every step.

They'd have to be interested in me to ask…

The comment made no sense at all. Tennessee was one of the most coddled, spoiled people he'd ever met. Her parents gave her everything she wanted; she lived in a mansion; her family had *servants*, for God's sake. He couldn't think of a set of parents more invested in their child, other than Moose, of course.

Not interested? That was Levi's dad. He didn't give a shit about Levi, except as a source of alcohol.

Tennessee...her parents paid for music lessons and a new car and attended all of her music recitals and sent her all over the country to compete in competitions and had paid for her four-year college degree.

Those were not the actions of parents who didn't give a damn.

Levi followed slowly after the enigma that was Tennessee Rowland. Damn girls. They never made sense.

Maybe another weekend by himself on his lumpy couch wouldn't have been so bad. At least, it wouldn't have been so confusing.

CHAPTER 6

TENNESSEE

*T*ENNY HURRIED AWAY from the probing eyes of Levi, feeling his gaze on her every step. She felt wrung out, used up, and totally worthless. She didn't know how to put up a tent; her parents were the very epitome of smothering; and she said *way* too much around Levi that she didn't say around anyone else. Did he have some sort of magical hold over her?

This was *not* a positive development.

Georgia looked up with a big smile, one that faded once she saw Tennessee. "Is everything okay?" she asked as Tenny neared the two lovebirds.

Dammit. She'd been stupid enough to let her emotions show on her face for a moment. She was really starting to lose it.

She smoothed her face into the appropriate lines, sending Georgia a bland smile. "Of course," she said. "The tent is up. What can I help with next?" *Because I was such a giant help with the tent.*

She pushed that thought down, too.

"Well, it's getting late and I don't know about you, but I'm starving," Georgia said. "I was going to move all of the sleeping bags and suitcases inside of the tent now that it's up – thank heavens it's such a huge tent, right? – if you and Levi want to get to work on tonight's dinner."

Tennessee found herself torn between wanting to say, "That tent? That tent over there? It's huge?" and "Levi? Really? Can't I help *you* with dinner?"

But she shut her mouth. Whining and complaining wasn't going to get her anywhere. Just because the tent they were all going to be sleeping in that night was roughly the size of her closet and just because Levi thought she was a completely worthless, spoiled brat didn't mean that it was okay to whine and complain.

And anyway, no one wanted to listen to it. Her parents had taught her that a long time ago.

Levi spoke up right behind her, almost scaring Tenny out of her skin. "Sure, we'd be happy to. What are we having for dinner?"

"I packed everything we needed for tinfoil dinners," Moose said. Tennessee blanched. Tinfoil? For dinner? Wasn't that dangerous? "You don't eat the tinfoil!" he said quickly, catching the look on her face. "You wrap the food up in tinfoil."

"Of course," she said regally, as if that was totally something she knew before he explained it. "Where's the food?"

"Over in the coolers," Moose said with a jerk of his head towards some blue-and-white coolers sitting underneath the shade of a pine tree.

Tennessee took off walking towards the coolers and then realized that if she got there first, then she'd have to pull the food out, and then she'd have to admit that she had no idea *what* food she was pulling out, and she'd already looked like enough of a fool for one day, thankyouverymuch, so a much better strategy was to fall into line next to Levi and then let *him* pull the food out. Once it was all out and spread out on the card table Moose had set up over by the campfire, it'd be self-explanatory from there.

She slowed her pace and shot a brilliant smile up at Levi. If she just flirted with him enough, he might forget to notice that she knew virtually nothing at all. Well, at least, nothing at all that was helpful on a camping trip. She could lay out the silverware for a proper meal in the correct order and she knew how to arrange a vase of flowers for the most visual *oomph* possible, oh and she totally knew how to dicker with saleswomen at high-end department stores to get the best deals possible, but…

Yeah, nothing useful for a camping trip.

"Isn't the John Deere dealership busy this time of year?" she asked as Levi knelt down next to the coolers and began pulling food out, handing it up to her. Her brilliant plan had worked. She gave herself a mental pat on the back for that one. "How are you able to take Monday off?"

He shrugged, his shirt pulling tight across his delicious muscles as he continued to dig. The food just kept coming so Tenny had to turn sideways so she could continue to drool over him as he worked, but that view? Totally worth it.

"I've been there long enough that Rocky pretty much lets me set my own hours," he murmured distractedly, rifling through the cooler with a muttered curse. Before Tenny could question him on that – Moose had never had that sort of latitude and it was his father's dealership – Levi pulled out a bag of carrots triumphantly. "There you are, you little buggers." He started to hand it up to her when he actually took a good look at her. "Oh, whoa!" he said, scrambling to his feet and beginning to unload her arms. A sack of potatoes, a bag of celery, onions and garlic and a few more items later that she didn't even recognize, he could finally look her in the eye again.

He stared down at her for a moment, and then let out a small laugh. "If I'd handed you those carrots, where, exactly, would you have put them? On top of your head?"

She shrugged, which was considerably easier now that he'd taken half her load away. "I still had a pinky free. I was going to hold it with that."

He shook his head, kicking the cooler top closed with his booted foot and then heading back towards the fire. "It's okay to complain, you know," he said as they walked. "You can say, 'Levi, I'm drowning in food over here.'"

A second card table had appeared from somewhere, pushed up together with the first one, and they began laying out the food. As they did so, Tennessee contemplated his words. They were a foreign concept, to say the least. Complaining about something just meant that she'd have whatever it was piled on top of her twice over. Hate practicing the piano? Butt-on-bench time would be doubled from two hours a day to four. Hate caviar? That's all they'd eat for a week until she could learn to swallow it without grimacing.

Before she could think of how to respond to his comment – *if* she could even think of a good response to give – Levi held out a short knife to her. "Are you good with chopping up celery?" he asked, clearly worried that her complete lack of camping knowledge also extended to cutlery.

"Absolutely!" she said, snatching the knife out of his hand and getting to work on the green stalks. Knives? Now there was something she knew something about.

He stopped, mesmerized by her quick and efficient strokes of the knife blade, and then murmured, "Hidden talents," before starting in on cubing the potatoes.

She hid her smile of triumphant. Maybe she didn't know jackshit about tents or camping in general, but she wasn't *completely* worthless. Too bad there wouldn't be a chance for her to show off her ability to put together a smashing menu, paired with just the right wines. Maybe she could be in charge of the menu next time.

Next time…

It had a nice ring to it.

CHAPTER 7

LEVI

*T*HE CAMPFIRE WAS CRACKLING, sending sparks up into the gathering twilight and adding a homey cheer to their camp-out. Levi'd never admit it out loud, of course, but his favorite part of camping was the campfire. It chased the darkness away, casting a circle of light where staying inside of it meant safety and security.

Hmmm…

What was it that made him love camping so much, other than the campfires, of course?

Sitting next to Tennessee, who was busy trying to get pine sap off her fake fingernails and muttering about the lack of civility out in the wilderness, he thought back over his childhood. Maybe he hadn't been camping since he was old enough to walk – yeah, okay, that was an exaggeration – but he had been camping since he was pretty young. Moose's family would take him along with them, even Linda joining in on the fun, and they'd spend a week up in the mountains, away from the stress of the world. Rocky Garrett wasn't one to take much time off from the dealership, but he was always willing to go camping.

And then it hit Levi – the realization so obvious, he felt like an idiot for missing it before.

My dad never took me camping.

That was it.

Never, on a single camping trip, had Levi been beaten black and blue, screamed at, backhanded, or called names, because his dad was never there with him. Why leave his recliner and his blaring TV and his alcohol, all to go sit in a tent up in the wilderness?

No, camping was a Steve-Scranton-free zone, which made it…wonderful.

On the other hand, Rocky Garrett had always been kind to him, treating him like a second son, and yeah, maybe he'd been hard on Moose and what had happened with the dealership wasn't cool, but…well, Rocky still had Steve beat to pieces. He was practically ready for sainthood in comparison, even if Moose didn't see it that way.

Moose didn't understand what it was like to *truly* have a shitty father, and Levi was simultaneously glad for it, and jealous as hell.

What would it have been like growing up to know that he was going to be eating dinner every single night? What if he could've known that he could always count on heat coming out of the ducts during the wintertime? What if he'd been able to have someone wash and dry his clothes for him, rather than having to scrub things out in the bathtub and hanging them up over the shower curtain rod to dry?

Heaven. Heaven on earth.

Moose had been spoiled absolutely rotten, and he didn't even know it.

"What are you thinking about?" Tenny asked him, startling him out of his thoughts. He quickly recovered, though – hiding his thoughts was what he did best. He turned and flashed her a smile in the darkness, scrambling for an appropriate topic to give to her as an answer. One that didn't involve Steve Scranton or belts or trying to sleep at night while his stomach was eating through his backbone.

"I was just remembering the ghost stories that Moose and I used to tell each other while we were up here camping," he said, shooting Moose a huge grin across the sparks of the campfire. "Around junior high or so, we started coming up here and camping together, just him and me, and some of the stories we came up with..." He shook his head, laughing. "I can't believe we didn't piss our pants."

Moose laughed. "I was always too cool to admit that I was scared spitless, of course. We'd sit around the campfire for hours, adding in the goriest details, and then we'd crawl into our sleeping bags and I was *just sure* that there were monsters outside, about to come in and eat us alive. I'd spend the whole night shaking in my sleeping bag, and then, we'd do it all again the next night."

Georgia let out a belly laugh at that. Moose leaned down to whisper something in her ear, and sure enough, the spit swapping commenced.

Levi rolled his eyes and turned pointedly towards Tennessee. "Wanna hear a ghost story?" he asked loudly over the slurping sounds.

The edges of her lips twitched for just a moment, and then she nodded regally. "Of course," she said as the moans of desire commenced. "I'd love nothing more."

As Levi started into one of his favorite ones, finally pulling Moose away from Georgia's lips long enough to add his own gory deets into the mix, Tennessee's eyes got wider and wider and she began scooting closer and closer to him on the log they were sitting on.

Levi figured if he kept this up, she'd end up on his lap soon enough. The idea was...an interesting one. At least, according to his dick.

He casually rearranged the front of his jacket.

When the story finally came to a bloody end, both Tennessee and Georgia were letting out little whimpers of panic. He grinned down at Tenny, her soft body plastered against his side, her arms wrapped around him. Turned out, telling ghost stories to Tenny was even more fun than telling them to Moose.

Huh. He'd finally found something – other than

the view, of course – to recommend taking a girl on a camping trip.

He looked up and caught the horny gaze of Moose, who was currently eating Georgia up with his eyes. Moose stretched oh-so-casually and then said, "Well, we should probably go to bed. Uhhh…you guys can stay up if you want to," and then he was carrying Georgia to the tent, her squeals of laughter ringing out into the night forest.

Levi looked down at Tennessee, who, sadly enough, had moved away just a bit to start poking at the fire again with her stick. He said softly, "So, we should probably stay out here for a while longer. Seems like they're needing their privacy."

Tenny let out a light laugh even as a blush so brilliant he could see it in the darkness began to climb her cheeks. "I'm pretty sure Georgia would never speak to me again if we headed into the tent just now."

"Probably not," Levi agreed dryly. "I think Moose might even invent some new swear words for the occasion."

They lapsed into silence, just the crackling of the fire and the hooting of a distant owl and the rustling of the insects over the fallen leaves and pine needles to be heard.

Levi tried to remember the last time he felt this comfortable around a girl. High school with Georgia? Probably. It was hard to remember that far back. They'd started drifting apart as soon as they left to their separate colleges, so it certainly hadn't been during that phase of their relationship, and sure as hell not after Georgia turned him down flat when he'd finally gathered up the courage to propose to her.

But being this comfortable around *Tennessee Rowland*? Bizarre.

"So, what's it like to work for the almighty Rocky Garrett?" Tenny asked, laying the fire stick down and turning towards him on the log.

He shrugged. "Rocky...he's not the easiest guy in the world to get along with, but I'm also lucky enough that I'm not his son. He's always been hard on Moose, but me? I think I had the good luck of not living in the Garrett home." *As much as I would've loved to.* "He didn't have to argue with me about whether or not I'd done my homework or if I was staying out too late at night, because I wasn't his child. At times, it felt like I was 'cause I spent half my childhood at the Garrett home—" *something you do when your father is the town drunk and more interested in beating you than feeding you,* "—but I never lost that special shine that came with the fact that Rocky hadn't had to potty train me."

"You really think that Rocky potty trained Moose?" Tennessee asked with a laugh, her brilliant white teeth glinting in the firelight. "I'm pretty sure Linda took care of that."

"Good point," Levi said dryly. "Anyway, Rocky paid for TIG welder training for me so I'd come back to the dealership once my certification was done, and so...well, I've been there ever since. Even though I wasn't his kid, he was kind enough to pay for my schooling, so I can't pay that back by being disloyal, you know? I'll probably be at the John Deere dealership for life. So," he hurried on before she could ask him any more personal questions, definitely one of his least favorite topics on the planet, "what about you? I know you've played in a lot of piano competitions around the US. Are you thinking you're going to become a professional piano player?"

"'Pianist' is the official term and dear God in heaven, I hope not," she said seriously. She began twirling a lock of her hair, refusing to look at him, her other hand dancing around, refusing to settle down into one spot.

He'd originally thought her hands fluttered around when she was lying, but now he was starting to think she did it when she was nervous.

At least, that was his working theory. Further study would be needed to know for sure.

For that reason only, he should keep his eyes glued to her face, watching her every move and blush and sigh.

No other reason, of course.

"Why, dear God in heaven, not?" he asked, mimicking her words. "I've heard you play – you're good." She'd played at every talent show in elementary school and had been one of the few students participating who could actually claim any talent.

When they'd hit high school, she'd entered into

every beauty queen competition in the valley, and Moose had dragged Levi to them all, claiming that sitting through something like that without someone there to keep him sane would mean the death of him. Levi hadn't minded them like Moose had – who complained about girls dressing up in evening gowns, and (even better) swimsuits while walking around in high heels on a stage?!

Tennessee's talent for these competitions had always been the piano, too. She'd won every one of them that she'd competed in, making her the Homecoming Queen, the Prom Queen, the winner of Junior Miss their junior year, and Miss Sawyer three years in a row. She'd even come in second at the state level, making her Miss Idaho 1st Runner Up.

And yet, here she was, sitting next to him, Levi Scranton, on a log up in the wilds of Idaho.

Sometimes, life was a little on the bizarre side.

She didn't answer his question. He nudged her in the side softly. "Do you not like playing the piano?" he asked, trying to prod her into answering. That obviously wasn't it, but maybe it'd make her tell him something.

"I hate it."

She whispered her confession into the darkness. The flames had died down a little, making it hard for even Levi – who had excellent night vision – to see what she was thinking.

He turned the shocking words over and over in his

mind, trying to make sense of them. *Hate?* But she'd been playing the piano since…

"When did you start playing the piano?" he asked, realizing that he couldn't remember a time that she hadn't played.

"Three. My parents decided that I was going to be a musical prodigy. They didn't base this on anything, like my natural aptitude for it or an innate desire to play; they just decided that's what would happen." She was rigid; a piece of steel carved into a beautiful impersonation of a woman.

"You know what's really funny?" she asked sarcastically. "Virginia loves music." Virginia was Tenny's younger sister, and if Levi remembered right, she played some sort of violin instrument. He'd honestly not paid a lot of attention in high school to his girlfriend's cousin's younger sister, but that seemed vaguely correct. "Ginny loves it all. Her music teacher told her that if she keeps it up, she could end up at *Juilliard*."

She turned and squinted up at him. He was quickly sorting through his mind, trying desperately to come up with a meaning for the word *Juilliard*. He wasn't quick enough, though, because she saw his confusion and clarified, "It's one of the most prestigious music schools in the country. You know what my parents said when Ginny told them that? To hush up; they were talking about me just then." She let out a hollow laugh. "They're so focused on me and my music career that they don't care at all about the daughter who actually loves her cello and actually wants to play it. The irony…"

She shook her head and turned back towards the fire, staring at the orange coals burning brightly in the summer night. Levi wanted to reach out a hand and rub her back or pat her on the thigh or something consolingly, but touching Tenny…what if she didn't want him to?

She was – quite literally – a beauty queen. He was nothing. She wouldn't want him to touch her, and he couldn't blame her at all for that.

Conflicted, trying to figure out what to do, he realized that the hushed groans and moans and cries from the tent had finally died away, so he stood, holding his hand out to Tennessee to help her up. "I think they're finally…uhhhh…done. You want to help me put the fire out?"

She looked down at the glowing coals and back up at him, confused. "Why? It's so pretty!"

"Yeah, but if a wind comes along and whips the fire back up, we could start a forest fire without even knowing it. You should only leave a fire burning if you're there to watch it."

"Oh. Right. Of course."

They poured water on the fire, the steam and smoke curling up in the sky, popping and crackling its discontent at being doused into oblivion. Once it was full out, Levi verifying that by pushing the dirty gray ashes around with Tenny's fire stick, they headed for the now-quiet tent.

As he removed his boots and shucked off his jeans under the cover of darkness, quickly pulling on a pair of sweatpants before crawling into his sleeping bag, he thought over the day's events. Maybe it wasn't nice of him to make that comment about Tenny needing servants to dress her, but the longer he was around her, the more he was starting to realize that it had been a little more true than even he'd wanted to admit.

Left to her own devices, she'd have no tent or sleeping bag to sleep in, but that's okay because she'd have a forest fire to keep her warm.

He sighed to himself.

She could only survive in an environment where she was being coddled and taken care of every moment of the day. Not that her life was especially easy – it was true that having overbearing parents wasn't exactly a walk in the park – but it also didn't prepare her for the real world.

Like a porcelain doll, she could sit there and be beautiful, but never more than that.

CHAPTER 8

TENNESSEE

*T*ENNESSEE AWOKE to something doing its best to rearrange her spine. With a groan, she rolled over, finally free of the giant lump she'd spent the night sleeping on. She opened her eyes and looked around the tent blearily, realization that she was in it by herself belatedly registering in her mind. She could hear the chatter and quiet laughter of the other three outside so, with a sigh, she pushed her way out of her sleeping bag.

Instantly, the cold of the mountain morning hit her and her teeth started chattering.

Soooo…coollldddd…

She shoved her hair out of her face and unzipped the tent, fumbling around for her slides before finally managing to shove her feet into them so she could hurry outside and over to the warmth of the campfire sure to already be roaring.

Which was when she spotted Levi crouched next to said campfire, dressed in only a pair of sweatpants.

She gulped.

Hard.

Muscles everywhere, a thin smattering of chest hair, pecs to die for…

Where was a shopping cart when she needed it? Her skin was still freezing but her insides had warmed right up. She was twirling a strand of her hair nervously when Georgia came up and whispered in her ear, "You should wipe that drool off your chin," as she handed her a cup of coffee.

Tenny's eyes flew to her cousin's, mortified that it was that obvious. Georgia just winked.

Tenny barely suppressed a groan as she took a sip of the hot liquid. She hadn't brushed her hair or her teeth, she was wearing her flannel PJs with dancing puppies all over them, and her teeth were chattering while her stomach was a glowing tangle of worms.

No wonder her mother had warned her against camping so stridently.

Moose looked up from his spot next to the propane stove. "Good morning, sleeping beauty!" he called out, flipping a pancake over. "Ready to eat breakfast?"

"Sure," she said, walking over to the cooking set-up to see what there was to eat, which was when she spotted it…pancakes with butter and syrup, and bacon.

Are you kidding me?!

Her eyes shot over to Georgia's, panicked yet again. Surely they couldn't expect her to eat that many carbs and fat all in one meal. But Moose was already pushing a loaded plate into her hand. "Here's a fork," he said, plopping the fork on top of it all.

A coffee mug in one hand and enough calories to feed a small country in the other, Tennessee made her way over to the campfire. Someone had found camp chairs at some point, so with a happy sigh that she didn't have to sit on a sappy pine log, she lowered herself into a chair and then stared down at her plate.

She couldn't eat all of this. She just couldn't.

She began pushing it around with her fork, taking the occasional bite, hoping that no one would notice how little was actually going into her mouth. Moose and Levi were discussing where they wanted to go fishing after breakfast, and Tenny could only be happy that these plans didn't seem to include her. At least, not that they were mentioning. Maybe she could stay back at camp and...suntan? Stare at the pine trees?

Huh.

What, exactly, did a person do while on a camping trip that didn't involve spearing and drowning innocent creatures? She had no cell phone service up here, so her iPad and iPhone did her no good at all. She really needed to do her hair but so far, no one had pointed out a place to plug in her curling iron or blow dryer, so she was guessing that a braid was going to have to do.

There was no piano for her to play, no

cosmetician to do her nails, and no shops to buy clothes or handbags from. Which meant that everything she was good at? None of it counted. Not up here in the endless wilderness of pine trees and mountain streams and rocky hillsides.

She looked up to find Levi's eyes focused on her. She had the oddest feeling that if she asked him, he could accurately tell her how many bites of her food she'd taken thus far. With an internal groan, she ate another bite, the sweet, buttery pancake filling her mouth with yummy goodness.

So, she ate another bite.

Only to please Levi, of course.

She wasn't about to put up with him accusing her of being anorexic. She'd struggled with that in high school but she'd long since left that particular mental disease behind. Nowadays, she was just careful about what she ate, which was absolutely a different thing. If her teenage, anorexic self could see her now, she'd be horrified. Tennessee had gained 35 pounds since the height of her anorexia, and no matter what her teenage self would think, it looked good on her.

She just didn't need to make it 36 pounds, was all.

She snuck another peek. Levi was still watching her.

She took another bite.

Damn, this was good. She couldn't remember the last time she ate bacon. Had it always been this good? Or was it just bacon cooked over a campfire that tasted this amazing?

If she'd known how tasty it was, it would've been a lot harder to give up all those years ago, but their cook had always made turkey bacon, and…well, turkey bacon was easy to pass up, to put it politely.

"Are you going to come down to the lake with us?" Georgia asked, interrupting Tenny's worshipful eating of the crunchy bacon.

"Uhhh…" Her eyes flicked over to Levi's, although honestly, she had no idea why – it wasn't like they were there together. As a couple. On a date.

She forced herself to look back at Georgia. "Sure, why not?" She could work on her suntan down at the lake just as well as she could work on it here at the campsite, and, bonus points, she wouldn't have to feel guilty about letting her cousin down.

"Good!" Georgia said. "Let's get ready for the day and then take off." She stood up and headed for the tent, and with a longing look back at her mostly empty plate, Tennessee followed her. It was shockingly hard to leave those last few bites of syrup-soaked pancake behind.

No chocolate for a month. Not even any Pierre Marcolini chocolates.

Forget 36 pounds. If she kept eating like this, it'd quickly become 50.

Georgia showed her how to take a sponge bath using facial cleaner wipes. "As long as you hit all of the, uh, important parts," she said tactfully, "you'll be surprised by how long you can go without a shower with these things." After they were finished with their spit baths and had dressed, Georgia told her to grab her toiletry bag and follow her outside.

Tennessee pulled out the lime green bag from her Louis Vuitton suitcase, and hefted it over her shoulder.

"Is that your toiletry bag?" Georgia asked her, eyes wide.

"Yeah. I made sure not to pack anything but the necessities," Tennessee reassured her. She was kinda proud of how far she'd been able to pare down her makeup bag, honestly.

Georgia just nodded mutely and headed for the Rubbermaid water dispenser on the table at the edge of camp, her tiny bag clutched in her hands. Tennessee looked at her cousin's bag and sighed. She probably packed a toothbrush and travel-sized toothpaste and called it good. Tenny loved her cousin, but sometimes, she was just too practical for her own good.

"Okay, so pull out your toothbrush and hold it under the nozzle here," Georgia said, demonstrating with her own toothbrush, "and push this little button – out comes the water. You only need a little bit; water conservation is super important while you're up camping because it's not like you can exactly run down to the corner store and buy more, right?"

Tennessee looked around at the idyllic forest setting and realized her cousin was right. She hadn't really thought about it, but not only was there no electricity, there was no running water, either.

Why do people do this on purpose again?

"Once your toothbrush is wet," Georgia continued, happily ignorant of Tennessee's less-than-impressed views on camping, "then you brush your teeth, and spit into the bushes. When you're done brushing, you rinse your toothbrush out – being careful about the water again – and you're done!"

Tennessee nodded, getting to work on setting up her own toothbrush as Georgia began brushing away. Someone else would've been offended by Georgia's instructions, maybe feeling like she was talking down to them, but Tenny was just profoundly grateful. It never would've occurred to her to spit into the bushes. She would've started brushing, and then probably would've ended up swallowing instead, not knowing what else to do.

And being careful with water usage? *Definitely* wouldn't have occurred to her. She usually just turned on the water at home and kept it running until she was done. It was…weird not to do that here, that was for damn sure.

Once they'd finally finished their tooth care for the day, Georgia asked, "Do you want me to braid your hair for you? Just to keep it out of the way. There aren't any outlets up here, so obviously curling your hair is out of the question."

"I've realized that now," Tenny said dryly. "I wish I'd thought about it beforehand; I wasted a lot of room packing my curling iron and blow dryer and straightener."

Georgia's eyes grew wide. "Well," she said, her voice a little higher than normal, and then she cleared her throat, "where's your hairbrush at? I'll brush out the tangles and then get it braided for you."

"Oh, sure," Tenny said, rummaging around in her toiletry bag. A movement caught her eye and she looked up to see Levi watching them. As soon as she looked up, he glanced away.

What is he thinking about? He had a...funny look on his face.

She pulled out her favorite hairbrush and a hair tie, handing them over to Georgia and then sitting in a camp chair by the smoldering campfire. Georgia brushed through her hair gently, and then began braiding. "Your hair is so gorgeous," she murmured as she worked. "Super thick, too – so unusual for blonde hair."

"Thanks," Tenny murmured, self conscious about the compliment. Normally, they didn't faze her much but Levi was still there and she could just tell he was listening to every word.

What did he think about her?

And why did she care?

"All right, all done!" Georgia announced. "Everyone ready to head to the lake?"

Tenny stood up, touching her braid self-consciously. She couldn't remember the last time she'd braided her hair. It felt like a little kid thing to do. And on top of that, she wasn't ready to head to the lake yet – she hadn't put on any makeup! She looked around the camp and saw Levi carefully pouring water on the fire to make sure it was completely out, while Georgia and Moose were gathering up the fishing supplies. When Georgia had said, "Let's head to the lake," she didn't seem to mean, "Let's head to the lake in an hour, after Tenny has finished getting ready for the day."

With a reluctant sigh and one last longing glance at her lime green toiletry kit, Tennessee followed the group down the trail to where she assumed the lake was, fishing poles bouncing on everyone's shoulders except hers. She might as well have been naked; she felt like she was, anyway, without any makeup on. She knew one thing for sure – if Levi hadn't known if he liked her before or not, he sure as hell wasn't going to like her now. Without eyeliner and bronzer and blush and eyeshadow, she didn't stand a snowball's chance in hell with him.

Which is really too bad, she thought admiringly as she watched his casual, loose-hipped swagger that all cowboys seemed to adopt as soon as they learned how to walk. She could bounce a quarter off that ass, she was sure of it.

She was also sure she wanted to try.

Keep your mind out of the gutter. Especially considering how ugly you are right now, he wouldn't touch you if you paid him to.

Once they got to the lake, everyone started hooking their worms, laughing and placing bets on who would catch the most fish and the biggest fish while Tenny discretely searched for a rock to sit on. She'd just stay out of the way, watch them have fun, and…that was it.

It still felt like a weird thing to do – absolutely nothing at all – but then she shrugged to herself. Relaxing was a thing, right?

"Want to fish for a bit?" Levi rumbled in her ear. "You can borrow my pole."

There was something very sexual about that question. Or maybe it was just the way he said it. Or how the sound of his voice made her feel. Or how close he was standing to her when he asked.

Yeah, any one of those things.

"I've not fished before," she finally said, turning to look up at him. His Superman curl was especially curly this morning and she had to clench her hands into fists by her side to keep from running her fingers through it. He had the most touchable hair of any guy she knew.

"I didn't figure you had," he said, a light laugh in his voice. She glared up at him. She really hated it when people laughed at her. Plus, he hadn't picked up on the unspoken half of that sentence: I haven't fished before *and I don't want to start now*.

But he was still just standing there, unmovable, waiting for her answer, so with a sigh, she agreed to try. It was a sad statement on her life that peer pressure absolutely worked on her. She thought she'd become more immune to it when she graduated from high school, but that day hadn't come.

Yet.

She trailed him down to the sandy shoreline where he plucked a wiggling worm out of a small container full of dirt and held it out to her. "First, you put the worm on the hook."

She took the wiggling creature between thumb and forefinger, gulping as she stared at it. Did it have to move so much? Why couldn't she spear some dead worm?

"Does it matter which end?" she asked faintly. *Please, God, don't let me pass out. Please. I'll be good from here forward, I promise.*

"Not at all," he assured her cheerfully. She glared back up at him. Did he have to sound so happy about this?

Finally, with a gulp of air, she pushed the worm onto the hook and then frantically threw the hook into the water. She was panting, the world going a little black around the edges.

"You just threw the hook into the wat…Listen, that's *not* how you cast out," Levi said, disgruntled, spinning the round thingy on the rod and zipping the hook right back up so it was dangling in front of them, the worm squirming and wiggling in front of her eyes.

"Really? Again?" she muttered.

"Okay, so hold the rod here," he said, wrapping his arms around her so he could properly show her what to do. "Now, you're going to trap the line underneath your finger, right up against the pole, like that. Good. Next, you're going to open the bail…"

Except, standing in the circle of his arms, she couldn't breathe again and this time, there was certainly no shopping cart between them. No *room* for a shopping cart between them, or even a piece of paper. His warm breath was in her ear and his muscular arms, rippling from years of welding and working with his hands, were encircling hers. She became transfixed by the light sprinkling of hair on his arms, springy and ticklish against her skin, his deep tan dramatic against her light golden skin, the same color she always got to no matter how long she lay out in the sun. He had a smattering of freckles – or were they moles? – down by his wrist and she began imagining tracing them with her tongue. She could—

"Are you paying attention?" Levi asked grumpily, pulling her back to the present.

The overwhelming nature of it all – him, right there, breathing in her ear, his arms around her, feeling his heartbeat through his thin t-shirt – washed over her, smothering her, and she immediately became defensive. Her defenses were her last resort – the only way to protect herself from him and whatever…*this* was.

She ducked out of the circle of his arms and stood off to the side, hands on hips, glaring at him. "Why did you ask me to come if I annoy you?" she demanded tartly.

He pulled the line back in and then laid the rod down on the sand. Hands freed, he crossed his arms over his chest and glared down at her. "You don't annoy me," he rumbled, looking annoyed.

She glared harder.

"Don't lie to me," she snapped back. "I'm a big girl – I can take it. Why did you ask me on this camping trip if you don't even like me?"

He sucked in a breath at that, his whole body frozen as he stared down at her. Finally, he reached his hand out, brushing her elbow with his calloused fingertips. "I never said I didn't like you," he said softly.

And then, it was her turn for the world to freeze.

CHAPTER 9

LEVI

*H*AD HE JUST SAID those words out loud? Based on the look on Tenny's face, he was going to guess that he did.

Dammit.

The thing was, he *did* like her.

He liked the way her hair shone in the sunshine. He liked making her laugh. He liked talking to her when her guard was down. He liked how her ass looked in a pair of short shorts. He liked how she was gorgeous when her hair was done and her makeup was perfect, and he liked how she was equally as gorgeous (but in a totally different way) when she was up here, camping, her hair in a braid and no makeup to be found anywhere.

And he liked how being around her made him feel.

He liked her too damn much – that was the problem.

She was biting her lower lip as she stared up at him, and he wanted to snap at her to stop. Stop looking at him with those huge eyes. Stop worrying about what he's thinking. He was just the son of the town drunk. He shouldn't even be talking to her, and she certainly shouldn't be looking at him like…like *that*.

His defenses sprung into action. He needed room from her – space. Mental space to breathe properly. She was still looking at him like *that* and his self control was crumbling in the face of it. He couldn't let that happen.

"You know what your problem is?" he asked rhetorically, nastily, bitterly. "You care too much about what other people think."

Her giant blue eyes – they were blue now, against the deep blue of the mountain lake – snapped open in irritation and anger. Without a word, she spun on her heel and stomped away, back towards camp.

Away from him.

His heart hurt as he forced himself to pick up his fishing pole from the sandy shore. *Good. I can get some fishing done now. I didn't want her here anyway. Asshole Moose, dragging Georgia along, forcing me to take Tennessee.*

Girls and camping don't mix. Everyone knows that.

He was pissed.

Well, he was happy that Tenny was gone and had left him alone, of course, just like he wanted, but he was pissed, too.

He was pissed because...well, he wasn't exactly sure why. He just was.

What he wanted to do was tear into Moose for forcing him into this disaster of a weekend. What the hell had he been thinking? He hadn't, that's what. Moose'd been thinking with his dick, the only part of him that had been reliably working since he and Georgia hooked up. Levi wanted his best friend back; the one who could think about something other than the shape of Georgia's ass.

He wanted—

Huh. Speaking of Moose and Georgia, where the hell are they?

Right in the middle of his mental tirade, just as he was really starting to get into it, he realized that he hadn't seen the two lovebirds in a while. Finally, he spotted them down the beach a ways, wandering towards him, holding hands and chatting. He watched the way they laughed together, and his gut twisted. Moose looked up and saw him staring down the beach at them. "Hey, catch anything yet?" Moose called out, his face happy and open and cheerful.

Levi was pretty sure he wanted nothing more than to stomp on Moose's foot with one of his work boots.

"Not yet," he called back tightly, turning back to the lake and casting out his line again. He'd forgotten what he was even doing there for a minute. He jiggled the line impatiently. He hadn't had so much as a nibble yet. Maybe he should move down the beach a little.

Or, to the next state over. There probably weren't that many Tennessees in Montana, right?

"Are you okay?" Moose asked as soon as they reached his side, his concern apparent as he skimmed Levi's face.

At the same time, Georgia piped up, "Where's Tennessee?"

Levi decided to ignore Moose's question. If his best friend really cared about his feelings, he wouldn't have forced two girls onto him. "She went back to camp," he said to Georgia. Well, at least, that's where he guessed she'd gone. She didn't seem like the type to go on a day hike by herself, but she also hadn't exactly announced her destination as she'd stormed off.

Of course, he never would've guessed that she'd agree to go camping either, so maybe he didn't know a damn thing after all about Miss Tennessee Marie Rowland.

Georgia went off in search of her cousin while Moose stayed behind, obviously not willing to have his questions ignored.

Dammit all.

"What's going on?" Moose asked quietly. "Are you upset about Georgia and I dating?"

Levi opened his mouth to automatically brush off that concern – it was *obviously* not true – when he stopped.

Actually, it really *wasn't* true. After years and years of carrying a torch for Georgia, dating her, being in love with her, proposing to her for God's sake…he really was fine with Moose and her dating.

He really wasn't jealous or upset at all.

It was like walking on a newly healed foot – he expected the jab of pain to be there, and it just… wasn't.

"I'm over her, honest," he said, pulling his gaze back from the lake to stare Moose straight in the eye as he said it. Moose was one of the few guys who was just as tall as Levi, which meant that Levi really was staring him *straight* in the eye.

No guilt, no shame, no worry that he had to hide his true feelings…he really was over Georgia Rowland.

Huh.

That felt surprisingly good to figure out.

Moose nodded slowly, his shoulders relaxing. He believed Levi. "So why the attitude?" he asked softly. "You've been…difficult this whole time."

Levi shrugged, his eyes flitting away to the gorgeous green forest surrounding the lake. "I'm not used to having girls on our camping trip," he finally said tightly. The camping trip they'd taken together every single year since they'd turned 14 and could finally drive by themselves. The camping trip that'd been just them, or just them and a couple of other guys, that whole time. The camping trip where they'd made a million memories, and caught at least that many fish.

Of course it was hard for him to have Georgia and Tennessee tag along this time.

Of course.

"Hmmm…" Moose said noncommittally, and then headed back towards camp, leaving Levi on the shore to fish all by himself.

Levi reeled his line back in and then cast it out. Good. He liked being alone. This was just what he wanted. Just him, the mountain air, the impossibly blue water, and his fishing pole.

He didn't need anything – or anyone – else.

"SMOKE FOLLOWS BEAUTY," Moose said.

"What?" Tennessee asked, coughing as she waved her hand in front of her face in a desperate attempt to get a clean lungful of air. She and Georgia scooted their chairs to the right, and like magic, the smoke of the campfire followed their movements perfectly.

Mother, I'm sorry I didn't believe you. I'll never question your judgment again. Except when it comes to caviar. You're wrong about that. I don't care how many times you make me eat it.

"Smoke follows beauty," Moose repeated. "Everyone knows that. When you're sitting around a campfire, the smoke always wants to drift towards a beautiful person. That's why you'll never see my ugly mug choking on the stuff."

Tennessee sent him a dry look through the smoke. "Are you sure this isn't just a way to make someone feel better who is currently contracting a case of lung cancer?" she asked sarcastically.

Moose let out a belly laugh. "You know, I like you so much better, now that I'm not dating you."

"Funny – I feel the same way about you," she retorted with a saucy grin.

"We should go for a walk," Georgia said through a coughing fit, finally abandoning her chair and escaping to stand outside of the ring of smoke. "We could hike and take some pictures – see some scenery."

"Sounds great! Let me go ask Levi if he wants to go with us," Moose volunteered and without waiting for them to agree to his plan, he stood and headed down the trail towards the lake.

Tennessee also stood up and moved out of the line of fire…errr…smoke. She wasn't entirely sure why Moose had been so insistent on building one as soon as he followed her and Georgia back to camp; she guessed it was so he had something to do to keep himself out of the way while her and Georgia had some "girl time" together. Either way, the campfire was functioning better as a camp*smoker* and if they'd needed to send a smoke signal to someone, well, they would've been set.

Too bad smoke signals had stopped being a thing like 150 years ago.

"Are you okay with Levi coming with us on the hike?" Georgia asked, her finely arched eyebrows creased with concern. For the hundredth time, Tenny sighed inwardly as she looked at her cousin. She really was pretty and would be upgraded to knockout status if she took more than five minutes on her appearance every morning. Her naturally thin eyebrows, her beautiful clear eyes, cheekbones Tennessee would kill for…some people just wasted their potential.

"It'll be fine," she told her pretty-but-not-as-pretty-as-she-could-be cousin. "He was just being a… a guy," she said, waving her hand around dismissively. "And he's right. I should stop caring so much about what other people think. I just…it's easier said than done. Also, he can certainly say things like that in a less dickish tone of voice."

Before they could rehash his comments in great detail, dissecting every one of them down to the nth degree, Moose and Levi showed up on the edge of camp, slightly sweaty from their hike from the lake.

Tenny's eyes were automatically drawn towards Levi, the dappled sunlight hiding and then highlighting his cheekbones and heavy eyebrows. For the thousandth time, she wondered how on earth her cousin could've possibly picked Moose over Levi. Not that she was complaining – Georgia had saved her from a lifetime of unhappiness – but *seriously!* Looking at the two guys side by side…once you got past the fact that they looked enough like each other that they could've been brothers, it wasn't hard to see who was the *real* heart stopper of the bunch.

Moose was handsome, sure, but Levi…Levi was at a whole other level. He had the kind of good looks that deserved a warning sign to be attached to his chest at all times. *May cause heart palpitations. Proceed with caution.*

"You guys ready?" Moose asked as Levi poured water over the campfire, finally putting it out of its misery. Georgia grabbed four backpacks from the bed of the truck with water hoses and snacks already packed inside of them – she was entirely *too* organized some days – and handed them out, while Levi and Tenny studiously avoided each other's eyes. Tenny busied herself with the straps on the backpack, trying to pretend that getting them *just right* was a terribly difficult ordeal.

Finally, Moose and Georgia took off down a side trail that Tenny hadn't noticed before, so slowly, dutifully, she followed along behind them. They never let go of each other's hands, and even kept sneaking kisses from each other. *Blech.* Did they have to be so lovey-dovey all the time? It was like hanging out with 14-year-olds who'd just learned how much fun it was to kiss.

As they hiked higher and higher up into the hills, she began to work up a sweat, even in the cooler mountain air. She took a drink off the hose attached to her Camelbak with a happy sigh. All right, maybe her cousin's need to be prepared down to the nth degree was useful after all. Tenny knew *she* certainly couldn't have gone on this trip by herself. She'd packed her favorite pillow, 20 changes of clothing, her hair dryer, curling iron, straightener, makeup, and the only pair of tennis shoes she owned as her sole provisions for this trip.

And, let's be real, the only reason she owned a pair of tennis shoes was because she'd bought them a couple of years ago when Georgia had pestered her into running with her, telling her that she'd grow to love the sport.

Tenny looked down at her virtually brand-new shoes with a small chuckle to herself. She'd gone running with Georgia once. After that, she pretended she'd sprained her ankle for weeks on end, until Georgia finally gave up pestering her.

Running had involved sweating and exertion, two of Tennessee's least favorite things. She had not, in fact, grown to love the sport.

It was one of the few times when Georgia Rowland had been dead wrong about something. This trip being the second time that happened. *Come along and have fun with us!* she'd said. *Levi will love it!* she'd said.

Tenny laughed to herself without humor. No, this was one time when Georgia was *dead* wrong.

"What're ya laughing about?" Levi asked, his deep voice rumbling through her like a freight train aimed straight at her. It was the first words he'd spoken since they'd taken off walking, and they startled her. She'd *almost* managed to forget he was walking there alongside her.

Almost.

"Nothing. Inside joke." She waved her hand

dismissively. She really didn't want to have to explain to Levi about Georgia's obsession with running, and Tennessee's obsession with not running, and how she'd come prepared for this camping trip like a toddler could be relied upon to prepare themselves for a trip to the North Pole. Left to her own devices, she would've starved to death, possibly before or maybe after she froze to death.

And anyway, he didn't really care about any of that, she was sure. Who'd care about something like that about her? *Don't bore your boyfriend*, she could hear her mother say. *Always focus on him. People like to talk about themselves. No one wants to hear about you.*

"Do you mind?" Levi asked abruptly, apropos of absolutely nothing. She glanced over at him, confused. "About Moose and Georgia dating, I mean?" he clarified.

The question was so startlingly ridiculous, it made her laugh. "Absolutely not," she declared firmly. Without saying a word to each other, they instinctively slowed their pace, letting the lovebirds get far ahead of them. It just didn't seem right to talk about them within hearing range. "I've been trying for years to figure out how to get out of that whole disaster," she said, once she was sure they couldn't hear what was being said. "I'd never been so happy as I was the night that Moose told me he wanted to break things off. I thought he'd come over to propose to me, and if he had, I probably would've thrown up all over his shoes, right before saying yes. It was…awful. The whole thing."

"Why would you say yes if you didn't want to marry him?" Levi asked, looking at her aghast. No, not aghast – he looked positively horrified, like she'd just started detailing her plans for human sacrifices under the next full moon. "I mean, isn't that a slogan – 'Just say no'?"

She jerked to a halt, the anger building up inside of her.

She wanted to knee him in the nuts.

She wanted to storm away like she had before but she was *supposed* to be participating in this damn hike.

So instead, she looked him straight in the eye and said icily, "It sure would be nice to live in a world where everything is so damn black and white. Never having anyone have any control over me; never doing anything I didn't want to do. Just live footloose and fancy free. Yeah, it sure would be nice to be *you.*"

She crossed her arms over her chest defensively and brushed past him, following her cousin and her former boyfriend, tears of frustration building up in the corners of her eyes.

She hated crying when she was angry. She wasn't sad – she was *pissed*. There was a difference, dammit. Too bad her eyeballs didn't know it.

Right then, she thought about the one thing she had left behind at her house – her knife. She'd left it behind intentionally, but the urge in that moment… she wanted her knife in her hand.

Levi grabbed her arm, jerking her to a stop and spinning her in a half circle to stare up at him. He could obviously overpower her so she decided that rather than fight him, she'd just glare at him like death couldn't come fast enough. The jackass deserved it.

Her mother's training – years of being taught to "act like a lady" and not let someone get under her skin…it was falling to pieces around him.

It wasn't a development that Tenny exactly saw as progress.

"I'm sorry," he said stiffly. "I'm not used to people caring about what I do. My dad…he couldn't give a shit about me. If I'm not bringing him Pabst Blue Ribbon beer, then I'm worthless to him. I quickly figured out as a kid that the less I was underfoot, the better. My old man…he wasn't exactly the doting type."

She nodded, wiping discretely at the corner of her eyes, wanting to get rid of the telltale wetness that'd pooled there. "We're like the three bears," she said bitterly. "My parents care too much—" *if you can count smothering and controlling to be caring*, "your parents cared too little, but Georgia's parents are just right. Do you know how many times I wished I'd been born to Shirley and Carl Rowland? To have them as parents…"

She shook her head ruefully and began wandering back down the trail again, this time her steps a little slower. A little less pissed. She was still uptight inside, wound up like an eight-day clock, but she tried to let the anger and resentment go.

People didn't understand what it was like to be the oldest daughter of Robert and Roberta Rowland. She needed to cut them some slack. She needed—

"You'd want to be the child of Carl Rowland, the *younger* brother?" Levi asked incredulously, breaking into her thoughts as his long strides caught him up to her and then he began matching her, step for step. "But...but they live in that 1970s shoebox of a house," he protested, "and they both work at the school district. I mean, just think about everything you'd give up—"

Which was when she spun in a half circle and stormed back down the path towards camp yet again.

Forget it. He was a blithering idiot and there was no hope for him and she was sick to death of trying to get it through his thick skull that living in a mansion didn't automatically solve all her problems.

No, not even anywhere close to it.

CHAPTER 11

LEVI

*L*EVI STUTTERED TO A STOP. *What the hell…?*

He spun around to face back down the trail, where Tennessee's swinging blonde braid marked her progress back towards camp. One minute he'd been asking her perfectly logical questions, and the next minute, he was talking to no one at all and she was storming off again.

Did she pull this stunt all the time, or was he the only "lucky" one in her orbit? He didn't remember her being this prickly before. Had she changed and he just hadn't noticed?

He chased her back down the path, letting Moose and Georgia continue on without him. They probably wouldn't even notice for another half hour that half their group had disappeared.

He grabbed Tenny's arm and jerked her to a stop. "What the hell is your problem?" he demanded. Her blue-green eyes were glowering up at him, dark and stormy and angry as a wet cat. "Who pissed in your Cheerios this morning?"

"Hey, you're the one who told me to stop caring about what other people think. Well, I'm starting with you." She shrugged off his hand and kept on going down the path.

He hurried after her, his long legs eating up ground, and this time, he got a better grip on her, spinning her in a circle to look him in the eye again. Except, this time she was refusing to; instead she was staring at the ground, her cheeks flushed a brilliant pink.

"I'm sorry," he said gruffly.

She snorted her disbelief.

He took a few deep breaths. "I'm sorry," he said again, softer this time. How many times had he already apologized to her? It seemed like half the words he'd said on this camping trip were, "I'm sorry." It wasn't something he liked doing, that was for damn sure, but there was something about Tenny that meant he was constantly shoving his foot into his mouth. He never knew what was going to set her off, and even if he didn't understand some of her frustration, a part of him felt bad for causing it anyway.

But despite his 1938th apology this trip, she still just stood there, the seconds ticking by until he began to wonder if she was simply going to pretend he didn't exist until he finally left her alone, and maybe he deserved that but it didn't mean he had to like—

"You're not the first person to think that being rich solves every problem," she finally said, speaking so softly that he found himself stooping to hear her better. "It doesn't. I've been rich all my life and I have more problems than ten other people put together. So yeah, I'd *much* rather be the daughter of Carl and Shirley Rowland than Robert and Roberta Rowland. Maybe Carl didn't inherit all the money, but he also didn't inherit all of the assholishness either, so…" She trailed off, shrugging.

She still wasn't meeting his eye, but he hardly noticed that as he stared off over her shoulder. What she was saying just didn't make sense to him. The only people who said that money didn't matter were the people who had loads of it. When he'd grown up having to earn every dime he could to keep himself clothed and fed, when he'd had to do work far beyond his years just to keep from starving to death because the only thing that mattered to his father was where could he get his next case of Pabst beer?

Yeah, money meant a hell of a lot.

"You only say that because you've never been without money," he said softly, trying to point out the obvious without pissing her off again. "If you don't think that money matters, try going two weeks without using any money from your parents. Then we can talk again about what matters and what doesn't."

"I can't do that!" she protested, her eyes finally snapping back up to his. "I don't have a job! How am I supposed to—"

"Exactly my point," he broke in. "How many other 26 year olds do you know who don't work at all, and just live at home, mooching off their parents?"

At the word "mooching," her spine stiffened so fast, she resembled nothing so much as a human porcupine in that moment. She was pissed again. It was contagious, and Levi instantly found himself pissed, too.

The tentative truce had lasted just moments, and then it was gone.

"Is there *anything* I can do to prove to you that I'm not a spoiled rotten child?" she ground out.

"Nope," he said, his mouth popping the *p* in exaggeration. "Not a damn thing."

Crack.

Her open palm smacked against his cheek so hard, his ears were ringing from it. This time, when she stormed back down the path towards camp, he didn't follow her. Instead, he cut off through the woods and took a shortcut over to the lake. He didn't have his fishing pole on him, but at least down at the lake, he could be by himself. He needed some space from Tennessee – the most annoyingly beautiful, spoiled rotten human being he'd ever met.

Why was she getting under his skin like this? He rubbed his jaw ruefully as he walked. He'd known Tenny all his life – they'd all graduated from high school together and being Georgia's cousin and Moose's girlfriend, he hadn't exactly somehow overlooked her – but she'd always been on the cusp of marrying Moose, so he hadn't ever looked at her as being more than that.

She'd been knock-out gorgeous her whole life, even through the awkward teenage years when everyone else looked like a potato that'd contracted the chicken pox, covered in red acne on every conceivable surface.

So yeah, being in love with her would've been like being in love with a Greek goddess.

Equally as gorgeous; equally as untouchable; equally as unlikely to result in a relationship.

Now, she seemed to be *right there* all the time, and equally as frustrating, she seemed to be completely ignorant of what a blessing it was to be rich. To have the kind of money that she'd always had…it was life changing.

Even now, making good money as a TIG welder, there was a part of Levi that felt like it'd never be enough. He could never have enough in savings "just in case." He could never add enough to his retirement fund to ensure he didn't end up eating dog food when he retired. He couldn't pay his mortgage down fast enough – owing money to the bank on that balance was slowly eating away at his insides, and hell, even after he paid it off, he'd still always owe taxes to the government for it.

He could still somehow end up penniless, living on the streets.

The fact that Tennessee didn't know that fear? It made her completely ignorant of what the *real* world was like, and for some reason he couldn't begin to name, that bothered the hell out of him.

He picked up a rock from the shoreline and tried to skip it across the water but it instead sank with a splash, sending ripples through the still water.

She was a spoiled rotten child and he shouldn't care that she didn't know what the world was really like.

He just didn't know how to stop.

CHAPTER 12

TENNESSEE

S O DINNER WAS...FUN.

And by "fun," she meant the most torturous thing she'd ever lived through. After their fight on the trail – well, and their *other* fight on the trail – she and Levi weren't exactly on speaking terms. Georgia had tried to pry the story out of Tenny but she'd refused to talk about it. She knew if she told Georgia, then Georgia would tell Moose, and for all she knew, Moose would tell Levi.

And if she wanted to talk to Levi, then by damn, she'd talk to Levi. But she didn't, so she wasn't talking to anyone at all.

After the quietest dinner humanity had ever suffered through, and Tennessee was even counting the Rowland Family Sunday Dinners in there, Georgia and Tennessee cleaned up while the guys built up the fire to a roar that lit up the world for miles around, or at least, it seemed like it. Happily, this time it seemed more flame than smoke, a real improvement in Tenny's opinion.

During the whole washing up, Georgia kept sending her sidelong glances. Tenny knew it was just killing her not to ask yet again what was going on, but Tennessee didn't say a word to her. If she wanted to talk, she would.

But she didn't, so she wouldn't.

After dishes were done and Tenny and Georgia went over to the fire to settle down into the two remaining camp chairs, Levi ducked inside the tent and came back out carrying a small guitar. He must've stuffed it into his duffel bag when he brought it up here, since she surely would've noticed him carrying a guitar case out of his house when Moose had picked him up. After a few practice strums, he began singing and the anger swirling around inside of Tenny melted just the tiniest bit.

Tiniest, itsiest bit.

Turned out, Levi's singing was as gorgeous as his face, which was really saying something. Deep and melodious and husky, he was singing some song she'd never heard before about love and heartache, and how sometimes, love was worth giving everything else up for, even life itself.

Yeah, it was a cheesy love song, but...

They caught gazes and in the dancing flames of the firelight, she couldn't shake the feeling that he was singing those words to her. Which just crazy. He thought she was a spoiled brat, and she thought he was an asshole. He was *not* singing a love song (cheesy or not) to her.

Not

Possible

Soon, the stars were popping out on the deep, dark sky overhead, and Moose and Georgia were saying their goodnights and heading for the tent. Tennessee knew better than to follow them, even though this new Levi was making her wish she could. She liked Levi better when she thought he was an asshole. It was better that way. Less dangerous. This Levi…he made her want to tell him her thoughts. Tell him what she wanted in life, and how – even more scarily – she didn't really know what she wanted in life.

She couldn't blame her parents from holding her back if she didn't even know what she wanted to do. Right?

Probably.

"What are you thinking?" he asked softly.

He'd stopped playing. When had he stopped playing?

"That I don't know what I want to do with my life," she admitted. It was dark and the firelight was cozy and the singing had been soft and sweet…it all conspired together to make her feel safe. Safe enough to tell someone the truth.

Even if she would regret it later.

"You mean, you don't know what you want to do as your career?" he asked, his normally dark eyes completely unreadable in the firelight. She could only tell that they were trained on her.

But what did he think about her?

And for the millionth time, why did she care?

She pushed those thoughts away for the moment, choosing to focus on his question.

"I guess…?" she said finally. "Honestly, I was never meant to have a career. I was meant to marry Moose and have ten little Garretts and throw dinner parties. I didn't have a purpose other than that. Now, none of that is going to happen and even though I'm glad, it's also a little scary. And I have no idea why I'm telling you this."

That last part just slipped out and she clapped her hand over her mouth, mortified. Levi shrugged and then focused on the first part of her statement, ignoring her inadvertent admission. *Thank God.*

"Well, your career can be whatever you want it to be," he said, his dark eyes flashing with the flames of the campfire. "You can be or do whatever you want."

She laughed scoffingly at that. "C'mon, that's what elementary school teachers tell their students," she chided him. "Like the idea that any of us could become president of the United States. It's just a fairytale. Think about it. Could I actually become president? Or…or…a welder?" she asked, naming the most outrageous idea she could think of. She probably had a better chance of becoming president than she did of becoming a welder, honestly. "Can you just see it now? Flamethrower in my hand, sparks going everywhere?"

He laughed, his deep chuckle making her feel things in parts of her body that she preferred to pretend didn't exist. "I like the fact that you think I use a flamethrower to weld with! That makes my job seem a lot more exciting than it really is."

"Don't you use a flamethrower to weld with?" She'd seen welding happen before, when she'd gone down to the shop to ask her father a question and had seen a worker over in the corner, sparks going every which way like there was a 4th of July celebration happening just for the Rowland family.

"Nope. In fact, the kind of welding that I specialize in – TIG welding – uses light in the parts of the spectrum that are almost invisible to the human eye. If you watched me work, you would hardly be able to see a thing and might think I was just pretending to be doing something. There are other kinds of welding – MIG welding and stick welding – that are visually a lot more exciting."

"Oh." She felt stupid. She had no idea that there were different types of welding. She hated feeling stupid. She instinctually wanted to pull back – change topics or go to bed or something – but she forced herself to be a little vulnerable instead.

Just a little bit.

"I didn't know there were different kinds of welding," she admitted. "What's the difference?"

There. That didn't kill you.

Not yet, anyway.

"Well, in order to be a welder, you really have to know how to weld everything, so I can do stick welding *and* MIG welding *and* TIG welding. But I specialize in TIG welding, which is just a fancy way to say that I can weld aluminum."

"Welding aluminum is different than welding other kinds of metal?" Her head hurt. How was she the daughter of a farmer and yet knew absolutely nothing about welding? Or farming, for that matter?

Because your parents have kept you inside of the house, playing the piano and putting together menus.

"Oh yeah. Aluminum welding is a beast. It's like going from college basketball to the NBA. It's a totally different level of difficulty. There's this oxide coating that makes welding two pieces of aluminum together a real bitch–I mean, really hard to do." His face flushed, and she could tell he was embarrassed to have said a swear word in front of her.

Which just meant that he didn't know Robert Rowland at all.

"Swear words don't offend me, I promise," she told him dryly. "If they did, I would've spent roughly 98.2% of my life offended. Have you *met* my father?"

He laughed a little, but she could tell that he wasn't convinced. "Well anyway, so no, no flamethrower at work. And honestly, you *could* be a welder." At her snort of derision – *Mother would kill me if she heard me making such an unladylike noise* – he hurried on. "I'm not shitti–I'm not kidding you. There are female welders out there. And carpenters. And firefighters. And—"

She cut him off before he could name another 50 male-dominated professions. The "You can be anything you want to be" speech was cute, and completely impractical. "Speaking of being a firefighter," she said smoothly, "how did you end up on the Sawyer City Fire Department? One day, you and Moose were just suddenly on the fire crew. All I could think was that I'd graduated from high school with you two, so knowing that you would be the ones to save me from a burning building…it was a little weird, to say the least."

"Weird?" he gasped in mock outrage. "Are you doubting my ability to sweep you off your feet and carry you around?"

Her eyes flicked to his bulging muscles, highlighted by the slowly fading flames of the campfire, and swallowed hard. "No," she said in a strangled whisper. She cleared her throat. "No, I don't doubt that. I just…firefighters were always older than me growing up, so it was strange when suddenly, they were the same age as me."

He shrugged. "Well, I joined because of money, honestly," he admitted. "I know you don't like to talk about it, but money does make the world go round and—"

"I never said that I don't like to talk about money, and I've never said that money wasn't helpful," she broke in, anger on the rise again. Was Levi always this dense, or just on days that ended in Y? "My point is simply that it doesn't solve every problem you encounter in life. There are a whole *shit* ton," she stressed the swear word just because she could, "of problems out there that money does not help with at all. Just because my parents are rich doesn't mean that I live this perfect life without a care or stress in the world! That's not how it works. But is money useful? Of course it is. Any idiot with two brain cells to rub together could tell you that. But it isn't a magic potion."

She was back to glaring at him again and had half a mind to go to bed right then, whether Moose and Georgia were done going at it or not, when Levi held up his hands in surrender. "You're right," he said quietly. "You're right. I've been poor for so long, it's easy for me to think of it as fairy dust, making everything in sight even better. But," he heaved a sigh, "it doesn't make life perfect."

Her shoulders relaxed just a little. "No, it really doesn't," she whispered. She straightened up, suddenly feeling vulnerable. She didn't want to make this about her. "If it did make life perfect, do you think we'd have any celebrities ever commit suicide? If money equalled perfection, then no one in Hollywood would ever kill themselves," she pointed out. The cuts on her upper arm pulsated for just a moment but she ignored that, too. "Anyway, you were telling me about joining the fire department, and how the money was your enticement?"

He nodded, apparently willing to go along with her blunt hint to leave their money discussion behind. "You know that Rocky didn't pay Moose well when he was an employee at the John Deere dealership, always telling him that he was putting 'sweat equity' into the business in preparation for taking it over. Well, Moose had worked on the fire engine a couple of times at the dealership since it's hard to find a mechanic's shop that's large enough to repair something like that, you know? Tractor dealerships are one of the few places that have the equipment to work on shit that big. Anyway, one time as the old fire chief was picking it up after repairs were done, he mentioned to Moose that he could volunteer and make money on the side if he wanted to. We talked it over and decided what the hell, why not. It was a better side gig than working the drive-thru at McDonalds."

"But, there is no McDonalds in Sawyer," Tenny pointed out, confused.

"Exactly! And now you can see why fighting fires was a better side gig than that," he answered, his white teeth flashing in the firelight.

She laughed and shook her head. "All right, true enough. So you two decided to start risking life and limb for a few extra bucks?"

"Well, honestly, no one ever says, 'I can't wait to go fight that fire over there and die in the process!' You like to think that you'll be able to do it without dying; at least, we all hope so. Unfortunately, the old chief – did you know Chief Horvath?"

She shook her head mutely. She knew *of* him, of course, but considering that he was older than her father, they hadn't exactly hung out together on the weekends and painted each other's toenails.

"He wasn't the best at keeping up with paperwork or budgets or training or things like that. Jaxson, the new fire chief who came in at the beginning of this year…damn, he's been such an improvement. I'd only ever worked under Horvath so I guess I didn't really know what I was missing until Jaxson took over. We have trainings regularly now, he's working hard on getting our equipment upgraded, he's trying to get the hydrants around town fixed…if your house caught fire, there's a pretty good chance that I could actually get you out alive. There's still a long ways to go – don't even get me started on our radio system – but at least, now we're making moves in the right direction."

He lapsed into silence and she realized with a start that he'd just said more words to her in a row than he ever had before in the history of their friendship. He wasn't normally one to talk a whole lot – he was pretty quiet in general, except when telling her all about how wonderful her own life was, of course – so that many words, strung together into a paragraph…

She wasn't sure if it should freak her out to hear him talk that much, or make her feel privileged.

Before she could decide which, he spoke up again.

"Maybe your parents did raise you to be a china doll – to sit in the corner and look pretty – but Tenny? You can do so much more than that. You can *be* more than that. You can be whatever you want to be. Just look at me. I should be holding down a stool over at the bar, throwing back beers all day and telling anyone who'll listen about how horrible my life is, and how no one cares about me. That is, if I was gonna be just like my daddy.

"But instead, I make pretty good money as a welder and I have a real nice job with good benefits and I own my own house. Well, it'll be mine once I pay the bank off, anyway. And my truck is *my* truck. I paid it off and no one can take it from me. Rocky Garrett may be a bastard to Moose, but he's changed my life. Believing that I could be anything I wanted to be, he made my life possible. You're smart and you're beautiful. You can be whatever you want to be. Don't let anyone tell you otherwise."

She nodded tremulously, surprised by his faith in her. She wasn't entirely sure that she believed everything he'd just said, but the fact that he'd been willing to say *any* of that to her, a beauty queen who really was supposed to be nothing more than a china doll to sit up on a shelf and then ignore…

It was fooling her into thinking that maybe he was right.

That maybe she could be more than just the future mom to a passel of children; the hostess of grand parties; the player of pianos.

But *what*? She tried to think of something that got her blood pumping – something that would get her up in the morning with a smile on her face. She could…

She could…

Huh.

It was kinda scary that she couldn't come up with a single thing that she was just dying to do. Even in the now very dim lighting of the campfire, Levi must've been able to read her expression because he whispered, "You don't have to figure it all out tonight. It's late and it's getting cold." He pushed himself to his feet. "Plus, the grunts, groans, and screams of ecstasy have faded away, so we're probably okay to go into the tent now."

She let out a snort of laughter at that, and Levi looked up from the campfire, where he'd been carefully pouring water over the flames. "Did Tennessee Rowland just *snort*?!" he asked in a dramatic whisper, clearly finding this development hilarious. "What would your mother say…"

"Let's not find out," Tennessee whispered back, feeling delightfully naughty.

After the fire was well and truly out, they made their way over to the tent where Moose and Georgia were snoring away, and got changed into their PJs under the cover of darkness. It felt weird to strip out of her clothes and put on her PJs with Levi *right there*, even if it was so dark, he'd need night vision goggles to see anything.

Plus, her PJs were not anything to get excited about, unless he had an owl fetish. This particular pair of fleece PJs were covered in adorable fluorescent pink and lime green owls, and they buttoned all the way up to her neck. She'd always struggled with sleeping – she got cold way too easily and could never sleep while she was an ice block – so her PJ repertoire was more suited to a 10-year-old girl than a 26-year-old woman.

This had never been a problem before, considering she'd never slept with a guy in the same room as her, but as she crawled into her sleeping bag, trying to warm up inside of its cottony embrace, she realized that for once, she wanted different PJs.

And she wanted to model those PJs for Levi.

And they needed to have significantly less owls and significantly more lace.

And preferably not button up to the bottom side of her chin.

She fell asleep and somewhere in the middle of the night, their hands clasped together and she slept better than she had in a really long time.

Maybe her whole life.

CHAPTER 13

LEVI

*L*EVI LET OUT a huge yawn while scratching his balls, staring blearily into the fridge. He really needed to make something to eat for dinner, but that seemed complicated as hell so in the end, he settled for a loaf of bread in a can – aka, a beer.

He sat down on the couch with another huge yawn, grabbing the remote from the coffee table and blindly turning on a documentary about…something. The Titanic? Baseball? He wasn't quite sure. After getting home from their camping trip late last night, it'd been back to reality that morning when his alarm had unforgivingly gone off at 6:45 in the morning.

He'd been out of it all day, even screwing up a weld when the memory of Tenny stretching flashed across his mind, her every curve perfectly shown off by her thin t-shirt…

Yeah, that weld had been total shit.

He settled down further onto his lumpy couch. He should really take a shower or something, but he'd go do that in just a minute…just a minute and then he'd go clean…

Knock knock

The unexpected sound jerked him into an upright position on the couch.

What just happened? His mind scrambled to remember.

There was a loud noise.

Oh, someone had knocked on the door. He remembered that now.

He squinted across the room at the clock ticking on the wall. 7:22 pm. He really was turning into an old man if he was falling asleep at seven in the evening.

He pushed himself off the couch and stumbled over to the door. Dollars to donuts, it was Moose wanting to hang out and play video games for a little while before going home. Levi could definitely get behind spending some quality time with his best—

"Tennessee?" he said, staring down at her in shock. He ran his hands through his hair and then rubbed at his eyes, trying to push away his sleepiness. He opened them up again. Yup, she was still here. "What are you doing here?" His eyes ran up and down her body, taking in her holey jeans and grungy shirt, and the handkerchief over her hair, which she had in two braids down her back.

His eyes went back up to hers. *What the hell?*

"You said I could be anything I wanted to be and could do anything I wanted to do," she reminded him. "So, I decided I want to learn how to weld, and I'm here to learn."

"Oh."

If she'd just announced that she wanted to take up pole dancing, he wouldn't have been more surprised. When he'd said that she could be a welder, he'd meant it of course — she was physically capable of it — but he also didn't expect it to actually happen.

"Right. Of course." He stepped back from the doorway, belatedly welcoming her into his house. "You, uhh, you wanna start right now?"

"I'd love to," she said with a grin. "I've only got so long before my parents come looking for me."

"Your parents don't know you're here?" he asked, panic welling up inside of him again. They didn't know she'd slept in the same tent as him; they didn't know she was at his house…this seemed like a *real* good way to get his ass fired from his job. One word from her dad to his boss and his ass was grass.

"I told them I was volunteering down at the food clinic, which if they knew anything at all, they'd know was only open on Wednesday evenings, not on Tuesday evenings. But, since my parents have all of the altruistic impulses of a modern-day Scrooge, they'll never realize the truth." She shrugged. "So, are you ready to teach me?"

"Yeah, of course." He looked down at his filthy clothes and ran his hands through his hair again.

Even in her trashed clothes and braided hair, Tenny looked ready to grace the cover of a magazine, maybe a DIY one, while he looked…well, he probably looked exactly like what he was: A kid born on the wrong side of the tracks. "Ummm…let's start on the easy stuff. I've got a MIG welder in the back – an old piece of shit but it does the job when I need to do a small project." He winced when he realized that he'd cursed in front of her again but she was just smiling at him, waiting patiently for him to lead the way, seemingly unaware – or at least uncaring – about his cursing.

It wasn't that she'd ever protested about hearing swear words from him or anyone else, it was just those huge blue-green eyes, paired with the longest eyelashes he'd ever seen…it made her look like an angel.

And you just shouldn't swear around angels.

They stepped out onto his back patio which, with her in tow, he suddenly realized needed to be cleaned. He'd left some beer cans behind the last time he'd sat out there with Moose, and dead leaves were piled up in the corners, needing to be swept out…

She put her hand on his arm. "I'm here to learn how to weld, not to critique your housekeeping skills," she said quietly, "but for the record, you actually have a pretty clean house for a guy."

"'For a guy'?" he repeated, laughing. "Is there a compliment in there somewhere?"

"Absolutely." She winked at him.

Teasing.

Tennessee was teasing him.

Tennessee wasn't a stranger to him, obviously. Over the years, they'd gone on a hell of a lot of double dates together, but back then, she'd been matched up with Moose and Levi had been matched up with Georgia.

But in all that time, he'd never seen her *teasing* someone else. She'd always been beautiful, and nice, and everyone had wanted to be around her, but she'd never been *funny*.

Was she coming out of her shell?

Or was he just seeing what he wanted to see?

He shook it off and made himself focus.

"Safety first, right?" he started. "The good news is, I tend to hoard helmets and gloves just in case I lose a pair or break something, so although I'm not gonna promise they're the best lookin' things on the face of the planet, I at least have a set for each of us." He rummaged through the pile of crap that he kept meaning to organize "someday" and plucked out two pairs of gloves and a welding helmet for each of them.

He gave her the nicer ones of the sets, and was gratified that she didn't turn her nose up at them, despite their…less-than-stellar appearance.

He put his helmet on his head, keeping the shield flipped up, and, turning so his back was facing her, he showed her how to adjust the knob on the back of the helmet until it was snug up against his skull, but not painful. "Okay, your turn," he said, supervising her tightening of her helmet as she turned her back to him. Her blonde hair was shining, even under the cover of the back porch, making it hard for him to really concentrate. He wanted to touch the shimmering strands but dammit all, that'd be creepy as hell. He scrounged together a modicum of self-restraint and forced his hands to stay by his sides.

Once they got all of their gear in place, he found an old rusty piece of angle iron that he'd kept meaning to throw out. It'd be perfect to learn on. He set up two sawhorses and then laid a piece of plywood on top of them to create a flat work surface, with the angle iron resting on top of that.

He usually didn't weld much at his house, but he didn't want to make a special trip out to the shop with her in tow, so just for tonight, he'd ignore the fact that welding on top of plywood would probably guarantee that the plywood would be on fire at some point.

Well, what was a little learning without a few flames, right?

He started out by showing her how to draw a bead down the metal, how to angle the head, how to hold the welder, and then let her go at it.

The first round was...well, chicken scratch, to put it mildly; the industry phrase for "total shit." There was no worse insult than to refer to someone's welding as being "chicken scratches" and Tenny's first round was pretty much the textbook definition of it.

Huh.

"How did I do?" she asked eagerly, pushing her

visor up on her head. He hesitated for a moment; he didn't want to burst her bubble. It was a good first try, after all. Just not somethin' anybody but your momma would appreciate.

"It's…a good start," he told her truthfully. "Next time, you need to move a little slower. See how there's metal spatterings all over the place? You were moving too quick – impatient to get on with it."

She nodded, biting her lower lip in concentration as she looked down at the rusty piece of metal. He felt his groin tighten at the sight. He'd never seen a more gorgeous, enticing sight in all his life than Tennessee, wearing a welding helmet and biting her lower lip.

He had visions of her in bed, wearing nothing at all. He groaned.

"Are you okay?" she asked worriedly. "Did I screw up that bad?"

"Oh no, you're good," he assured her. This was *not* the time to be sporting a boner. Too bad his dick didn't agree. "Eyes," he said, and she obediently pulled her helmet down along with him, and then began drawing another line of bead along the metal. He watched her progress intently, realizing that this was just about the most fun he'd ever had welding. Not that they were messing around – messing around and welding were two things that just didn't mix – but simply being there with her…it was a damn sight more fun than working with Farmer John staring over his shoulder.

The torch turned off and she pushed her helmet

back up on her head. "Does this look any better?" she asked. He quickly pushed his helmet up too, forcing himself to concentrate on something other than what Tenny looked like while biting her lower lip.

He looked down at the rusty metal and let out a surprised whistle. "Well, I'll be dipped in pig's shit," he said wonderingly.

"What? What's wrong?" she asked. "Did I screw it up?"

"This is why women make better welders than men," he told her bluntly. She looked at him, disbelieving. "Seriously. It took me a whole spool of wire to get that good. It took you five minutes."

"Are you pulling my leg?" she asked him, a little defensively.

"Tenny, I make jokes about a lot of things, but welding ain't one of them. You're a natural. Now, let's try a couple of other techniques…"

CHAPTER 14

TENNESSEE

*N*EERRRVVOOOUUUSSSS...

She drew in a deep breath, rubbing the palms of her hands on her jeans. She was on Levi's front porch yet again, but this time, he knew she was on the other side of the door. Well, he knew she was going to be on the other side of the door. Unless he'd been peeking out the front window when she pulled up, he probably didn't know she was there at that very moment.

Focus, Tennessee!

She'd spent the day watching YouTube videos on welding while hiding in her room, other than her two hours of required piano practice, of course. Someday, her parents were going to give up on her being a world-famous pianist, and if she was lucky, that day would be soon. But in the meanwhile, she could continue to play by their rules.

Ha. Play. She'd made a punny and hadn't even meant to.

She raised a trembling hand and knocked on the door, schooling her features into their normal bland expression. If she didn't show her nerves, then he wouldn't know they existed and as long as she had everyone else fooled, that was all that mattered. Right?

Right.

He opened up the front door, and today…

Her mouth went dry.

She'd surprised him yesterday, which she'd totally done on purpose, and he'd been filthy then from his long day at work. Strangely enough, though, he'd been filthy in a really sexy way. Not in a I-want-to-kiss-my-way-up-his-legs way – he'd had too much grease and dirt splattered on him for that – but in a I-am-a-man-and-can-take-care-of-you way.

Tennessee was an Idahoan through and through, even if she didn't always act like it, and a prissy man who wore business suits every day and had his fingernails buffed and manicured…no, thank you. She liked men who had dirt under their fingernails and knew how to swing a hammer.

Levi had been the very embodiment of that yesterday.

Today, he still had that vibe, but a cleaned-up version of it. The five o'clock shadow was gone, along with all of the grease and dirt, and his clothes didn't look like they'd been rescued out of the trashcan after a hobo ditched them there.

Not that they were fancy clothes – just jeans and a wife beater that read, "I flexed and the sleeves fell off" – but they were certainly cleaner than the ones he'd been wearing yesterday.

Overall, he was, quite literally, breathtaking.

She'd never really understood people being nervous around her because she was beautiful; she was just Tennessee and there wasn't a good reason to be nervous around *her*. But now that she was drooling over Levi, she suddenly had pity for people in that situation. To be around someone who looked like he'd just stepped off the pages of a magazine…

It was hard to keep from drooling.

"You were flexing, eh?" she said in lieu of a greeting, unable to tear her eyes away from his chest. His kissable, delectable chest. He made that shirt look way better than it had any right to.

He looked down at his shirt like he couldn't remember what it said, and then laughed. "This was a gag gift from Moose one year for Christmas. He dared me to wear it to school; I lost that dare. If I remember right, I ended up having to pay him back for losing by bringing over a case of beer, which we promptly drank together."

"So in other words, a terrible consequence?" she asked, laughing.

"Yeah, just awful," he said dryly. "Stores aren't supposed to sell alcohol to kids who are underage, of course, but everyone in town knows who my dad is, and they all knew that if I didn't bring back the beer, he'd beat my ass, so they'd sell me Pabst on the side. I just might've taken advantage of that a time or two in high school."

She threw back her head and laughed even harder. "Man, I must've missed all the fun parties," she said ruefully. "What the hell was I doing when y'all were getting drunk?"

"Practicing the piano?" he suggested.

"Yeah, probably."

They stared at each other for a moment, the laughter dying down between them.

"Oh, you should probably come in!" he said, stepping back from the door. "I didn't mean to keep you standing out here the whole time. You ready to get to work on welding right away?"

"Sure," she said. *Unless my other option is making out with you.*

She kept that thought to herself.

"Well, I thought I'd up the difficulty level today, since you did such a great job yesterday. I've never had anyone take to welding like you did, honestly. Like watching a duck take to water."

She blushed and shrugged. She was used to compliments ("Your hair is so beautiful!" "Your eyes are such an unusual aquamarine color." "You play the piano beautifully!") but Levi's compliments? They *meant* something to her. She knew how to make herself more beautiful with the use of makeup, sure, but the basic bone structure and features weren't something she got to choose when she was born. She didn't work hard in order to deserve them. They were just given to her, part of her DNA coding.

And piano…piano was a guilt-ridden anxiety-inducing disaster zone. She was good, sure, but she'd never be great and what was more, she didn't really *want* to be great. It certainly didn't register on her list of things to do that'd get her out of bed with a smile on her face, that was for damn sure.

But welding? It was all hers – it was her secret. Her parents didn't control it; didn't even know about it.

Some kids did drugs in order to rebel against their parents. Tennessee welded.

Her mother probably would prefer the drugs if given the choice.

"What are you smiling about?" Levi rumbled, looking up from getting the welder ready to go.

"That my first act of rebellion in my whole life is to weld metal together behind my parent's backs," she answered truthfully.

Which, the fact that she'd actually told him what she was thinking? That was its own form of rebellion. It'd been drilled into her since birth – no one cared what she thought. When asked questions, give blasé answers, and immediately change the subject back so it focused on the other person again. Women were to listen to men, not complain to them.

Sometimes, Tennessee had a hard time remembering which century she lived in.

"I do have to say that it is an...unusual form of rebellion," Levi said with a laugh. "Tattoos, drugs, alcohol...that's the normal way to rebel. Not welding. Okay, are you ready to give this a go?"

She nodded, pulling her helmet (the extra one he let her borrow) into place and pulled his leather gloves onto her hands. She had long fingers for a girl (something every piano teacher she'd ever had remarked upon) but they weren't wide, so the gloves were obnoxiously oversized. She needed to buy a small pair as soon as possible. Not being able to easily and fully control her fingers wasn't the ideal way to weld, for sure.

He stepped behind her so he could guide her arms, wrapping his long arms around her, easily embracing her smaller form. Their helmeted heads knocked together, which wasn't exactly the most romantic thing in the world, but the rest of his body...she could feel every square inch of him.

Speaking of the rest of him, she brushed against his hardened dick accidentally with her ass, and instantly sucked in a quick breath. Yeah, she could feel *every* square inch of him.

He backed away, yanking off his helmet and flipping off the welder.

"Tennessee," he began, but she pulled off her helmet and cut him off at the pass. Leaning up on her tiptoes, she pressed her mouth to his. He froze for a moment and then with a groan, he pulled her tight against his chest, crushing her against him, their hearts pounding together as his tongue swirled and dipped inside of her mouth.

She was kissing him. After years of lusting after him, the forbidden fruit that she wasn't allowed to touch because she was marrying Moose…he was right here. And he wanted her.

Breathing, thinking, analyzing…it was all swept away. It was just him and her and the desire to tear his clothes off with her teeth.

But finally, she forced herself to pull away. She was completely out of breath, like she'd just run one of those godawful marathons with Georgia, but this one was a *fun* marathon.

They were staring at each other, not blinking, trying to read each other's thoughts, when she broke the silence. "If you still think I'm nothing but a spoiled brat," she said softly, "then it's time to leave me alone and let me get on with my life. Neither of us are the kind of people to play games, so right now? The ball is in your court."

She spun on her heel, hurrying back through the house and out the front, back to her hot pink convertible VW Bug. She'd finally worked up the guts to tell Levi what she was really thinking – a *guy*, even – but after that…well, it was up to Levi if their relationship would move forward or not.

She drove off with the top down, pressing her fingers to her bruised lips the whole way home.

CHAPTER 15

LEVI

*H*E WAS STANDING on the imposing front steps of the Rowland home, yellow roses in one hand, his knuckles of the other hand posed over the door. He just needed to knock.

His hand hung there in mid-air.

Any minute now…

He wondered if he'd throw up on their peonies, and if he did, what he'd do after that. He could run off to Mexico and never talk to the Rowlands again. That was totally an option. He could pretend Idaho didn't exist, and just be a surfer bum on the beach and wear his hair in dreadlocks and learn Spanish.

In that moment, this plan seemed absolutely like a logical one, even if he didn't throw up on their peonies first. Maybe he should just leave for Mexico that night. Screw it – right now. Make a run for the border.

Then his hand was knocking, almost without his

knowledge or control, and after two raps on the door, he yanked it down, strangling the bouquet of roses with both hands for lack of something else to do. He couldn't make a run for it now – they would spot his truck driving off and know it was him.

He was stuck.

His breath was coming in short gasps.

He hadn't been this nervous since he had to give a history report in 4th grade on Lewis and Clark. Not exactly a comforting idea, considering that report ended prematurely with him puking into the teacher's trashcan.

"Hello?" Roberta Rowland said, opening the front door and peering out into the evening light. "Can I help you?" Her eyes flicked up and down him, bluntly assessing him. He'd worn his best pair of Wranglers – new, without a single hole in them – and a button-up shirt that he usually reserved for weddings. No tie because he didn't own one, and a beat-up pair of cowboy boots, but at least they weren't his work boots, right?

She didn't seem to appreciate his efforts, not if that look on her face was anything to go by.

"I'm here to see Tennessee," he said, his normally deep voice registering in the mid-range instead. For him, this was positively squeaky. He cleared his throat. "Is she home?"

She just stood there, openly studying him, clearly deciding whether to lie to him or not when they both heard Tennessee's voice behind her. "Levi! What a pleasant surprise," she said formally, ducking out past her mother's stiff body, which was when she spotted the roses in his hands. "Oh, beautiful!" she gasped, and this time, her voice didn't have that fake, Stepford Wives quality to it.

He realized in that moment that there were two Tennessees – the front that she showed the world, especially when her mother was there to witness the performance, and then the real Tennessee, the one he saw when it was just the two of them together.

He tucked that bit of information away along with her fluttering-hands tell for later contemplation.

"I heard that you loved yellow roses," he said, holding them out for her to take. She buried her face in them, breathing in deeply, and looked up at him, her blue-green eyes sparkling.

"Was it a certain Deere Garrett who told you that?" she asked a little breathlessly. It took him a moment – he so rarely heard Moose being called by his real name that he almost blurted out, "Who?" – and then it registered.

Your best friend, you dumbass.

"Well, he may have given me a hint or two," Levi said with a wink.

Mrs. Rowland cleared her throat loudly. Tennessee turned back to her, roses still tightly grasped in her hands. "Momma, this is Levi Scranton. He works for Rocky Garrett as the dealership's head welder. Levi, this is my momma, Roberta Rowland."

"Pleased to meet you," she said cooly, holding out

her hand to shake his, her fingers as limp and dead as three-day-old fish.

Levi was back to considering that run for the Mexican border. She looked about as pleased to meet him as she would be to find a dead horse's head on her front doorstep, Mafia-style.

Tennessee was undeterred. "Let's come inside and sit in the drawing room," she murmured to Levi, her Stepford-Wives persona firmly in place. Her mother, realizing that it would be much too rude to physically block his way into her house, finally moved off to the side, allowing them to enter.

Levi followed Tenny over the threshold and then all breathing stopped.

Dear Lord above, what had he gotten himself into?

In high school, on their numerous double dates, the four of them (Moose, Levi, Tennessee, and Georgia) had always ended up at Moose's house afterwards. It wasn't really a choice they contemplated but rather was just what happened. Rocky and Linda were like a second set of parents to Levi; they were Moose's parents; and they had a large basement where they let all of them hang out without much hovering, thus making it a damn ideal place to spend their Saturday nights.

Levi sure as hell didn't take anyone back to his house to just hang out. Even if his father had somehow started the evening being okay with the idea, it still would've ended with beer cans being thrown at their heads – empties or full ones – and being told to stop bothering him.

But because they'd always ended up back at the Garrett's house to hang out and watch movies, Levi had somehow never been inside of Tennessee's house. He'd seen the outside hundreds of times, waiting out in the car as Moose went in to fetch Tenny, or to drop her off afterwards, but inside?

It was even worse than he'd imagined.

Marble columns and fancy chairs that'd probably break just by him looking at them sideways and a giant-ass staircase that led up to the second floor that was so grand, it seemed like he could drive a team of horses up it, oh and don't forget the chandelier hanging from the ceiling that was quite literally dripping with gold and crystals and…

"C'mon, in here," Tenny said, grabbing his arm and pulling him into what must be the drawing room. She closed the double doors behind her quietly, and then spun around to look up at him, the formality gone, the happy Tennessee in its place. "You came for me!" she said with a huge grin, burying her face in the roses again. "It's been a couple of days. I thought maybe you'd decided…well, not to come for me."

It had been five days. Not that he'd been counting; he just happened to know that.

It'd taken him five days to screw up the courage to actually show up at the Rowland home.

Well, and to get a dozen yellow roses from Happy Petals. After quizzing Moose on what Tenny loved, he'd gone down and talked to Carla, enlisting her help in getting the most gorgeous, the most fragrant yellow roses in that she could get her hands on.

God bless Carla. Despite his obvious nerves, she'd walked him through the whole process without talking down to him once. There was a reason everyone in town loved Carla.

"It took me a while to get the roses," he finally settled on saying, leaving the rest out. She didn't need to know what a mess he'd turned into. Or the fact this house wasn't helping, not one bit.

"So does this mean that you see me as more than a spoiled rich brat?" she asked softly, staring up at him through the blooms she was still holding up to her face, almost like she was using them as a shield against the world…? He tucked that observation away for future contemplation also.

He hesitated before he answered, looking around the room they were in. There was a baby grand piano in the corner, and although he didn't exactly consider himself to be a connoisseur of pianos, grand or otherwise, it wasn't hard to make the educated guess that this piano probably cost more than his whole house did.

And that wasn't even taking into consideration the rugs on the hardwood floors – probably handwoven, imported from Persia or some such insanity – and another chandelier here in the drawing room, just slightly smaller than the one in the foyer…

She lowered the flowers until they were hanging

listlessly by her side. "Thank you for the roses," she said formally. "I find that I am quite busy this evening, though, so if I could see you out now…?"

She began to open the double doors back out into the foyer.

"No!" he said urgently, stopping her by putting his hand over hers. They both froze, the electricity arcing between them so violently, it was almost painful. "Please…your house is just…it's a lot to take in."

"I am not my parent's house," she said. No emotion. Her eyes were flat. She was hiding herself from him.

"I know." He drew in a deep breath. "I know. And I'm sorry. I know that for you, this is all normal…I just need you to give me a minute." He didn't know how to say, "Your family's money is smothering me alive" because what if she got angry about that? It seemed like the only time they saw eye to eye was when they *weren't* discussing money. "You're so much more than this house, or your parents," he said softly.

Her shoulders relaxed. Just a smidge. "Are you just saying what you think I want to hear?" The heartbreak in her voice hurt his heart. And he hated that. He hated having her be this serious and this worried.

"Well, yeah," he drawled ever-so-casually.

It took her a second to realize what he'd just said but before she could knee him in the nuts in retribution, he laughed. "I'm just kidding, of course," he said, reaching out and tucking a blonde strand behind her ear. "Believe me, if I could guess what it was that you wanted to hear, we'd be arguing a lot less often."

She glared at him for a moment and then shrugged. "Fair enough," she allowed primly. He laughed. She smirked a little. "Were you always this awful?" she asked him baldly. "Somehow, I don't remember you teasing Georgia this much in high school."

"That's because you and Moose were always too busy making out," he volleyed back.

"We were…we did not!" she contested hotly, her cheeks flaming a bright red.

A flustered Tennessee. It was almost as sexy as a lip-biting, welding-helmet-wearing Tennessee.

And that was really saying something.

"You ran out on me during our last welding lesson," he reminded her needlessly. He mostly just wanted to see her cheeks flush pink again, as she remembered what they'd been doing right before that lesson ended. "Didn't even give me the chance to show you the Fillit Weld."

"The Fillit Weld?" she repeated.

"Yeah. You use it to fill between two pieces of metal."

She laughed. "Very creative name," she said dryly.

"Welders never claimed to be creative," he reminded her. "All we do is weld giant machines back together when they break out in the field. Creativity isn't part of the equation."

"Oh, that reminds me!" she exclaimed. "Hold these – I'll be right back." She thrust the flowers into his hands and slipped out of the drawing room, closing the door behind her quietly.

While she was gone, Levi decided to wander around a bit, looking over the imposing bookshelves that lined every wall, figurines and ancient books and pictures of Tenny and her younger sister Virginia gracing every shelf. Tennessee had been a looker ever since she'd been born, as far as Levi could tell. He hadn't really appreciated it as a kid – girls were icky and had germs when they were seven, of course – but now, looking at her childhood pictures, he could see the Tenny she was going to grow up to be. Why didn't she become a supermodel instead of playing the piano? She was certainly gorgeous enough for it.

"So," she said breathlessly, hurrying back into the drawing room and pulling Levi's attention away from the pictures, "I've been working on these in the evening. I was trying to think of what I could weld together, and it came to me – what does every farmer out there have about a bajillion of? Old shovels. So I thought it'd be fun to make garden creatures out of them." She held the drawing notepad out to him.

He took it and began flipping through, his breath sucking in as he looked.

"Shit on a stick, Tenny, you're good," he murmured. "Bolts for eyeballs; shovels for heads; rebar for legs…it never would've occurred to me to do this." The creatures she'd drawn were quirky and fun and lively, almost jumping off the page. Mixed in were flowers, some monstrously large while others were life-sized.

"Well, it's just some sketches," she said, waving her hand dismissively. "But I don't know if I have the talent to actually create these in real life, you know?"

"Not just some sketches, Tenny," he said seriously. "I'm not kidding when I say that I'm not a very creative guy. I am good at fixing things; I'm not good at *making* things. It takes a different way of looking at the world to see a pile of scrap metal and come up with these creatures. I just see scrap metal that I can use to repair something if needed. Hey, you want to go weld with me?" he asked impulsively. That was *not* on the agenda for that evening; he'd been planning on wining and dining her. But after looking at these drawings…he had a feeling that she'd enjoy welding more. "But we need to do it out at my shop, not at my house."

"You have a shop?" she asked, surprised.

He nodded. "It's on the outskirts of town, over by the airport. I do repair jobs on the side for people, so I have a full shop where I can run saws and welders to my heart's content without pissing any neighbors off. It isn't much, but I have a whole pile of scrap metal that you could look through—"

"I'll be right back!" she broke in, not even waiting for him to finish. Clutching her drawing pad to her chest, she rushed out of the drawing room and up the stairs to where he assumed her bedroom was.

He looked around the drawing room again, the oppressiveness of it settling over him like a blanket made of lead. They were from two different planets, her and him, and every instinct in him told him to make a run for it before he got in over his head.

The problem was, he was already in over his head, and sinking fast.

CHAPTER 16

TENNESSEE

*T*ENNESSEE CLICKED to the next blog post, her head swimming from it all. She really should be taking notes, but honestly, she didn't know where to start. Although the internet was a marvelous thing in many ways, it also had its drawbacks – mainly, that nothing was organized. She could wander around in circles, picking up tips here and there, but this was such a major undertaking, she needed more than tips.

She needed a lifestyle makeover.

Books! Of course.

There were probably tons of books on how to become more frugal, with step-by-step guides.

With a big grin, she clicked over to Barnes and Noble and began filling her online shopping cart with title after title. She'd have them sent to Georgia's house so her parents wouldn't see the box and ask what it was; they'd long ago stopped paying attention to her credit card bill that they paid in full every month, but they would definitely notice a giant box of books showing up on the front doorstep.

Except…

She groaned. She was hopeless, she really was. Here she was, trying to learn how to be more frugal and she was going to be spending…she looked up in the corner of the screen – $172.49 to do it?

Was she ever going to stop thinking of money as the way to solve a problem? No wonder Levi had thought she was a spoiled brat.

Think, Tenny, think. How can you get these books without actually buying them? The idea of holding up a B&N and stealing the books flashed through her mind, and she laughed a little to herself. All right, so maybe a lifetime behind bars wasn't exactly a valid plan of action.

Oh! She could ask Georgia to buy them for her. Georgia would do it, especially when she heard what Tenny was wanting to learn about…

Urgh.

Turning into a mooch off her cousin really wasn't any better than being a mooch off her parents. Tennessee had been *pissed* when Levi had called her a mooch on that camping trip but she'd had the weeks since then to realize, like it or not, that he was right.

She hated to admit that – in fact, she still hadn't said it out loud and probably never would because admitting that he was right was just a downright awful idea, in her not-so-humble opinion – but she *had* been a mooch off her parents her whole life. Maybe it was excusable when she was a kid – not too many three year olds were required to earn their keep – but ever since she graduated from high school, and especially from college?

She could've started standing on her own two feet.

She just hadn't, and honestly, her attempts to start doing it now weren't exactly going well.

"The library!" she exclaimed, jumping up from her chair, and then she clapped a hand over her mouth. She hadn't meant to say that out loud, but of *course*! She could go down to the library and borrow the books from there – no payment needed, and no gun either. A lack of black-and-white horizontal stripes for the rest of her life did hold a certain appeal, if she did say so herself.

Horizontal stripes just weren't flattering.

Did she still have a library card? She couldn't remember. She'd been required to get one as part of some school project but that'd literally been over a decade ago, so…

Yeah, no idea.

Well, even if she did have a card, the chances were that they'd changed computer systems since then anyway, so she'd need to get a new card no matter what. She grabbed her purse with her driver's license in it and her keys and headed for the garage, using a back hallway that her mother hated because of a lack of windows in it.

Note to self: If I ever do manage to marry someone and

have kids someday, do not tell them which parts of the house I absolutely refuse to ever go into. It's only begging for them to exploit that loophole.

Seriously, some days, it was just a little too easy to pull one over on her parents.

When she walked into the library, she saw Marian behind the front desk. She was a few years older than Tenny and they'd obviously hung out in different groups in high school, but she'd always seemed nice. It was good to see a face that Tenny actually knew. She felt so far out of her element, she was like a fish that'd just been asked to climb a tree.

So she did what she always did in awkward social situations – she hid her feelings. She'd had decades of practice by this point, so she was pretty much at the black-belt level by now.

"Hi, Marian!" Tenny said cheerfully, putting her rhinestone-covered purse on the counter. "I'd like to– Mari?" she said, catching the nametag pinned to the librarian's chest. "Sorry, I always thought you preferred Marian."

Mari laughed, her green eyes twinkling. "Well, after I got a job here at the library, I decided to go by Mari instead. Too many people singing to me," she said with a conspiratorial wink, as if that explained everything.

"Oh right, of course," Tennessee said easily, without blinking an eyelash. She had absolutely no idea what Mari was talking about, but she also wasn't about to admit that. "So, I was wanting to check out some books on being frugal. Do you have any books on that topic?"

"Of course!" Mari assured her. "That's always a popular subject. Let me see what we have in right now." She did a few quick searches on the computer, scribbled down some numbers on a piece of paper, and then took off for the shelves, Tenny trailing behind her. "I'm surprised to see you come in here," Mari said over her shoulder. "I didn't know you were a library patron. I must've missed seeing you before."

"Oh, I haven't been since I was in high school and was required to check a book out of here as part of a history project my junior year. I'm...ummm...trying to...expand my horizons." Which sounded much better than *I'm trying to learn how not to be a mooch and thus far, failing horribly.*

Yeah, just about anything sounded better than that.

"Well, I'm glad you came in," Mari said with a genuine smile, coming to a stop in front of a bookshelf. "Now, we organize using the Dewey decimal system, which means any books with these numbers on their spines," she pointed to "640.42" and "332.024" written on the scrap of paper, "will probably have some useful information in them. The stacks wind back and forth, the numbers getting bigger as you go that way," she pointed at the far wall, "so you should be able to wander through and find some books that look interesting. If nothing works, tell me and we can see about doing an interlibrary loan."

Leaving the scrap of paper behind, Mari headed for the front desk again, leaving Tenny by herself.

Stacks? Interlibrary? Dewey?

She wasn't sure if Mari had been speaking English that entire time, but she tried her best to follow the instructions. She quickly realized what Mari had meant by "numbers on the spines" – every book had a little typed-up number at the base of its spine, making it easy to see where she was at in the number line. She began wandering through, gathering books as she went, forcing herself to not look down her nose at some of the ones that had been printed several decades ago. Maybe they were oldies but goodies. She wouldn't know until she sat down and really looked through them.

Once her arms were full to overflowing, she made her way over to a table and began spreading the books out, flipping through them one by one. Some looked amazing, while some looked…less than inspiring. She set those off to the side, leaving her about a half dozen to take home.

She looked down at her pile with a grin on her face. She felt accomplished – she was getting her hands on organized, useful material, and she wasn't spending a dime to do it. Maybe she wasn't so awful at not being a mooch after all.

She gathered the books up that she planned to borrow and made her way to the front. She had some shopping bags out in the car from Victoria's Secret and J. Crew that she could use to sneak the books inside the house. Her mother would freak out if she knew Tenny was doing something as low-class as borrowing books from a library, so this would have to be her little secret.

Secret #402 of Tenny's short life.

It was a good thing she was great at keeping them.

CHAPTER 17

LEVI

*I*T WAS STUPID OF HIM to have even tried.

"If I wanted some damn water, I'd walk to the sink and get some!" his dad hollered, throwing the bottle of flavored water straight at Levi's head.

Well, he'd tried to aim at Levi's head. Luckily, his speech wasn't the only thing affected by his drunk-off-his-ass condition; his aim was shit, too. The plastic bottle hit the far wall and exploded on impact, the carbonated water shooting out everywhere.

They both ignored it.

"Dad, I'm not bringing you Pabst anymore. I already told you that." He sounded weary. Exhausted. And he felt it too.

Looking down at his father's bloated form – skin that appeared to be turning yellow before his eyes, broken blood vessels across his nose, watery blue eyes – he wondered for the millionth time where he'd come from, what with his dad's blond, thin hair, scrawny height, blue eyes, pot belly…

No, he didn't look a damn thing like his father. His mother and his father must've been a hell of a pair. She'd probably been able to scoop Steve off his feet and carry him wherever she wanted, like a slightly oversized doll.

Except unlike a doll, his father was absolutely no fun to play with.

Splat!

Jerked out of his thoughts, Levi looked down to realize that one of the burgers he'd brought over was sliding down his chest, and then with a plop, fell to the floor. His dad started laughing maniacally. "You don't think you're such hot shit now, do you?" he crowed as what appeared to be a hundred cats started swarming the floor, all desperate for the food.

Something broke inside of Levi.

Broke and twisted and shattered apart.

I don't have to care about this man, no matter what blood we might share.

He turned and headed for the door, the cackles quickly turning to anger. "Hey, come back here!" his dad shouted. "I didn't tell you you could leave! Damn you! Where's my Pab…"

The wind whistling past the decrepit house pushed the words away, sending them spinning down the street. Levi climbed inside of his pickup but instead of making his way home right away, he pulled out his phone.

"Hey Moose," he said when his best friend answered, "wanna come over and just hang out for a while?"

Moose hesitated and Levi knew, just knew, that Georgia was there and Moose was debating who to choose and Levi's chest hurt because dammit all, he needed someone to want *him*, and then Moose said, "Absolutely. I'll be right over, pizza in hand," and then hung up.

Levi shoved the key into the ignition and started up the truck. It was time to leave Steve Scranton behind, father or not.

CHAPTER 18

TENNESSEE

"*T*ENNESSEE," her mother's voice floated up the stairs, "I need to talk to you."

Dammit. She froze, her hand over her pad of paper, the partial drawing of a metal bear still waiting to come to life on the page. She dropped the pencil into a cup and with a sigh, headed to find her mother. Whatever it was that she wanted, it wouldn't be good, Tenny was willing to bet money on that. Her mother didn't call her downstairs to tell her she'd done a good job arranging that week's flower arrangement.

Her mother was standing in the drawing room, her hands clasped behind her back. Tennessee spotted Virginia on the couch in the corner, watching the whole thing, her eyes wide, and Tenny sighed again. Her younger sister didn't need this kind of drama in her life – she was a teenager; she had enough drama already – but her mother wasn't one to consider that sort of thing and Tenny didn't want to make her younger sister feel unwanted by asking her to leave.

Plus, she also just wanted to get this over with.

Whatever "this" was.

"Yes, Mother?" she asked politely, also clasping her hands behind her back. She felt like she was a soldier being inspected by the general, and would be expected to salute at any moment, but she stuck with the pose anyway. She'd found long ago that playing by her parent's rules only helped her cause, never hurt.

"What is *this*?" her mother demanded, pulling a book from the library out from behind her back and shaking it accusingly at Tenny.

A small, snarky (thankfully inner) voice wanted to reply, "How to Save Big Bucks Each Month – Painless Personal Finance Tips to be Frugal and Live Fabulously," but Tenny kept that particular thought to herself. She was pretty sure her mother didn't want a reading lesson.

"How did you find that?" she demanded instead, feeling like a rebellious teenager whose parents had just found a stash of weed under her bed.

"I have my ways," her mother replied imperiously, which was absolutely code for, "The maid found it."

Dammit all. I really thought I'd found a good hiding spot this time.

Every time the maid came over to clean, her mother would "miraculously" discover something Tenny had tried to hide from her. A part of her wondered if the maid was being paid per contraband item, like a really bizarre version of a salesman's bonus.

"I'm trying to learn how to be more thrifty," Tenny said, deciding that sticking to the truth could only help in this case. Plus, it wasn't like she could say, "I'm taking up gardening!"

"I already put that part together for myself," her mother said sarcastically. "What I cannot figure out is *why*. First, camping like a hobo and now wanting to live like a poor person...Oh, it's that Scranton boy, isn't it!" she exclaimed, waving the paperback around wildly. Her eyes were gleaming with the triumph of having figured it out.

"Levi—"

"I told your father – I *told* him he was bad news!" her mom exclaimed, cutting Tennessee off at the pass. "Well, whatever the reason for your actions, it'll all be coming to an end soon anyway. Now that you're not marrying Moose like you were supposed to, your father has been on the lookout for someone new. He met up with a farmer from Washington whose son is single, and I do believe that they're having talks right now to settle things up, but he's not going to want to marry you if you're going to be doing things like reading...reading *trash*!"

The world wobbled around Tennessee for a moment, the edges turning black as she stumbled forward, grabbing onto the back of the chaise lounge and staring up at her mother. "You can't...I can't..." She couldn't make her mouth work right. "You can't marry me off to a stranger!" she finally got out. "You *can't!*"

She could hear Virginia's gasps of horror behind her, but they were quiet and far away, as was her mother's voice. It was like the world had suddenly ended up underwater – hazy and indistinct and garbled.

"You'll meet him before you marry him – we're not barbarians," her mother snapped, but it was a far-away voice because Tenny just couldn't seem to bring anything into focus.

"You're going to sell me off to the highest bidder," she said hollowly. Even her own voice sounded far away.

"Do you think it's cheap to live like this?" her mother thundered. Tennessee's eyes snapped up to her mom's, and suddenly, it all came together, in one horrendous, awful answer:

Her parents were poor.

Or, at least, they were spending more than they were making, which Tennessee was discovering from her illicit books, meant the same thing. The late nights of quiet arguing, the larger-than-normal stacks of credit card bills coming in, the one time their electricity got turned off three months ago or so, and her mother had yelled and harangued the poor Idaho Power employees to within an inch of their lives for *their* mistake.

It wasn't their mistake.

Her parents hadn't paid the bill on time.

Her parents were poor.

Tenny started laughing. Laughing and laughing and laughing, until tears were streaming down her face. She could see her mother's mouth moving but had no idea what she was saying and even more importantly, didn't give a damn.

She finally straightened up, wiping the tears from her eyes. Her mother was still talking, but Tenny was done listening. She took her iPhone out of her back pocket and laid it on the Chippendale end table.

"Virginia, if you want to talk to me," she said loudly to her younger sister, boldly ignoring her mother who promptly sputtered to an indignant stop, "call me at Georgia's house. Mother," she said, swinging back to the woman standing in front of her, spitting angry at being the second one to be addressed, "if you want to talk to me...don't."

She plucked the frugal book out of her mother's hand and swept past her and up the stairs. It was time to leave. It was time to stand on her own two feet.

She pulled her Louis Vuitton suitcases out – three, a matching set, of course – and began throwing clothes into them with abandon. Her mother chased her up the stairs, her chest heaving with anger or exertion from running, Tenny didn't know.

And didn't care.

"Just wait until your father gets home!" she yelled from the doorway, the veins popping out in her forehead in a very unladylike way. "You'll wish you hadn't done this."

Tennessee looked up at her and laughed dryly. "Mother, you've already made me wish I wasn't born. At this point, there isn't much else you could do to me."

"We've given you *everything*!" her mother protested. "Music lessons and college and a credit card and a convertible godawful Pepto Bismol pink car and—"

"But no love," Tenny said, looking her mother straight in the eye.

No, she wasn't her mother. Simply the human being who'd happened to give birth to her.

"You've never given me love," she repeated softly. "I have been a thing to use to get what you want — more cash by selling me off to the highest bidder after you and Father blew through Grandpa's estate. How long did it take you two to spend those millions?" Even as she challenged her mother, something she'd spent virtually her whole life trying to never, no *never* do, she continued to pack, grabbing everything she could get her hands on.

She could do this. She could walk away and never come back. She could.

"You have no idea how expensive children are," Roberta said, her tone suddenly wheedling. "All of those shopping trips to the mall — do you think we got that money off trees?"

"No, I stupidly thought you grew it from the ground in the form of mustard seed and wheat and corn and potatoes. You know, Father's job as a *farmer*."

"Farmers only make so much," her mother sniffed. "We couldn't possibly live on just *that*."

"Father is the largest farmer in Long Valley County," Tenny pointed out. It was a fact that he liked to slip into a conversation whenever possible, so yeah, basically every time he talked to someone. "If you and Father cannot make it on his income alone, how the hell does anyone else pay their bills?"

"Language!" Roberta snapped.

"Roberta," Tennessee said, admittedly enjoying using her biological mother's first name a little too much and watching her eyes grow wide with shock and anger, "I am 26 years old. I can damn well say 'hell' anytime I want to." She zipped the three suitcases up and began wheeling the first two down the stairs, thumping carelessly down. each. step. as. loud. as. possible.

"You're going to mar the wood!" Roberta yelled down the stairs. "Stop that this instant."

"I find it fascinating that wood on the staircase is what you're worried about right now," Tennessee said dryly, parking the suitcases next to the door out to the garage. "And oh-so-telling." She ran back up the stairs to grab the last suitcase, wheeling it past ~~her mother~~ Roberta with a sarcastic smile. "I'll bring the car by later. Perhaps you two can sell it and use the money to pay off some debtors."

"The car? But…you can't not have a car! How are you going to get around?"

Tennessee pulled her wallet out of her purse and

began laying all of her credit cards down on the counter with a snap.

Snap. Snap. Snap. Snap. Snap.

Her mother had kept giving her new cards, telling her that they had better rewards, and Tenny had taken them every time with a shrug. It hadn't mattered to her which card she used. But now, because of her frugal books from the library, she was beginning to realize that her mother was trying to move balances between credit cards to stay one step ahead of the bill collectors.

Just how in debt are they?

She pushed the thought away. Not her monkeys, not her zoo.

"I will drive my own car around *when* I earn the money to buy it. Until then, I walk." She opened up the door to the garage and began wheeling the bags out one by one, pitching them into the backseat of the open top car.

"Walk?! I will *not* have my daughter walking around town like some...some hobo!" her mother spat from the doorway. Tenny slid into the driver's seat as she tossed her purse into the passenger seat, and then looked over at the woman with a dry smile.

"Well then, I guess it's good that I don't consider you to be my mother any longer." She hit the garage door opener on the visor of the car, waiting for the door to open and let her out, and give her freedom. Freedom from restrictions and lies and expectations.

Freedom from her parents.

She pulled out of the garage and swung around to head out down the road. She spotted Virginia at the front door, waving madly as Tennessee drove past, and Tenny waved back, her heart soaring.

She'd done it, she'd really done it.

Now she could only hope that her cousin didn't mind her being a mooch for just a little while.

CHAPTER 19

LEVI

*K*NOCK KNOCK

Two swift knocks on the front door jerked Levi out of his Saturday afternoon nap. He'd been staying up late a lot lately, which meant that afternoon naps were becoming almost habitual. But it was worth it – hanging out every evening with Tennessee, Moose, and Georgia was an absolute blast because this time, they were paired off into the right couples, instead of everything feeling so forced all of the time.

Moose and Georgia still spent way too much time sucking face with each other but not surprisingly, Levi found that he didn't mind it nearly as much now that he had someone of his own to make out with.

Funny that.

He opened up the front door to find a package lying there, the mail carrier already halfway down the block, ponytail swishing as she went. "Thanks!" he hollered at her retreating back, and then grabbed the package and walked back inside.

What the hell? He couldn't remember ordering anything lately from an online retailer and it wasn't like he had relatives who'd be sending him a care package. He flipped the small box over in his hands and looked at the From address.

YourAncestryRevealed.com?

"What the..." he muttered, pulling his knife out of his pocket and using it to slit the package open. Out came a welcoming letter, telling him congratulations on choosing to research his ancestry, and reassuring him that the process was painless and simple.

"What process?" he asked his empty house. As he pulled out the swabs and containers, everything neatly sealed in plastic to keep them from being contaminated, it slowly started coming back to him.

The night that his father had used him as burger-throwing target practice, he and Moose had played video games until the wee hours of the morning, and then Levi had collapsed onto the couch to fall asleep, drunk as a skunk. But he couldn't sleep and instead, he'd spent hours channel surfing, until he stumbled across an informercial running about YourAncestry-Revealed.com. The idea that he could have his DNA tested and figure out where the hell his mother had come from had been really appealing to him, probably even more so in his inebriated state than it normally would be.

He turned the cotton swabs over and over in his hands, sterile, ready to be used. Just a couple of swipes of the inside of his mouth, and he could finally have a few answers. More answers than he had right then, anyway.

He couldn't believe he was going to do this, but as the welcoming letter made abundantly clear, he'd apparently already paid for the test. There wasn't much point in throwing his money away, right?

He settled down at the kitchen table and began to read the instructions.

CHAPTER 20

TENNESSEE

JENNY FLIPPED THROUGH the pages of the Boise State University catalog, hunting for something – anything – that looked like a career she could do. The fact that she was looking at attending a state university instead of a private college...the very thought made her smile. Her parents would have a conniption fit if their daughter was attending something as low-brow as a publicly funded college, but then again, what they thought didn't really matter, right?

She technically had a Bachelor's degree in Liberal Arts, which, as far as she could tell, qualified her to preside over state dinners, or work the drive-thru at Burger King. She certainly hadn't learned anything of real value at the private college her parents had sent her to, unless learning how to fold cloth napkins into swans counted as being valuable.

She flipped the page in the catalog, her eyes

skimming down it automatically without finding anything of interest.

She could be a teacher…except she knew nothing about children and really didn't relish the idea of being a human Kleenex to a bunch of five year olds all day.

She could be an accountant, except numbers made her eyes cross.

She could be a policewoman, except she couldn't exactly fathom yelling "POLICE!" at the top of her lungs while breaking down doors. Hmmm…maybe she could break down doors and then offer the women inside a makeover. A new kind of police officer!

Yeah…no.

What she really wanted to do was to make the world a better place. Which sounded cheesy and hippie as hell and would have her mother diving for her smelling salts if she heard it, but it was true. Tennessee had spent her whole life doing nothing but worrying about her hair and nails and clothing and how to best highlight her cheekbones. She wanted to do something for other people.

She wanted to make them smile.

She wasn't about to become a stand-up comic, so…

Tennessee Rowland, you are an idiot.

Duh.

Big, fat, whomping "What the hell was she thinking?!" duh.

She could make yard art for people.

Right?

That was a "thing," right?

Plus, she wouldn't have to take out student loans to make it happen. She was learning more every day with Levi as her tutor. Sure, some of their lessons ended in make-out sessions and so they didn't exactly get a shit ton of learning done then, but for the most part, when they concentrated, she was learning fast.

As quickly as her excitement came, though, it began to disappear. The old adage, "You need money to make money" flashed through her mind. How would she buy metal to use? She couldn't just keep "borrowing" Levi's scrap metal. Borrowing implied that you gave the item back, and unless he wanted oversized bumblebees on stakes to stick throughout his yard…yeah, he wasn't getting this metal back.

Not to mention that his scrap pile was quickly dwindling, and anyway, this needed to be her job, which meant she couldn't be a charity case. She'd already moved into her cousin's spare bedroom; she'd already borrowed countless pieces of metal from Levi, plus a welder and gloves and a helmet and a workshop space…

She needed to stand on her own two feet. She just didn't know how. Had everyone else been sent to Adult School when she hadn't been looking? Had everyone else learned how to make adult choices during a phase of their lives that she'd somehow skipped?

She groaned, burying her head in her hands, hot tears pricking the edges of her eyes. She needed to stop being so needy. She needed to be a grownup. *Stop relying on everyone else to solve your problems for you, Tennessee. Levi and Georgia aren't your mother, and the woman who did happen to give birth to you is a bitch.*

You're on your own; no one else is there for you.

Stop being a baby about it.

Such a baby.

Crybaby.

The pressure mounted, pounding on her, the panic swirling. Yeah, her mother was an awful human being – and her father too – but as the worry washed over her in drowning waves, smothering her, she began to think that maybe she shouldn't have left home. Hell, maybe the guy in Washington wasn't so bad. How would she know – she hadn't even given him a chance. She didn't even know his name. Maybe she could grow to love him. After a while. People had been suffering through arranged marriages for centuries.

What made her so special? She wasn't special.

Just ask her mother.

Hot tears were dripping off her chin and plopping onto the catalog, the cheap ink smearing everywhere.

Even as her hands went searching for the cool metal, she knew she shouldn't. She had to stop. She just...life was too much. It was just a thing she did to help. She could stop anytime she wanted.

She just didn't want to right now.

CHAPTER 21

LEVI

*W*HEN HE SAW THE EMAIL in his inbox, his stomach flipped with delight and not an insignificant amount of panic.

He'd done it. He was about to find something out about his family. His heritage. Everything his father had always refused to tell him.

He clicked on the email and began scanning through. When he got to the end, he paused, completely confused. He scrolled back up to the top and began scanning through again, more slowly this time.

What

The

Hell…

The percentages were all there. Apparently, he had some English in him, and then a mix of Italian and Spanish for the rest.

The one thing he was not? Scandinavian.

This doesn't make any sense.

It couldn't be right. Had they mixed his results up with someone else? Was that possible?

An email notification popped up in the corner of his screen – he'd received a second email from the company. *Thank God!* He clicked over to it, just sure that it'd be a "So sorry – don't know what we were thinking; here's your real ancestral information!" email.

Instead, it was entitled, "Levi Scranton, did you know there's a relative in your area?"

Everything slowed down. He felt like he had when he was a kid and had jumped on a trampoline for too long – dizzy and off balance as his body tried to re-acclimate to the world around it.

No, this was not possible. Absolutely, positively not possible. Levi knew almost nothing about his family's background, but he did know that Steve and she-who-shall-not-be-named mom had moved to Long Valley a couple of years before he was born. His father had gotten a construction job in Franklin, so they'd moved here from somewhere in Colorado.

Instead of a fresh start in a new area, though, his dad had fallen off a ladder after only a couple of weeks on the job, and hadn't worked a day since. He used disability and Social Security payments to live on, along with a settlement from the construction company for providing "unsafe working conditions."

Levi only knew that story because his father repeated it so many times, usually with a choice swear word (or seven) about how stingy the construction company had been in its settlement, and if they'd only been willing to give him more, he could've had a much better life from there forward…

Which, of course, meant an easier time being able to afford as much Pabst as he wanted.

The one and only other thing Levi knew for sure about his heritage was that his dad was Scandinavian. It's why he claimed he shouldn't go outside very often – he had fair skin that burned easily. Why, if only he wasn't Scandinavian, he could've gotten another construction job but between his fair skin and his bad back, well, no one could expect him to work.

Levi had always had to bite his tongue at that ("Sunscreen – it's a new invention! Try it, you'll like it!") but arguing with his father was like wrestling with a pig in mud: The pig would only enjoy it and in the end, they'd both end up filthy.

Yeah, arguing with his dad never worked out well.

But all of that meant that 1) He should absolutely *not* have any relatives in the area, and 2) He should be at least 50% Scandinavian.

He forced himself to click on the relative email to open it up. Just staring at it for hours on end wouldn't give him the answers he wanted, as tempting as that seemed in that moment.

He began skimming down it. About halfway through, he found the info he was looking for: He was related to a Florence Garrett who'd registered in the system a little over two years ago.

Florence Garrett?

*Florence **Garrett**?!*

No.

No.

No.

He couldn't be a Garrett. *Moose* was the Garrett. Levi was the Scranton. Didn't YourAncestry-Revealed.com know these things?

Florence Garrett…

Florence Garrett…

The name echoed in his mind as Levi tried frantically to match it up with something, anything, but he was coming up empty-handed. After all these years, Levi had never heard Moose mention a Florence. Maybe it wasn't the same family. Maybe it was all a huge coincidence. Maybe they'd sent him the wrong test results.

With a trembling hand, Levi picked up his cell phone and called Moose. As soon as his best friend picked up with his customary greeting, "Yo! What's up?" Levi blurted out, "Who's Florence Garrett?"

CHAPTER 22

TENNESSEE

TENNESSEE WALKED DOWN the sidewalk of the residential street towards Levi's house, the heat waves rolling off the black asphalt under the baking summer sun. Tennessee was basking in the heat – glorious, wonderful summer was the only time of year she could count on not needing to wear a jacket or wool socks in order to get through the day – when she noticed Moose's truck in the driveway of Levi's house.

What the hell?

Not that she minded seeing Moose – in fact, she rather liked hanging out with him, now that she wasn't going to have to marry him – but Levi and Tennessee had planned on spending the evening working on slicing metal into various shapes so Tenny could weld them together to create a piece of yard art. She was wanting to try that bumblebee idea today.

But none of this was something they'd usually do with Moose right there beside them.

Tenny hesitated. Maybe she should just walk back to Georgia's house. Call Levi later and see if he wasn't busy at that point. She shouldn't bother him when he was spending time with his bestie, right?

Don't be stupid. Moose probably just dropped by and surprised Levi. No doubt he'll be on his way soon. You're not bothering anybody.

But she couldn't completely suppress the niggling, panicky feeling spreading through her gut. *Something wrong, something wrong, something wrong...*

The chant kept time with her footsteps and her heartbeat, until she finally made it to the front door of Levi's house. She knocked and then stood back hesitantly when she heard a deep rumble of swear words that'd make her father proud.

The chant began to speed up. *Somethingwrong, somethingwrong, somethingwrong—*

Levi yanked the door open, his face flushed, his hair curling every which way in a mass of chaos that'd normally be an invitation for her to run her fingers through it, but not today. Not right now.

Somethingwrongsomethingwrongsomethi—

"Tennessee," he said, his voice breaking on her name. He sounded panicked? Angry? Worried? She couldn't tell. She couldn't read his tone, and that made her even more uptight. "Tenny, you gotta come in." He pulled her inside and practically pushed her towards the couch. "Sit," he ordered gruffly. "You're gonna wanna be sitting for this one."

Moose was at one end of the couch and she sent him a bemused smile as she settled down on the other end. Instead of giving her an encouraging smile in return, he looked...just as panicked as Levi?

What the hell is going on?!

"Tenny," Levi blurted out, "we think we're half brothers. Moose and I. We're related."

CHAPTER 23

LEVI

THE LOOK ON TENNESSEE'S FACE...

Well, it probably mirrored the look on his own, honestly.

"Moose," he said, turning back to his best friend – his brother?! – "we gotta go talk to your parents. Our dad? Oh God, I think I'm gonna puke."

It wasn't that the idea of being half brothers with Moose was such an awful idea, of course – if he could choose any person in the world to be his brother, it'd be Moose, hands down – but just that everything he knew was a lie.

Everything

Was his name even Levi Scranton?

He felt the bile rising up further in his throat, making it hard to breathe. It was all too much. A small part of his brain told him that he was going into shock, but he couldn't figure out how to stop it.

He knew Tennessee must be dying inside, wanting

to know what the hell was going on, but he wasn't sure if he had it in him to tell this story twice in ten minutes, let alone yet again to Rocky Garrett. And he sure as shit had to tell Rocky, if only because he wanted some answers.

Well, not Rocky. His father.

Rocky was his father. Not just his boss.

His stomach roiled.

He'd tell Tenny and Rocky at the same time. Two stones, one bird, and all that shit. Two birds, one stone? Maybe there's birds in the bushes. Or birds in his hand? Or maybe it's stones in his hand. It could be–

Tennessee laid her hand on his arm, jerking him out of his quickly spiraling panic. "It's okay, it's okay," she said soothingly. "Let's go over to…uhhh…Rocky's house. Talk to him. Get this all straightened out."

She said it so reasonably and calmly, as if talking about whether to go out to eat at a Chinese or pizza restaurant. He felt his body begin to shake.

Instinctively, protectively, like a momma bear protecting her cubs, his mind shut down and his body went into auto-pilot. He couldn't let his nerves get to him. He had to keep it together. One step at a time.

They walked out of his house and into the bright sunshine. He climbed numbly into the backseat of Moose's truck, not trusting himself to drive. He'd probably drive right into the side of a building without even noticing it was there. Moose and Tennessee chatted quietly on the way over to the

Garrett house but Levi couldn't make his brain concentrate enough to understand what they were saying.

Words were everywhere but they had no meaning.

Rocky is my father. Rocky Garrett is my father.

Who the hell is my mother?

It couldn't be Linda Garrett, that was for damn sure. Levi was two and a half months younger than Moose. Unless they were some bizarre medical miracle, he was pretty sure Linda didn't give birth to Moose in August and then give birth again to Levi in October.

Oh, and then choose to hand Levi off to the town drunk.

So who the hell is my mother?

They pulled up in front of the Garrett house and even through the haze and pain and overwhelmedness washing over him in waves, a small part of Levi's mind realized that Moose was probably about to see his father for the first time since he'd walked out in the middle of May and had started sleeping on Levi's couch.

What would it be like for Moose to see his dad after all this time? Levi reached out and put his hand on Moose's shoulder. Moose looked over at him, and they shared a look that said it all, guy style. No frills, no emotion, just the facts.

You ready for this?

Yeah.

Okay, let's do it.

Moose knocked lightly on the imposing front door and then opened it up. "Hey, it's Deere," he called out, pushing the door open all the way and ushering Levi and Tenny in behind him.

"Deere?" Zara gasped. She came sprinting in from the living room and threw her arms around her older brother.

Except, I guess I'm her older brother too.

Levi was beginning to suspect that eating lunch had been a bad idea.

"What are you doing here?" Zara demanded half-accusingly, pulling away and glaring up at him. In typical teenage girl fashion, she couldn't seem to decide if she was pissed or excited. "I didn't think I'd see you again...well, not for a while, anyway."

Moose patted her shoulder awkwardly. "Hey, are the parents home?" he asked, completely ignoring her question.

"Oh yeah. Mom's up in her sewing room and I think Dad's out back."

"Can you go get...Dad?" Moose asked, stumbling over the words. Levi's heart hurt. Last time the two of them had spoken, Rocky had disinherited Moose. He probably didn't know if he should even be calling him "Dad."

It was a really strange comment on the state of the universe that in that moment, Levi could honestly say that he was facing the same conundrum.

"Sure," she said slowly. Millions of questions were dancing over her face, but she bit her tongue.

"Be right back," she said and took off for the backdoor.

"I better go get my mom," Moose said, the words coming out much easier than when he'd called Rocky "Dad." "You two just hang out here."

He disappeared up the stairs, leaving Levi and Tennessee in the living room alone.

"Remember all the Saturday nights that we spent here?" Tenny asked quietly, breaking the silence. "I always thought of Linda and Rocky as being a second set of parents. I had no idea how true that was for... for you."

He gave her a wry smile that hurt to even push into place. "You and me both," he murmured.

"Levi?" Rocky said, coming in through the backdoor, pulling his gloves off as he came walking over, Zara trailing in behind him. He was sweaty and grass-stained — he'd obviously been working on the yard before they'd interrupted him. "How's it goin'?"

His boss reached out to shake hands.

"Dad," Levi said softly as he clasped Rocky's hand in his.

Linda, coming down the stairs, gasped as the world froze around them.

CHAPTER 24

TENNESSEE

IT WAS SO OBVIOUS, looking at the three of them. She felt stupid for having missed it before. Of course, everyone else had missed it too, but still…

She'd always joked that Moose and Levi looked like they could be brothers, but now, looking between Levi, Moose, and Rocky, she realized that Levi actually looked more like Rocky than Moose did. Moose had his mother's nose and eye color, while Levi…

Well, add on a few pounds, add in some gray hair and a couple of wrinkles, and he *was* Rocky. The same thick eyebrows, the same square jaw, the same dark eyes, the same deep, rumbly voice…

It was painfully, stupidly, ridiculously obvious, now that she was looking for it.

Rocky's gaze was darting between his sons and his

wife, clearly trying to decide what to say; what to admit to. Finally, he turned back to Levi.

"You're right."

The air was gone from the room, Tenny would swear it on a stack of Bibles. Or, at least, she was completely incapable of breathing. The world was going a little dark around the edges. *Don't pass out, Tenny, don't pass out. This is not the time or place for it. Breathe. Just breathe.*

"You are my son," he continued quietly. "I had an affair with my secretary, Jennifer Scranton – did Steve ever tell you her name?"

Levi just shook his head, not saying a word, his eyes trained on his father.

"I'm not proud of it, but…" He hesitated, and Tenny was just sure he was debating how much to admit to. As little as possible, if he thought he could get away with it. "Well anyway, once she figured out that she was pregnant – and based on some math, she was pretty damn sure I was the father – she wanted us both to get divorced and marry each other. Divorcing Linda…I may've been an idiot, but I'd never do that. I confessed to Linda what had happened, fired Jenn from the dealership, and then for good measure, I paid her some hush money to keep it quiet."

Rocky shrugged, glancing up towards the stairs where Moose and Linda were still frozen in place, and then back to Levi with an ashamed smile. "She was tall with dark brown hair…it would be easy to just assume that you took after her instead of Steve. It could've all worked out, except she ran through that money, and two years later, she was back on my doorstep. She wanted another bribe to keep it all a secret. I knew it'd never end if I kept paying her – she'd just keep coming back for more hush money – so the second time, I would only give her the money if she agreed to leave town and never come back. She was supposed to take you with her, of course, but she didn't. She left you behind with Steve. I don't know... I have no idea if Steve knows the truth or not."

He let out a long sigh. "I couldn't claim you as mine publicly; I couldn't get involved with Jennifer skipping town without people wanting to know why, so...I just kept quiet. When Deere first came home from school with you in tow...I'll admit, it was a little awkward at first, but we soon realized that you had no idea, so after a while, it was easy enough to just start taking care of you however we could. Linda may not be your momma, and she may have choice words for your biological momma and for me for my stupidity, but over the years, she's learned to love you as her own."

Tenny watched as Levi looked over at Linda standing at the base of the stairs, her hand over her mouth, her eyes filling with tears. She gave Levi a little smile and shrug that said without words, *Yeah, your biological dad's a bastard; what're ya gonna do?*

Tenny thought back to the years and years of Levi practically living at the Garrett home – the home-cooked meals, sleepovers, camp-outs; they had even sponsored him for high school football along with Moose because they knew Steve wouldn't pony up the dough so his son could play.

Except, he *wasn't* Steve's son.

Does Steve know? The question kept swirling around and around in her mind.

Jennifer had been married to him when she got pregnant. Maybe he really had no idea; maybe he truly believed Levi was his, and had still treated him that godawful all these years.

Tennessee looked back at the diminutive woman standing at the base of the stairs, Moose towering over her, his arm wrapped protectively around her waist. There had always been a special bond between Moose and his mom, and watching them in this moment, probably one of the worst moments of Linda's life...Tenny could see the love between them. Moose would stand up for his mom every time. She wasn't good at standing up for herself, even Tenny could see that, so she needed a champion in her corner. Tenny was glad that Moose was there for her.

Tenny watched as Levi turned back to his father – *oh, what a weird thought that is!* – and asked quietly, "So, is this why you paid for my schooling to become a welder?"

Rocky nodded. "Smart boy," he said with an approving chuckle. "Yeah, I couldn't claim you publicly, but I didn't want Steve's drinkin' to mean that you didn't have a chance in life. Paying for you to become a welder was easy enough to justify – after all, the official story was that I was just lookin' for a loyal and talented employee and since you was Moose's best friend, it wasn't real hard to make people think that that's how I got to know you. And in a way... they'd be right, anyway. All that time you spent at my house growin' up – that *is* how I got to know you." He paused for a moment, stroking his chin as he thought. "I have to ask – how'd you finally figure it out?"

"Your younger sister, Florence." Levi looked Rocky straight in the eye as he said it. No flinching, no accusations, just stating the facts.

Tenny couldn't be more proud of him than she was in that moment. In his shoes, she sure as hell wouldn't be keeping it together like he was. In fact, she *wasn't* in his shoes and she still wasn't keeping it together as well as he was.

"Flo? But...but she's dead." Now Rocky looked genuinely confused.

"You know how she was always doing genealogy stuff?" Moose asked, speaking up for the first time since his dad came walking inside. "Turns out, she liked taking DNA tests, too."

"DNA tests?" This did not seem to clarify anything at all for Rocky. Tenny almost felt sorry for the man in that moment, despite the fact that he'd done his best to force Moose to marry her and make both of their lives miserable.

The keyword being *almost*.

"Several weeks ago," Levi said, "I ordered one of those new DNA tests you see advertised everywhere 'cause…well, 'cause my da–Steve just don't look a damn thing like me." Levi shrugged, looking supremely uncomfortable. "I, at least, wanted to know what my heritage was. The results came back and they didn't make a lick of sense – no Scandinavian blood, but plenty of English, Italian, and Spanish."

"Yeah, Grandpa on my dad's side came from Italy; Grandma was from Spain," Rocky said, as way of explanation. "English was the other half of the family. I guess Jennifer must've come from the same places. I can't say as we ever sat and talked about it." He let out an uneasy chuckle and looked over at Linda, his face flushed.

Discussing your ex-mistress and mother of your illegitimate child in front of your wife couldn't be the easiest thing in the world to do. Tenny still found herself running short on pity, though. Maybe she just wasn't that nice of a person, but she couldn't look past him trying to force her into marriage with his son.

No, she wasn't overlooking that anytime soon.

"When the results came in," Levi continued, "they also said that I had a relative in the area who'd taken the test. That's when I was *really* confused because my parents were supposed to be from Colorado, not from around here. When it pulled up Florence Garrett…" He shrugged. "Y'all are the only Garretts I know, so I called Moose and asked him. At first, I thought that maybe Florence was my mom, but Moose told me that wasn't possible."

"No, Flo didn't have any kids," Rocky said,

shaking his head sadly. "Never did get married. Had some heart problems and knew she wouldn't be long for this earth. I think she tried to make up for it by researching our family history as far back as possible. She was obsessed with genealogy. I should've known she'd do somethin' like take a DNA test – it sounds just like her."

"Why hadn't I heard about Florence before today?" Levi asked. "I've been over here more times than I could count. How could you have a sister I'd never heard of?"

Rocky shrugged nonchalantly. "She didn't get out much, except to go stare at headstones or somethin'. When she passed, we had a little graveside funeral but she'd always been a pretty private person, so she didn't have many friends to come attend. We didn't hide her from you on purpose – why would we? She was just this quiet, retiring thing."

It was hard for Tenny to imagine Rocky having a younger sister who was a quiet, retiring, housebound ill woman. It was the exact opposite of the man in front of her. And yet…she was the key to forcing all of this out in the open. Tenny wondered for a moment what Florence would've had to say about that, if she'd been alive to see it. Would she have been happy to have found another branch of the Garrett family tree? Or would she have been horrified that her older brother had cheated on his wife and had fathered an illegitimate child?

Rocky shook his head again, this time with a small

laugh. "Well, now that it's all out in the open, why not do what I've always wanted to do from the get-go, right? Son, you oughta change your last name to Garrett, and then take over the John Deere dealership from me."

And just like that, all of the oxygen was gone from the room again.

"R̶ocky!" Linda gasped, horrified. "You can't—"

"What?!" Levi stared at his father, horrified, just sure he hadn't heard right. The universe had thrown a lot at him in the last three hours – understatement of the century – so maybe his brain was startin' to make shit up, wholesale.

Next, he was going to imagine that Rocky was actually the King of England and Levi was his heir.

Totally seemed possible in that moment.

"I always thought God had a real sense of humor," Rocky said, chuckling, seemingly oblivious to the astonishment swirling through the room at his idea. "I get three sons." He began ticking it off on his fingers. "One runs off and joins the military, one refuses to marry a beautiful woman, and one is a hard worker who says 'Yes, sir,' 'No, sir,' 'Right away, sir.' And guess which one I can't claim publicly." He shook his head ruefully. "And then the hard-working one is the one who ends up falling in love with the beautiful woman!" Involuntarily, Levi shot a glance over at Tennessee. How did Rocky know they were dating? Before he could reason that out or ask any questions, Rocky continued on. "You couldn't make this shit up if ya tried. So, as I figure it, God wants you to have the dealership."

Levi blinked, and then blinked again.

He was in shock again.

A small part of his brain knew it, even though it didn't exactly help to know it. His mind just spun around and around.

I'm in shock. I have a father and it isn't Steve Scranton. Rocky wants me to change my name. Rocky wants me to take over the dealership. I'm in shock. Is this what Alice felt when she fell down the rabbit hole? Why am I thinking about Alice in Wonderland *right now? I'm in shock.*

"Sir…Rocky, I can't…I can't take over the dealership," he finally sputtered out. "It's Moose's… he's worked his whole life for it."

"I am *not* giving the dealership to him," Rocky retorted, throwing a disgusted look at Moose, who was still standing next to his wife at the base of the stairs. "He defied me and made me look like a damn idiot in front of the whole town. Plus, he's gone off to work at *Massey-Ferguson.*" He said the name of the competing tractor company with a sneer. "No loyalty at all."

Levi's back snapped straight up. "That's where you're wrong," he retorted, staring his father straight in the eye, unflinching. Finally, the fog in his mind cleared enough for him to argue back against the worst idea known to man. "Moose is the best thing that's ever happened to you. He's worked his ever-lovin' ass off for you and that dealership. I'd *never* take it from him."

"You ain't takin' it from him 'cause it ain't his!" Rocky slammed his fist into his open palm. "I'd rather chop off my right arm than give the dealership to Deere."

"Then," Levi snarled, "you best get to work on choppin'."

He was done. His brain, his soul, his ability to think or breathe properly…he couldn't handle it anymore. He turned and headed for the door, his legs shaking, barely holding it together, the world closing in on all sides around him. A small part of his brain registered that Moose and Tenny were hurrying along behind him, but he had a hard time focusing on them. Focusing on anything at all.

"You'll change your mind!" Rocky called out. "Once you think about it, you will."

"Don't bet on it!" And with that, he slammed the front door shut behind them and then practically ran to the pickup, his heart racing, the anger pounding through him. How *dare* Rocky talk about Moose like that. Levi had known that Rocky and Moose had had a falling out – of course he'd known, Moose had slept on his couch for a couple of days after it had happened, until he'd been able to move into his own apartment – but still, there was a difference between hearing it secondhand and seeing it all upfront and personal.

To have a father talk about his son like that, his son who had done nothing but dedicate his life to Rocky and the dealership for years on end...it was sickening.

He sprawled, loose-boned, across Moose's backseat, his mind going a million miles an hour. Moose looked back at him when he got in. "Thanks," he said softly. He looked shook up. "I knew how my dad felt about me, obviously, but to hear it all again... it's like getting kicked in the gut."

Tenny climbed into the passenger seat, and quietly, they headed towards Levi's house, each lost in their own thoughts.

I am Rocky's son. I am Rocky's son. I have two brothers and a sister. I have a stepmom. I am not Steve Scranton's son.

I am not Steve Scranton's son.

He started laughing like a loon when they pulled up in front of his house. "Steve is not my dad!" he crowed in delight.

Moose turned back and looked over his shoulder at him. "No, he's not," he said quietly, and Levi sobered up. The pain in Moose's eyes...

It hurt to see.

"I'm sorry about what Rocky said," Levi said, putting his hand over the seat and onto Moose's shoulder. "That was a real dick move to make."

Moose shrugged, trying to play it cool, and if Levi

didn't have 18 years of knowing him, he might've even believed him. "Well, I'm gonna head home," he said casually. "Tenny, are you staying here or do you want me to drop you off at Georgia's house?"

Tenny looked over at Levi in the backseat, her blue-green eyes filled with concern and questions. "What do you want me to do?" she asked him. "I'm good either way."

The happiness and excitement that had filled Levi just moments earlier at the fact that he wasn't Steve's son all drained away, leaving anger in its wake. Maybe he wasn't Steve Scranton's son, but dammit all, his real father wasn't much better.

The whiplash between emotions made him feel off-balance, as if he'd just gotten off a Tilt-A-Whirl at the county fair. The world swirled and dipped around him at a dizzying speed. The emotional rollercoaster ride he was on…it wasn't fair to take anyone else on the ride with him.

"I'd like to be alone," he growled and then without another word, he pushed himself out of the truck, stumbling and hurrying for the front door, wanting to get away from Moose and Tennessee's gazes. He didn't want them to see him fall apart. He needed to get away from them – away from the world.

He made a beeline straight through his house and into the backyard, where he promptly began destroying every piece of wood he could get his hands on. "Everyone—" *crack* "knew—" *crack* "except for—" *crack* "me! Steve, Rocky, Linda, Jennifer…they all knew and they let me live this lie!" *Smash!* There went an old mirror he'd decorated his back patio with, shattered into a million pieces.

"Seven years of bad luck, huh?" he sneered down at the mirror pieces. "Bring it! I couldn't possibly have any worse luck than I've been having lately."

His shoulders and chest were heaving as he looked around the backyard, wanting to find something else to destroy, just like his life had been destroyed.

He spotted a piece of rotting plywood, tucked back behind his barbeque, and ripped it out, knocking his folded-up patio umbrella over in the process. "Bastards!" he yelled, breaking the board over his knee. "I hate you all!" He kept breaking the board into smaller and smaller pieces, throwing them across the yard when they got too small to break again.

The world was going black around the edges and he realized that he might pass out if he didn't stop and breathe for a minute. Just a minute. He put his hands on his knees and gasped for air, trying to get oxygen into his lungs.

The thought burst through to the surface, the one he'd been trying so damn hard to suppress:

He had to break up with Tennessee.

The heaving gasps for air turned to heaving sobs of pain. Even though the farthest they'd gone were some fairly heavy duty (and completely delightful) make-out sessions, he knew that for him, Tennessee Rowland was it. A part of him had loved her since he knew what love was, but then, he'd always known she was out of his league, too. Like falling in love with an A-list celebrity in Hollywood, loving Tenny would never go anywhere.

So he'd settled for Georgia, which in retrospect wasn't fair to her. He hadn't really thought of it as settling, except...he had been. Whether he'd wanted to admit to it at the time or not.

But regardless of how he felt about Tenny, what he had with her was fleeting. It couldn't last.

She was the feted and adored child of the largest farmer in the area.

He was the son of the town drunk.

Except, he reminded himself, it was even worse now – he *wasn't* the son of the town drunk. He was the bastard child of the John Deere dealership owner who couldn't keep it in his pants, and his secretary who was too dumb to know how to swallow a little white pill every morning.

He couldn't date Tenny and pull her into his disaster-zone of a life. He couldn't destroy her life like his had been destroyed.

He had to let her go.

Even if it killed him.

He picked up another rotting board and began breaking it to pieces, screaming with anguish as his world fell apart around him.

CHAPTER 26

TENNESSEE

TENNY SETTLED DOWN into the reading chair in Georgia's library with yet another how-to-be thrifty book. Although she was finding them instructive, of course, especially because so many of the concepts were as foreign to her as reading in Mandarin Chinese would be, they also weren't proving to be as useful as she'd hoped they would be.

They all contained one fatal flaw: They focused on how to *save* money.

Which didn't help Tenny much, considering she had no money to save. To save money meant having money, which usually meant a job. She didn't want a job, though, she wanted to make yard art. But yard art required that she have cash for the metal and supplies, which she didn't have, bringing her…

Right back to where she started.

She looked up from the book over to her ragged fingernails. Partial moons were showing above her nails – they were growing out and she'd need to get a new set put on and fast, or just go without.

She gulped. Hard. She couldn't remember the last time she didn't have fake nails on. It was one of the few battles in her life that she'd fought and won. Piano teachers were *not* impressed by her fake nails, to say the least. They'd often complained to her parents that she needed to get rid of them, but Tenny had refused. Real fingernails were ugly.

She groaned. She better get used to ugly real quick – a depressing thought that weighed down on her. Maybe Levi had been right during their camping trip – maybe she was a spoiled rotten rich kid.

She started flicking through the book, skimming pages as she went, looking for some magic pill or formula that could save her. She stopped on the clothing chapter. Now *here* was something she knew something about. She eagerly began reading, only to find the same ideas that she'd found elsewhere – buy from thrift stores or outlet malls. Buy off eBay. Never pay retail.

Ugh. Well, honestly, the one thing she didn't need more of anyway was clothes. She'd only managed to bring a small portion of her huge wardrobe with her when she'd left home, and the last thing she needed to do was go on a shopping spree for more.

Hold on… She stared down at the page unseeingly.

The one thing she had was clothes.

Lots and lots and lots of clothes. And handbags and shoes and belts and scarves and jewelry. Enough to keep a fashion model looking good for the rest of her life.

She let out a delighted laugh. *Oh Tenny, you're so stupid sometimes.*

She hurried through the house to find Georgia's landline, an arcane piece of technology that Tenny found rather delightful, the same way you find your Great Aunt Tilda to be delightful – in that quaint, aren't-you-adorable sort of way. She called her younger sister, Virginia.

"Ginny," she said, "I have a favor to ask of you."

CHAPTER 27

LEVI

*H*E COLLAPSED onto his lumpy couch, staring at the far wall without seeing a thing. He was exhausted.

Which wasn't surprising, considering it'd been a week from hell, but that still didn't mean he found it enjoyable.

On Monday morning, after the weekend's big reveal worthy of a reality TV show, Levi had walked into the John Deere dealership and dropped his keys on his boss' desk. "I'm done here," he told Sam. "If you wanna know why, you're free to ask Rocky. But I'm out."

He turned around and walked out of Sam's office while the man was still sputtering in disbelief, but Levi just didn't have it in him to stay and explain it all. His patience for the story and for the world as a whole was simply gone. He felt worn out, emotionally, physically, mentally.

But today was Day 4 of being unemployed, and he was already starting to regret his impulsiveness. Maybe he didn't have to quit the dealership after all. Maybe he could've just learned how to co-exist with Rocky and they could've moved on and eventually built some sort of relationship based on trust.

It was possible.

Highly unlikely, but possible.

Levi had been living frugally his whole life, and had plenty stashed away in his savings account that he could live off if need be, but the panic and worry was already starting to eat away at him. What if he didn't find another job for a long time? What if he lost his house? What if he became homeless? What if he became just like Steve – a drunk who blamed everything on everyone else?

What if…what if…what if…

He forced himself to take a few deep breaths. He'd be fine. A metal shop in town and a few farmers had been interested when he'd stopped by to talk to them. One of them was bound to hire him. He probably wouldn't be paid as well or have as nice of a benefit package, but he'd make it. He'd been in worse spots before—

Knock knock.

The sound jerked him out of his thoughts. *Who the hell is here?* Moose hadn't mentioned coming over tonight but maybe he'd wanted to surprise him. Levi pushed himself off the couch, swallowing his groan. He was tired, stressed to the max, and grumpy as hell.

He wasn't sure Moose deserved to be around him in that moment. No one did. He'd just have to tell Moose that they could hang out another day.

Except, he pulled the door open to find not Moose but Tennessee standing there, just as beautiful as ever.

No, scratch that. *More* beautiful than ever. His eyes searched her face and body hungrily, betraying him even as he was trying to force himself to tell her to go away. *I'm not good enough for you. I'm toxic. You have to leave me alone.*

She was wearing a short denim skirt, knee-high boots, and a drapey blue-green top that hugged her tits without making her look like a prostitute.

In short, she was stunning.

He opened up his mouth, trying to force the words out that'd push her away, that'd protect her from him, but only a croak came out.

"You stopped returning my phone calls," she said softly as she stepped deftly underneath his arm to stand inside of his living room. Stunned, he closed the door behind her on auto pilot, still trying to make his brain understand that she was standing right there, right in front of him. His hands itched to reach out and pull her into his arms. "I couldn't bear the idea of you being angry with me," she said, nibbling her bottom lip as she looked up at him beseechingly.

"I'm not mad at you," he responded instinctively, surprised by the mere idea of it. He couldn't stop staring at her, drinking her in visually. It'd only been five days since he'd last seen her, but it felt like a lifetime. A lifetime of pain and hurt and just having her here made that dissipate.

Just a little.

"I'm–I'm not good enough for you," he blurted out.

"Not good enough?" she repeated with a laugh. "Are you saying that because of Rocky and his inability to keep it in his pants?"

Levi had to laugh a little at the inadvertent mimicking of his own thoughts, even as he shook his head. "It's all of it. I'm a bastard, Tennessee. A literal *bastard*. You can't be with me—"

"Babe," she said, cutting him off, "the one thing you and I absolutely have in common is that we didn't get to pick our parents and if we had somehow been able to, neither of us would've picked the ones we've been stuck with. My parents are no prize. I mean, hell, they've been busy trying to sell me off to the highest bidder for years now."

She sucked in a quick breath and clapped her hand over her mouth, her eyes wide as she stared at him.

"Sell you off?" he repeated slowly, totally confused. When she'd moved out of her parent's house, she'd refused to tell him why, just saying that she'd had a falling out with her parents and that it was better for her to live with Georgia while she began working on standing on her own two feet. He'd applauded the idea, and anyway, he knew better than anyone that you may not want to tell every person you know everything that was happening in your life, so he'd accepted her decision not to share any other info with him.

But *selling her off*? That sounded huge. Not something they could just brush under the rug.

"What do you mea—"

And then, all thoughts of her parents and what they may or may not have done flew right out of his mind as Tennessee threw herself into his arms and began kissing him.

"I've missed you," she murmured as she kissed her way down his throat hungrily. "A girl can get addicted to someone like you, and then to have you just disappear on me…" She reached down and yanked his t-shirt off over his head and then leaned back so she could whistle appreciatively at the view. He felt awkward as hell having her just drool over him like that, especially since she was still fully clothed, so he decided to do some shirt removal work of his own.

It was only fair, after all.

Before he could get the clingy fabric off her, though, she pulled back out of range of his hands and bit her lower lip again. His groin tightened at the sight. Did she have any idea what she did to him when she looked at him like that?

"Let's go to the bedroom," she said softly, her huge eyes looking up at him as if he'd hung the sun, the moon, and the stars just for her.

All of the blood in Levi's body was going straight to his dick, making it hard for him to even understand what she was saying, let alone be capable of doing anything about it, but luckily for him, she took his hand and began leading him towards his bedroom. A part of him wanted to ask how she knew where it was – they'd always ended up on the couch before – but again with the whole talking thing…

Saying words other than *yes* and *please* seemed awfully complicated in that moment. He'd ask her later.

She pulled him into the bedroom, walking backwards, holding his hands as she moved towards the bed. It was dark; he'd left the blinds pulled, giving the room a distinct twilight feel.

"Window," he croaked out, wanting to see her body better but then she was pulling off her shirt and dropping it to the floor and he forgot why he'd even been asking about the window. The dim lighting of the bedroom did nothing to hide the beauty in front of him – she was delicate all over, like a fragile doll he might break if he was too rough with her.

Her short denim skirt and knee-high boots, combined with a lacy black bra…the world was going dark around the edges again, but this time not with anger but with lust. There was some reason that they shouldn't be doing this but it taunted him from the sidelines, refusing to reveal itself. *Something…something…*

And then she unzipped her denim skirt and let it pool around her feet and all thoughts were gone. She was wearing a black lacy thong that matched her bra, worthy of a centerfold spread in *Playboy*.

His restraint was gone, vaporized by the most beautiful woman he'd ever seen, standing in front of him, practically begging him to make love to her – a request he couldn't resist.

He swept her up into his arms and carried her over to the bed. "So gorgeous, so damn gorgeous," he murmured as he nibbled his way down her soft, golden thighs. When he met the top of her leather boots, he let out a growl of frustration, and she laughed.

"Here, let me," she said, and quickly unzipped them, kicking them off to the side. With a happy sigh, he began kissing and licking his way down her calves.

"I've wanted this all my life…" he moaned as he moved. "Watching you up on stage, competing in beauty pageants…I never understood Moose's aversion to watching you walk around in a bikini and high heels."

She let out a little laugh. "When you put it that way," she drawled breathlessly, "it does seem like a great way for a guy to pass a Saturday evening."

"I only had eyes for you," he said softly, pulling back from her delicious calves. "Even back then. Even when I was dating Georgia and in love with her…it was a self-defense thing. I knew I couldn't have you, so I wouldn't let myself really admit…"

She flexed her calves and the slight muscles rippled under her skin. All thoughts were gone again.

"Tennessee," he whispered, her name a prayer of love and devotion that came pouring out of him without restraint. He worked his way back up her legs and to the juncture of her thighs. She kept herself shaved bare and he couldn't help the shudder of desire that rippled over him at the smell and sight and softness of her mound. He began licking and nuzzling her, until he worked his way over to her clit, causing her to howl with pleasure, her back arching as she dug her fingers into his hair.

"Leeeevviiiiii…" she moaned and whimpered and shouted as tiny pinpricks of pain and pleasure shot through his scalp. She kept tugging and he kept licking and she kept moaning with desire and–

He couldn't handle it anymore. It had been too long. Much too long. He'd wanted to make her scream with delight again and again, but his self control had disappeared completely. With a shaking hand, he fumbled for a condom in his bedside table and rolled it into place and then with a groan of pure need, he slid inside of her…

And right through her virginity.

"Tennessee?!" he half shouted, his eyes popping open.

She looked up at him with a grimacing smile on her face. "Uh, yes?" she said in an all-too-innocent voice.

CHAPTER 28

TENNESSEE

*D*AMMIT.

She'd been hoping that the whole "A guy can feel it when he pops your cherry" thing was just an urban legend. Like the one about the lady who put too much hairspray in her hair and under the heat of the summer sun, her head caught on fire. Everyone knew someone's cousin's brother-in-law's great-aunt who had it happen to them, which was code for, "It wasn't a real thing."

But based on the look on Levi's face at this very moment, Tenny was pretty damn sure that being able to feel a girl's hymen via dick insertion was not, in fact, an old wives' tale.

"It's okay," she said, when he didn't seem like he was going to start moving again anytime soon. "Really. It didn't hurt." *Too much.* She kept that thought to herself. "Please, I was really starting to get into it." Before he'd slid inside, she'd been on another planet, gloriously and happily over the moon with pleasure, and sure, popping her cherry hadn't been the most fun she'd had all week, but the pain had already faded. She was ready and willing to get back to it.

She lifted her hips in the age-old move that silently begged for him to continue, but he shut his eyes and groaned instead. "But, you are…you *were* a…a…a *virgin*." He said it like he'd say that she had some sort of awful communicable disease. "How?!"

"I never had sex?" she said dryly, and then wiggled her hips again. Was there a jumpstart somewhere in here? A button she could push to make him go again? Talking about sex wasn't nearly as much fun as having it.

"You and Moose…for years…and you didn't…" He was sputtering and if she wasn't so damn horny, she'd probably laugh.

Seeing as she was as horny as a randy teenager, though, laughing seemed out of the realm of possibilities at that moment.

"No, we didn't," she finally said, deciding that answering his questions was the only way she'd be able to get back to the fun stuff sometime this century. "We decided when we were teenagers that we wouldn't have sex until our wedding night, and honestly, I'm gonna say that it was a pledge that was a little too easy to keep. Moose became this brother to me that I never had, and after a while, the idea of sleeping with him was just…yuck. No thank you.

"So no, we never had sex. We messed around a lot, but..." She shrugged and pulled him down towards her. "It's too late now to make me a virgin again, right? So, let's at least finish the fun." She began kissing her way up his chest, stopping at one of his flat nipples and flicking her tongue against it.

He growled, his self control breaking into a million little pieces in front of her eyes as he slammed back into her. She saw stars – glorious, beautiful, amazing stars, bursting overhead and flaming out into the darkness, lighting up her whole body.

If she'd known...if she'd had any idea that sex was this amazing, she *never* would've agreed to stay a virgin until her wedding night. Never.

The tingles ran up and down her arms as Levi howled his pleasure and Tenny shook and the world exploded and her voice joined Levi's as her back arched and the world swirled and dipped around them.

Yeah, her teenage self had *no* idea what she'd been agreeing to.

She didn't know how much time had passed when she felt him pull away, rolling over onto his side, away from her. She groaned and reached out her hand. "Don't..." she whispered, not ready to let him go. He flinched from her touch and she realized that he wasn't just rolling off her so she could breathe properly again.

He was pulling away from *her*. Emotionally, mentally, physically, he was withdrawing.

"Levi, where are you going?" she whispered. "You can't...what we just did...you can't leave me." She propped herself up on one elbow, the semi-darkness of the room not hiding his gorgeous body from her. She ran her fingers up his side and then back down over his glorious abs. He pulled in a hiss of air at her touch.

"Tennessee," he said formally, snagging her hand and keeping her from exploring further. "We shouldn't have...shouldn't have done that." He waved his hand in the air to encompass the whole room. "I'm not good enough for you. You can't—"

She put her finger over his mouth, shushing him with her light touch. "I already told you – I don't care about your background. You think I shouldn't be with the man I love because his biological father couldn't keep it in his pants?"

Levi sucked in a sharp breath at that and even in the faded light, she could see the wide-eyed look he was giving her at her words.

"Yes, love," she repeated, a grin spreading across her face. A joyful, happy grin because she was finally telling him the truth. "I've been in love with you my whole life, Levi Scranton; ever since I really knew what love was. Watching you with Georgia; being forced to date Moose...years of torture. Years. I never thought I'd actually get to be with you.

"And then you started fixating on my parent's wealth and I thought maybe, somehow, I didn't know you as well as I thought I did. Then, you showed up at my house with those yellow roses in hand, and my heart burst into a million little pieces of happiness. Having you with me because of *me*, not because your parents are guilting you into it or because you have to do it to inherit a tractor dealership – do you know how amazing that is?"

"I love Moose," Levi rumbled, apropos of absolutely nothing. Tennessee stared at him in the dark, trying to figure out where he was going with this and coming up with nothing at all. "Like a brother, which is ironic considering...well, you know." He waved his hand in the air dismissively and then dropped it back down on top of her side. He began playing with a curl of her hair, watching it wrap around his thick, long, calloused fingers. She waited patiently for him to continue. For him to struggle this much with spitting it out, she knew it had to be something important. Something huge.

"But him choosing Georgia over you...dumbest thing he ever did. Not that I'm mad about it – it gave me the chance to date you – but damn, he's an idiot. Georgia is fine – I loved her for a long time – but... she ain't you, Tenny. If I'd thought in high school, for just one moment, that I'd have a chance with you? I would've dropped her in a heartbeat and climbed Mt. Everest barefoot to make it happen. I just didn't think...I never dreamed..."

Tenny shook her head. "I was in love with you back in high school, Levi. I've been in love with you almost all my life, I think. But I wasn't strong enough back then to tell my parents no. I wasn't strong enough to forge my own path and tell them where they could stick their bullshit schemes for me. So it's damn good that you didn't know the truth in high school, because it never would've worked out. You would've grown to hate me for being spineless."

He shook his head in bewilderment. "Over the past couple of months, you went from being willing to say yes to Moose if he'd proposed, to moving out of your parent's house and dating me. I think you had more bravery in you than you knew."

She bent down and pressed a kiss to his strong jaw. "No, I didn't," she whispered in his ear. "You...you make me strong. You give me courage. Now," she said, pulling back and looking down at him seriously, "I need your help."

CHAPTER 29

LEVI

TENNESSEE TURNED OFF the flashlight and Levi stumbled in the darkness, letting out a string of curse words under his breath as he tried to figure out for the millionth time why it was that he'd allowed her to talk him into this. When she'd asked him, all big eyes and soft voice and her tits pressing up against his side, he'd agreed, of course. Saying no to her in that moment would've required the kind of self restraint Levi simply didn't possess.

As he tripped over a stone in the darkness and fell to one knee, he began to question that fact. If he didn't learn how to start telling Tennessee no when she batted her eyelashes at him, he was gonna end up in some deep shit.

As if he wasn't in exactly that right now.

"C'mon," she whispered, helping pull him back up to his feet. "Virginia is already at the window."

They both peered up at the window where

Tenny's teenage sister was waving wildly at them, as if she was worried they wouldn't see her, half hanging out of the second-story window of Tennessee's family home.

Well, mansion.

Levi pushed that thought away. He could be intimidated by her family's wealth another time. Right now was *not* the time.

As they neared the open window, Virginia ducked out of sight and then reappeared with a trash bag in her hands, ready to do her part. Once they got underneath the window, she let the bag go, nothing but the croaking of bullfrogs and discordant song of the crickets to hear in the still summer night.

Whoomp.

Levi caught the black garbage sack, filled with lumps of clothing and shoes and belts.

Whoomp.

The second bag landed in Tennessee's arms. Levi and Tenny took off for the truck, parked a block over, the garbage sacks slung over their shoulders like a midnight version of Santa Claus running down the street. Levi shortened his stride when he realized that Tenny's shorter legs were making it hard for her to keep up. Not everyone's legs rivaled a giant.

They slung the bags into the bed of his truck and then hurried back to the Rowland house. Levi tried not to groan out loud at the fact that if he were caught, he could kiss finding a local job goodbye. It was bad enough that he was trying to date Robert

Rowland's daughter; sneaking around and helping her steal her own clothes back from her parents was a whole 'nother kettle of fish.

When they got back to the Rowland mansion, Virginia was there, ready and waiting with another garbage sack to drop. As it came hurtling down towards him, he had to wonder, exactly how much clothing Tennessee owned. These were large sacks, and Ginny had already dropped three out of the window. Were they close to being done yet?

Tennessee caught hers with a smothered grunt and they took off for the truck again, their hurrying footsteps the only sound in the still summer night. Levi was happy that both Tennessee and Virginia were taking his warning to heart, and not saying a word as they worked. That and requiring Tenny to wear all black and cover her blonde hair with a black stocking cap were his requirements for actually going along with this scheme of hers.

Honestly, if they got caught, Tenny wouldn't be in trouble at all – her parents would never turn their own daughter over to the police for theft – but Levi's ass would be grass. He'd probably be locked away for life if the Rowlands had anything to say about it.

And yet, he couldn't tell her no, not with those big eyes looking up at him, and her small but perfect tits pressed against his side.

This was definitely going to become a problem. A problem he'd solve in the future; just not right now.

As the pile in the bed of the truck grew larger and

larger with every trip, Levi began to reassess Tennessee's spending habits. She'd told him that she'd been a big proponent of "retail therapy" as she called it, but this…

How was it possible for one human being to own this much clothing? And how did she make a decision every morning on what to wear? It seemed like she could spend the entire day dressing and undressing, all day long, all month long, all year long, and still have plenty of clothes leftover that she hadn't even touched.

"Last one," Ginny whispered, breaking her silence for the first time since the caper had started. "All jewelry – be carefu—"

The smaller bag slipped through Tenny's hands and landed with a clatter on the cobblestone pathway, metal and jewels spilling everywhere, glittering under the light of the moon.

"Shit!" all three exclaimed under their breaths at exactly the same moment, and then Ginny disappeared into the house, pulling her window closed behind her as Levi and Tennessee scrambled to find the jewelry in the dark. A light flipped on in the house and Levi heard some mumbled words drift through the summer air towards them. He didn't know what was being said, but he did recognize the voice: Mr. Rowland was awake.

"Shit, shit, shit," Levi muttered, snagging a few last glittering pieces and shoving them into his pockets. "Tenny, we gotta go!"

She nodded and scrambled to her feet, hurrying through the grass and down to Mansion Way, retracing the path they'd taken a couple dozen times already that night.

But this time, her gait was awkward as she tried to hug the jewelry to her chest, and she also seemed completely freaked out – incapable of making decisions like she should be in the heat of the moment.

Levi bit back his groan. He shouldn't have brought Tenny with him. He'd tried to convince her to just let him go alone, but she'd refused. She was sick of being a mooch, she'd told him. Her throwing his words back in his face had made him flinch, and then capitulate. How little he'd known about Tennessee during that camping trip. How much she'd grown since then.

But still, she wasn't a master thief and never would be.

They scrambled into his truck as Levi heard the front door of the mansion slam open and shouts ring out into the still night air. He started the truck and threw it into reverse, hoping that the blinding headlights shining out in the darkness would keep Mr. Rowland from being able to see his license plate, or much about his truck. He tore backwards down Mansion Way, his arm slung across the bench seat as he craned his neck around, concentrating on not taking out a parked car or telephone pole.

"You bastard!" he heard the man faintly call, the voice fading away. "I'll…"

And then his voice was gone altogether.

Levi backed up into a driveway, and then pulled out, heading forwards this time as they went back down the hill and into the streets of Sawyer proper.

"Holy shit, holy shit, holy shit," Tennessee chanted, and then began laughing hysterically. "I cannot believe we just did that!"

They began laughing together, the stress and relief rolling off Levi in waves as he made his way to his house.

"I can't either!" he said, looking over at Tenny with a huge grin. "My mastermind thief of a girlfriend, who used to be a beauty queen!"

Tenny shot him a huge smile. "One of the questions they always like to ask is if you win, what would you do. I'm pretty sure I wouldn't have won anything if I'd answered, 'Rob my parents!'"

"Probably not," Levi agreed dryly.

They pulled up in front of his house and quickly began unloading the bags of clothing and shoes and jewelry under the cover of darkness, the elation of having made a quick getaway fading away into the night sky. Even though Tennessee had treated it like a joke that she'd robbed her parents, the truth of the matter was, she *had* done that, and before he came along and ruined her, she never would've dreamed of doing something like this.

He was a kid from the wrong side of the tracks.

Instead of talking her out of pulling tonight's stunt, he'd helped her make it happen. Trip after trip into the house, his shoulders began to slump as the reality of what they just did washed over him.

He was an idiot. He never should've helped her. What if they'd been caught?

He wasn't good enough for her, and he never would be. Someday, she'd finally figure that out for herself, and then where would he be?

"Thank you for your help," she said quietly, sensing his mood. They stood back, both looking at the mountain of garbage sacks stacked up in the spare bedroom of Levi's house. "I couldn't have done this without you."

The words stabbed at him. Even she realized that he was enabling these poor life choices.

When was he going to learn how to tell Tennessee Rowland no?

CHAPTER 30

TENNESSEE

WHERE HAD HE GONE? He'd withdrawn in on himself; had disappeared despite being right next to her.

"Levi?" she asked, putting her hand on his arm. "What's wrong?"

"I shouldn't have helped you with this," he growled, his dark eyes flashing with pain. "Before, you never would've dreamed of doing something like this, and now look at what you're doing. You can take a rat out of the gutter, but you can't take the gutter out of the rat."

Tenny sucked in a breath at that. "Levi, you aren't a gutter rat," she said, stroking her hand up his muscled arm softly. He had a sheen of sweat on every inch of his skin, and she had the hardest time concentrating on what he was saying. Licking and kissing her way up his arm seemed like a hell of a lot more fun. "I've been a doormat all of my life," she reminded him. "I'm finally standing on my own two feet. This is a *good* thing, I promise."

"It's one thing to stand on your own two feet," he said, his eyes dark and hooded. "It's another to steal a bunch of clothes."

"*My* clothes," Tenny pointed out bluntly. "What, do you think my father was dipping into my closet on the weekends and playing dress-up? I would've just asked my parents for the clothes, but then they would've used them as a bargaining chip, forcing me to agree to their terms before giving me my own stuff. You kept me from having to play their game."

"I guess," Levi said, clearly unconvinced.

Tenny rolled her eyes and decided to change the topic. "You remember Sugar and Jaxson's wedding is tomorrow, right?" Jaxson Anderson was the new fire chief in town, and just months after moving to Sawyer, he'd fallen in love with Sugar, who worked down at the Muffin Man bakery. Tenny and Sugar had never been especially close even though they'd graduated from high school the same year – cliques exist even in the smallest of schools, and they had always run in different circles.

Despite that, they'd gotten along in that, "Hi, how are you? Good," sort of way, and Tennessee – a romantic sap to the bitter end – was thrilled that Sugar had found love, especially after her first disastrous marriage to Richard Schmidt. Sugar deserved all of the happiness she could get after putting up with that drunk asshole for six years.

And what with Jaxson being new to town and all, he'd asked Moose, Levi, and Troy to be his groomsmen at the wedding, all three firefighters for the city. Tenny had thought it was a really sweet gesture, but when Jaxson had asked Levi if he'd do him the honor of being in his lineup, Levi had grumbled that he wasn't fit to be in a lineup for a wedding. Moose, standing right there, had elbowed him in the ribs and told Levi that it was just good practice for when Moose married Georgia.

The look on Levi's face then…

Priceless.

Honestly, Levi didn't look much happier right now. "I was sort of hoping that they'd just forget to get married," he grumbled, walking into the living room and dropping down on his lumpy couch.

"Yeah, 'cause that's totally a thing that happens," Tennessee said dryly, sitting down next to him. "Hmmm…" she said, tapping her chin as she pretended to think hard, "I know I'm supposed to do something today…I just can't remember what…"

Levi grinned a little at that – just the slightest uptick of his lips – but Tenny felt a wave of triumph anyway. She'd never been known for her quick wit or her sense of humor, but apparently, that was coming alive in her now – another hidden part of her personality that she'd never known she possessed.

And all because of Levi…

"Did you pick up your suit from the tux rental place?" Tenny asked, running her fingers through his hair as they talked. He really did have the most touchable hair she'd ever seen. The dark curls just begged for her fingers to run through them, and now that she actually got to do it, she found it almost impossible to keep her hands to herself.

He shook his head. "Sugar and Jaxson are keeping expenses low so they can afford to throw a huge party down on Main Street to celebrate. No suits for the groomsmen and no fancy dresses for the bridesmaids. Clean jeans and a white shirt is all I have to worry about. They'll provide the tie." He rubbed at his neck as if already feeling the offending piece of fabric choking him.

Tenny couldn't help her small smile at the gesture. "Do you know how to tie a tie?" she asked, letting a chunk of dark hair curl over her finger. He looked good enough to eat, even sweaty and dirty from their midnight run.

Especially because of their midnight run, honestly.

He shook his head again. "Never worn one," he mumbled, looking embarrassed as hell to admit that out loud.

"Well, I'll tie it for you," she promised, before he could start worrying about how gutter rats shouldn't be wearing ties. "Moose hated them too so I always had to tie them for him. So, you'll come pick me up at nine at Georgia's house?"

Levi's eyes grew dark with lust as he looked over at her. "Or you could just spend the night…" he said softly, pulling the stocking cap off her head and letting her hair spill down over her shoulders. She probably looked like she stuck a fork in a light socket, but the look in Levi's eyes said that even if she did, he didn't care.

"Nope, no way," she said firmly. "Too much to do to get ready for the wedding in the morning and all of my stuff is at Georgia's house. But I promise to make it worth it."

She winked at him. He groaned. She laughed.

Yeah, she'd make it worth it, all right.

CHAPTER 31

TENNESSEE

S HE HEARD THE RAP on the front door and with one last pat of her dress, she hurried over to open it. She hadn't been this nervous since the night of the Miss Idaho Pageant.

She smoothed her features into place, and then opened the door, subconsciously standing as she had during the evening wear portion of the pageant – one leg forward, hand on hip, a smile pasted on her face. It was the most flattering pose possible, and at that moment, she wanted to look *good*. She wanted Levi's tongue to hang out of his mouth. She wanted him to drool. She wanted him to look at her like he wanted to tear her clothes off with his teeth.

The way Moose never, ever looked at her.

Levi's eyes went wide when he saw her, his gaze dropping down to her strappy high heels and working their way back up her body, past the thigh-high slit in her skirt, and up to the neckline that draped and dipped, showing and hiding her cleavage with every breath. The royal blue of the dress made her eyes turn a deep blue, without a trace of the green that could usually be found. As a final touch, the dress had these shimmery, sheer sleeves that cascaded down her arms, revealing and then concealing with every movement. As far as evening gowns went, it wasn't all that revealing, but it was the *promise* of skin showing that made it seem far sexier than it really was.

"That's it, we're staying here!" Levi burst out, practically jumping through the doorway so he could slam the front door shut behind him. "Jaxson will just have to get married without me."

Tenny couldn't help the huge grin that spread over her face. Different from the beauty-queen-pageant smile that she was used to pasting on, this grin said that she'd done exactly what she'd wanted to, and she knew it.

Ohhh yeeaaahhhh…

She grabbed her clasp purse from the side table, snagged Levi's hand, and started back towards the front door. "Come on, Levi, we gotta go."

She may or may not have brushed directly across the front of him as she moved past him. The hiss of breath told her that this move hadn't been lost on him.

Her grin got bigger.

"Ummm…shouldn't we wait for your cousin to finish getting ready? Drive her to the wedding?" Levi asked, his normally bass voice several octaves too high.

Tennessee smirked. She was used to being considered the most beautiful woman in the room, but still, there was something terribly satisfying about Levi's reaction. After years of indifference from Moose...

Yeah, she could stand Levi drooling a little.

"Nope, she's already at the church with Moose." Giving up on tugging him out the door – he'd somehow grown roots and was proving to be impossible to budge – she let go of his hand instead and slipped out the front door by herself, hurrying down the sidewalk to stand on the passenger side of Levi's truck. She knew he wouldn't let her just stand there all morning, so this was her best bet to get his ass moving.

"Ohhh," Levi groaned, his voice still higher than it was normally. Maybe he just had something in his throat, or maybe it had been the sway she'd put into her hips as she'd sashayed to the truck.

Hard to tell, really.

Reluctantly, Levi pulled Georgia's front door shut behind him, and then headed over to help her inside the truck. Once inside, she ever-so-casually rearranged her skirt, making sure that the end result was that it was gaping open at mid-thigh, and then reached past his head to grab the seat belt. He was stuck partially inside of the truck, his dark curls close to her lap, and as she snapped her seat belt in, she was

97.4% sure that he was contemplating kissing his way up her bared thigh.

Finally, he pulled out of the truck and let out a heartfelt groan.

"Are you okay?" she asked innocently, batting her eyelashes at him.

Levi closed his eyes and muttered a prayer under his breath as he hurried around to the driver's side.

As he settled into the driver's seat, Tenny took her sweet time looking him over, blatantly admiring him as they made their way to the Grace Valley Church. Even with the collar of the white shirt unbuttoned, he looked way more formal than he normally did, and something about seeing him in a button-up shirt…

He looked good enough to eat, that was for damn sure.

Levi kept stealing glances at her. "Are you cold?" he asked abruptly. "It's cold today."

It was already a blistering 91 degrees outside, and forecasted to only get warmer as the day progressed.

"You should put on a jacket," he announced without waiting for her to respond, rummaging with his right arm in the backseat as he kept his left hand on the steering wheel to drive. Without taking his eyes off the road, he pulled out a jacket and shoved it at her.

It would've been impressive…if he hadn't been shoving a greasy, torn plaid jacket into her lap.

"You should put it on," he suggested hopefully.

Uh-huh. Sure…

She picked up the edge of the jacket between her thumb and forefinger and dropped it back into the backseat.

"I'm not cold, I promise," she said blandly, hiding her laughter beneath her carefully constructed veneer she was so comfortable wearing. "But thank you for your thoughtfulness."

One should always be polite, right?

Levi gulped but didn't say anything else, gripping the steering wheel with both hands like it was a life preserver here to rescue him.

Before Tennessee could decide whether running her fingernails up his thigh would be great fun or a sure-fire way to end up in the ditch, they pulled up in front of the church and Levi cut the engine.

"I…you…" he stumbled, and then stopped, took a deep breath, and closed his eyes. "You-shouldn't-be-seen-in-public-with-me," he said in a rush, keeping his eyes tightly closed. "I-should-drop-you-off-and-then-leave-you-alone."

She waited quietly for him to get it all out, and then waited quietly for him to open up his eyes. The heat in the truck grew stifling but still, she just sat there, not moving a muscle, simply staring at him and waiting. He was stubborn, sure, but he'd never come up against someone like her. When she had a mind to, she could make mules look like pliable, easygoing animals high on muscle relaxants.

The silence grew and grew, and still, she sat and waited.

Finally, *finally*, he opened up his eyes and looked at her, haunted and scared.

His mouth was pleading for her to tell him to go away, that she didn't want to date him, even as his eyes begged for her to tell him that she loved him with all of her heart and soul.

She wondered if he knew how much his eyes were giving him away. As someone who was used to spending her time hiding every thought she had from the world, she knew what a huge chink this was in his armor. Unlike others, though, she swore to herself that she'd never use it against him.

"I'm here with *you*," she said softly, but with great feeling, stroking her hand across his smoothly shaved cheek. "There's no one in the world I'd rather be here with. I love you, Levi Scranton. I've always loved you."

He closed his eyes again and groaned, but he seemed to grasp the futility of arguing further, at least for the moment. He slid out of the truck, hurrying around to her side where he helped her out. She took a huge gulp of fresh air and then, looping her arm through his, they made their way up the front steps of the quaint, white church. Since Levi was part of the line-up, they had to be there early, and only a few dedicated souls had arrived before them, milling around and helping with the last-minute touches to the wedding arrangements.

Georgia spotted them and waved energetically, a huge smile gracing her lips. She hurried over. "Look at you two," she said admiringly. "Never saw a better-lookin' pair in all my life."

Levi pulled at his open collar, already looking like he was being choked to death by the tie he had yet to even lay eyes on. "Do you know where Jaxson is at?" he rumbled, his voice back in its normal bass range.

Tenny let out a little sigh to herself, disappointed to hear his voice back to normal. It really had been fun to mess with his mind.

"Yeah, back in the preparation area," Georgia said, pointing off to the left. "There's a guy's area and a girl's area, so make sure to pick the right door."

With a final squeeze of Tennessee's hand, Levi headed for the open doorway that Georgia had pointed to. Tennessee watched his loose-hipped gait with an appreciative sigh. Georgia grinned at her. "Now *that's* the sigh of a happy woman," she said with a laugh. "I know I'm hardly ever at home and we haven't had a chance to talk lately, so talk now – are things really going as well between you two as they seem like they are?"

Tennessee thought back to Levi's concerns about not being good enough for her and bit her lip hesitantly.

"Yes and no," she said finally. "He doesn't think that he should be dating me; that somehow he isn't good enough for me because of who his father is. To be honest, I'm not sure which was worse – Levi thinking that he was the son of the town drunk, or knowing that he's a bastard and the product of an affair. Neither are stellar choices, to be honest. It's... it's been a hard adjustment for him."

Georgia squeezed her hand. "Moose has been struggling with it, too," she admitted. "Not the part about knowing that Levi is his half-brother − I think if Moose could pick any person in the world to be his brother, it'd be Levi − but Rocky..."

Tenny nodded slowly, squeezing back. "I know," she said softly. "You weren't there that day, of course, but...if Moose didn't feel anything at all after that exchange, it could've only have been because he was dead. My parents aren't exactly top-notch but hey, at least, they aren't openly disinheriting me. Well, not yet." She sent Georgia a smile that was closer to a grimace. "After last night's escapades, though, I guess we'll see."

Georgia threw her head back and laughed. "Any word from them yet?"

Tenny shook her head with a sly smile. "I don't think my parents believe I'm capable of it. They'd probably prefer to believe some rando broke into the house and stole them all, rather than the culprit being their darling daughter. After all, I was always the good child who didn't cause any problems." She put her hands under her chin and fluttered her eyelashes angelically.

Georgia laughed. "It's always the quiet ones that you have to look out for," she said with a naughty grin. "They never see 'em coming."

People began filing in and the hubbub of the

preparations for the wedding moved front and center as Sugar, gorgeous in a simple white gown and gold-colored slippers, hurried around frantically, looking like she had a million things to do and absolutely no idea what order to do them in.

Tenny and Georgia volunteered to put out the bouquets and soon, Carla from Happy Petals was busy directing them, making sure that each vase was exactly where Sugar had requested it to be.

As Tenny watched guests file in as they worked, though, she had a painful realization: All of the women were wearing skirts or a dress, but not a single soul was wearing an evening gown.

Shit.

This was a morning wedding being held at a simple country church; this wasn't evening-gown territory. She'd been so focused on making Levi drool, she just hadn't thought about it.

Stupid, stupid Tennessee. People are really *going to think you're stuck up now.*

She knew that was the reputation that she had – more than a few people had stage whispered the phrase "Ice queen" as she'd walked by during her high school years and even afterwards. No one would say it openly to her face, of course, but that didn't mean that they weren't all thinking it, and today's stunt would only add to that misconception.

She ground her back teeth together, angry with herself. When would she ever learn and stop making dumb mistakes?

Her palms were sweating. She longed for the cool blade and weight of her knife in her hand. She could just—

But before she could do something truly stupid, Georgia grabbed her arm. "C'mon, Carla says that there's another load of flowers to bring in." Tennessee nodded obediently and followed her cousin to the front doors of the church.

It would be okay — it would all be okay. Maybe she'd overdressed for the occasion, and maybe people would think she was a snob because of it, but thoughts couldn't hurt her, right?

Sticks and stones may break my bones, but words will never hurt me.

She chanted the childhood rhyme to herself. It was a ridiculously childish rhyme, but it was also true. She just had to stay focused.

Words will never hurt me. Hurt me…

Still, she wished she knew where Levi was. Maybe one of his set-her-hair-on-fire looks would calm her nerves, or at least, give her something else to think about. But whatever Jaxson was having the groomsmen do, he was having them do it out of sight.

And then even Georgia disappeared; paired as she was with Moose, she was a bridesmaid for Sugar. Tennessee felt stupidly alone, every friend and relative she would've hung out with having disappeared into the back. She was good at mingling and small talk; she was good at being poised and even-keeled under pressure.

It didn't mean she liked it, though.

In what felt like years later, finally the organist was striking up a chord on the old pipe organ and Tennessee was craning her neck along with everyone else, watching as the wedding party began making its way down the aisle.

First up were two little boys who Tennessee guessed were Jaxson's children. They'd been tasked with throwing rose petals, and also holding onto the leash of the largest dog Tenny had ever laid eyes on. The older boy, his face serious and concentrated on his responsibility, had his hand firmly wrapped around the leash of the Great Dane, while his other hand was clamped firmly onto the shoulder of his younger brother.

The younger one, meanwhile, was *clearly* delighting in the idea of being given something to throw, and throw he did. Titters ran through the audience as he threw handfuls of rose petals directly at the guests in the pews. Tennessee bit back her own laugh. Someone should've been a little more blunt in their instructions beforehand; telling a 5-year-old boy to "throw rose petals" was really asking for it.

Halfway down the aisle, the Great Dane and older brother liberally covered in rose petals along with the back half of the audience, the little boy finally ran out of petals. His eyes got big and he tugged on the shirt sleeve of his older brother. "I don't got no more flowers, Aiden," he said in the world's loudest whisper. The tittering of the audience grew to outright laughter at that announcement.

Aiden's eyes flicked up to the front where his father was standing, waiting for Sugar to come down the aisle. "Daddy?" he whispered, just as loud as his brother. They'd stalled out in the middle of the aisle, the Great Dane sitting down next to them patiently, the collar made of flowers sliding around his neck as he waited.

"It's all right, boys, just keep coming," Jaxson whispered back, waving his sons forward. Aiden obediently tugged on his younger brother and on the dog, getting the group to move again down the aisle.

Well, "move" was a generous term for it – it had obviously been drilled into his head to walk s-l-o-w because the group's pace up the aisle resembled nothing so much as a herd of turtles doped up on sleeping pills.

Meanwhile, the organist, having finished the *Wedding March* before the bride ever even made an appearance, paused for a moment and then started up at the top again, heaving a loud sigh as she did so.

As the laughter grew and spread through the audience, Tennessee couldn't help thinking that at this point, her faux pas of wearing an evening gown to a morning country wedding probably wouldn't be the topic of gossip afterwards.

Thank God for small children, large dogs, and impatient organists.

The two little boys with the giant dog in tow,

finally made it up to the front where the younger boy threw his arms around his father's legs, clearly thrilled to be done with his part of the ceremony. "Can me and Hamlet go sit now?" he asked his dad anxiously.

Jaxson's dark eyes flicked over the group in front of him, obviously trying to decide what to do. Tennessee hadn't attended any of the wedding rehearsals, if they'd even had any, but even she could tell that this was not part of the plan. "Uh, sure," Jaxson finally said. "You guys can sit over there." He pointed off to the side of the stage.

"Yahooooo!!!!" the little boy whooped and took off, the Great Dane and Aiden following along behind him obediently.

The roar of laughter drowned out whatever the pastor was whispering to Jaxson, but Tennessee was pretty sure it was something along the lines of, "This is *not* appropriate behavior for a church." He was well known in the area for being a stickler for propriety and rules. In fact, Tenny was a little shocked that he'd let a dog into his church. The...*unhappy* look on his face made her think that perhaps someone else had agreed to this plan on his behalf without telling him.

The organist, who'd finished the *Wedding March* for a second time by this point and had clearly escalated to the Very Annoyed stage, started at the top again, louder than ever. Tenny was pretty sure that the organist was mentally pounding the wedding group into submission via the ivory keys, and was most likely wishing that she was wielding a whip rather than an organ.

Emma Dyer, Sugar's best friend in high school and the younger sister to the owner of the Muffin Man, was now hurrying up the aisle, Levi on her arm. Tennessee could tell that she was trying to pick up the speed to make up for Jaxson's kids, but Levi, who'd obviously been told to walk slowly up the aisle, apparently hadn't been let in on this plan and was now being dragged behind her as she speed-walked up to the front. Tennessee barely had a chance to feel even a flicker of jealousy at some other woman's arm in Levi's before they were splitting off at the front to stand on opposite sides of the stage.

Next it was Moose and Georgia, looking better together than she and Moose had ever looked. The way that he was staring down at Georgia...Tennessee was pretty sure a proposal would be coming soon and thank God, it wouldn't be coming to her. The way they looked at each other, like the other person was in charge of hanging the sun, the moon, and the stars – yeah, Moose wasn't going to be proposing to Tennessee anytime soon.

She thought back to her discussion with Levi when he'd called the two of them "puke inducing." It was funny – she'd agreed with him wholeheartedly at the time, but now...

Now, she was jealous. At least Moose claimed his girlfriend in public. Tenny was having a hard time getting even that far.

She snuck a glance up at Levi standing in the front, hands clasped in front of him, looking as casual and at ease as ever. Anyone looking at him in that moment would believe that he wasn't self-conscious; that he knew wherever he was at, that's where he belonged.

Which was all a lie, of course. He hadn't wanted to be in the wedding party because he didn't think he was the kind of person you'd ask to be in something fancy-schmancy like that. He also didn't believe that Tennessee should be on his arm, because he didn't believe he was worthy of her.

In other words, he had just as many self-worth worries and insecurities as anyone else; he just didn't show them to the world. At least, not to anyone but her.

The thought made her feel more loved than any mere words could possibly express. To be vulnerable with someone – *that* was truly expressing love. Love was believing the other person would never hurt you, and acting accordingly.

He looked up and caught her staring at him, and gave her a lascivious wink. His eyes were promising that later, he'd show her *just* how much he loved her.

Intentionally, she bit her lower lip as she sent him a look back that said how much she was looking forward to that. Yeah, the church was going to burst into flames around them, and she didn't even care.

Just then, everyone stood and Tenny belatedly followed, realizing that she must've missed Troy walking down the aisle with whoever he'd been paired with because now they were on to the main event – Sugar.

Here she came down the aisle, her simple white wedding dress put to shame by the sheer amount of happiness pouring from her. Tenny was surprised to see her on the arm of not her father, but rather Emma's father, Mr. Timothy Dyer. She'd heard that Sugar wasn't speaking to her parents any longer, not after they basically forced her to marry her first husband, Richard, but still...It was rare to see this kind of schism made so public.

Sugar and Mr. Dyer made it up to the front, and the pastor asked everyone to please sit down. After the rustling and noise died away, the pastor launched into a well-worn speech about the sanctimony of marriage and love. He didn't appear to believe a word of it, and Tenny's mind wandered, looking at the back of Mr. Dyer, Sugar's arm tucked in his, patiently waiting to be asked who gave this bride away. Tennessee had known that Sugar had been inseparable from Emma during high school, but now she wondered if the Dyer family had pseudo-adopted her, much like the Garretts had with Levi.

Of course, Rocky Garrett had had a secret reason for taking such a close interest in Levi, and Tenny was pretty sure that wasn't the case with Sugar and the Dyer family. But still, it made her wonder how many teenagers out there were finding refuge in homes outside of their own. After all, Tennessee had done much the same thing with Aunt Shirley and Uncle Carl – when she'd needed someone there for her, she hadn't gone to her parents. She'd known better. She went to Georgia's parents.

Before Tenny could figure out why it was that adults had children if they had no intention of liking them, she heard the pastor announce, "You may now kiss the bride!" Startled, Tennessee looked up and realized that her wandering thoughts had caused her to miss the entire wedding ceremony. After a tongue-dueling kiss worthy of a Hollywood movie, Sugar and Jaxson began making their way back down the aisle, so happy that they looked like they might simply float away at any moment.

"What about the rings?" someone shouted from the audience and the organist, who'd been happily pounding out the piano version of *Somebody Like You* by Keith Urban, hit a discordant note and then collapsed into silence, staring over at the pastor for a hint as to what she should do.

Sugar and Jaxson looked at each other and then back up at the pastor, and began laughing. "I can't believe we forgot that," Jaxson got out around his laughter. They turned around and headed back up the aisle, the roar of laughter from the audience drowning out whatever the pastor was saying to Jaxson. The look on the pastor's face...he wasn't finding this oversight *nearly* as funny as everyone else was.

"Aiden, bring Hamlet over!" Jaxson called out,

and the older son obediently headed for the altar, the small horse trotting alongside him.

Okay, so Hamlet wasn't *actually* a horse, but to Tenny, he resembled a horse more than he did any dog she'd been around.

The younger boy, refusing to be left behind, streaked over and stood in the cluster up at the front, loudly asking Sugar if they were done yet. As the bride did her best to placate the five year old – Tenny heard her call him "Frankie" as they spoke – Jaxson was busy wrestling with Hamlet, trying to get at his collar. Hamlet, really having fun with this game, was bounding around, barking, tail wagging, knocking vases of flowers over with every powerful whack.

Tennessee had never laughed so hard in her entire life, she was sure of it.

Finally, Levi, Moose, and Troy waded into the fray, pinned Hamlet and his gigantic tail down, and pulled a box off the collar. Troy led the dog down the aisle and outside, in hopes of getting the overexcited dog some space and room to calm down. Meanwhile, Frankie and Aiden, now that they were up at the front with their father and stepmother, were clearly having none of it when Levi tried to scoot them off to the side and out of the way.

In the end, Sugar and Jaxson exchanged rings with Aiden and Frankie holding their hands – a brand-new family and even sweeter because of it.

This time, they walked back down the aisle together and the audience laughed and cheered and clapped as they went, Jaxson picking up and carrying Frankie while Aiden held Sugar's hand. Tennessee had never attended such a raucous wedding in all her life and couldn't help the laughter and huge grin that she had plastered on her face as she watched the Anderson family make their way through the crowd of well-wishers.

Levi and Emma, who'd originally started to follow the newly married couple down the aisle arm in arm as had been planned out beforehand, quickly realized that all of their plans had been thrown in disarray and they instead split, Emma heading off to find someone while Levi headed straight for Tennessee.

The look in his eyes…Tenny gulped.

She'd wanted him to look at her like he wanted to tear her clothes off with his teeth. She just hadn't expected it to affect her so strongly when he did.

How was it that I stayed a virgin for 26 years again?

CHAPTER 32

LEVI

THERE WAS NO WAY she knew what she was doing to him. That was the only explanation for it. If she knew what seeing her in that dress would do to him, she would've taken pity on him and not worn it.

Right?

Just as he reached her side, the crush of the guests pushing in from all directions, he heard a loud whistle and looked up to see Jaxson standing on one of the pews, waiting for everyone to quiet down and listen to him. Levi wanted to let out a bark of laughter – Jaxson standing on one of the pews inside of a church made this day complete – but he stifled it. He grabbed Tenny's hand and tucked it up against his side as he waited for the announcement.

Maybe he wasn't worthy to hold her hand, but if she was saying yes...

Well, who was he to say no?

"Just to make sure everyone heard," Jaxson shouted, the sound of his voice instantly quieting the last of the raucous crowd, "there will be a break until five this evening," he continued in a normal speaking voice. "I hope at that point that you can make it down to the street dance – we're holding it on Main Street, right in front of the Muffin Man. Desserts and snacks will be available inside of the bakery. Come ready to dance!"

And with that, he jumped off the pew and was swallowed up by the crowd of well-wishers, all wanting to congratulate him and Sugar.

Levi looked down at Tenny, his mind on repeat.

We have until five tonight. We have until five tonight. We have until five tonight.

He began tugging her towards the door, his hand clasped like a vise around hers. He would let her go right around the time he'd agree to chop off his left nut.

She tucked in right behind him, letting him part the crowd in front of him like the parting of the Red Sea, something that he found surprisingly sexy. She trusted him to lead the way. She trusted that wherever he was going, she'd want to go, too.

Who knew that trust was such an erotic thing?

Finally, they made it out the front doors of the church and into the bright heat of the July sunshine. Without missing a beat, he headed for his truck, his hand still clasped in Tennessee's while using his other hand to pull on his hated tie. Having never worn a tie before, he could now categorically state that they were just as awful as he'd thought they would be, and he never wanted to wear one again.

Well, that was, unless Tennessee wanted him to for some big occasion. He'd do it for her if she really, really wanted him to.

Oh Levi, you've got it bad.

He helped her into the truck, managing to *mostly* keep his hands to himself, and then hurried around to the driver's side.

"Ready?" he asked rhetorically, already throwing his truck into reverse.

"Anytime," she said softly, running her fingernails up his thighs.

He gulped.

Hard.

"You don't have your nails done," he said, his voice squeaking like a pre-teen who's just seen a girl in a bikini for the first time.

He didn't give a damn about her nails, of course, other than they were straying *dangerously* close…

They drifted across his dick for just one glorious moment and then she was back to having her hand on his thigh.

He gulped again.

Don't pass out, don't pass out…

"Yeah," she said ruefully, pulling her hand back and looking down at her nails with a glare. Levi wasn't sure if he was thrilled that he could breathe again, or devastated that her hand wasn't on him anymore. "It costs too much to get them done all the time, so…" She shrugged, trying to play it off as being no big deal, but he was starting to be able to read Tennessee Rowland a little better than she probably wanted him to be able to. "I started painting my nails instead." She spread her fingers out on her lap, staring down at the pearl pink nails. "After years of wearing fake nails, it'll take a long time for my real nails to come back."

As they pulled up in front of his house, he flicked his gaze over at her hands splayed out on her lap. He'd never tell her this, of course, but he never really understood why girls thought that fake fingernails were so amazing. But, whatever made her feel pretty was what he cared about, and if fake fingernails were it…

And then they were hurrying up the sidewalk to his house and all thoughts about fingernails, fake or otherwise, fled from his mind. Thinking at all seemed like a real stretch at that point, considering all of the blood in his body seemed to have gone south, at least for the moment.

They tumbled through the door, hands and lips and teeth already in the mix as they did their best to simultaneously undress each other while kissing, sucking, and licking every inch of skin within reach.

Finally, Tenny pulled back and gasped, "Let's go to the bedroom." It took Levi a moment to not only hear the words but understand them, and she was already busy tugging him down the short hallway back to his bedroom before her words fully registered.

"Whatever you want," he groaned, his dick aching for some relief. If she told him in that moment that she wanted to have sex on the kitchen table while wearing a monkey suit, his only question would be where to get the monkey suit.

With trembling hands, he helped her undo the clasp at the nape of her neck and then stood back as the dress slid down her body to pool at her feet. Standing there with her back to him, high heels, a strapless bra, and a thong the only pieces of clothing left on her, Levi was having a hard time processing everything. Was this beautiful woman *really* willing and excited to have sex with him? The teenage boy inside of him was letting out war whoops even as he reached with trembling hands towards her gorgeous body.

"Just a moment," she murmured, and stepped over to the window where she drew the blinds. "I don't want the neighbors to be able to peek inside," she told him as she moved back towards him, an extra sway in her hips as she moved.

Levi opened his mouth to tell her that the bedroom window was angled so that it was almost impossible for anyone outside to see inside but the sway of her hips...

What was I going to say again?

Whatever it was, it wasn't important. Not as important as getting his hands on Tenny's body. He picked her up easily and she wrapped her long legs around his waist, clinging to him as he plundered her mouth while carrying her towards the bed.

I love this woman so damn much.

Which turned out to be the last coherent thought that he had for a very, very long time.

TENNY SHOOK HIS SHOULDER, slowly pulling him up through the layers of sleep. His eyes fluttered open to find her laying on her side, her hair flowing in a tangled mess over her body, hiding and exposing her body to his gaze much as her dress had done, except now, she looked thoroughly loved.

If asked, he would've sworn earlier that it was impossible for Tennessee to be sexier than she had been there in the Grace Valley Church, but looking at her now…

He realized he would've been wrong. Hair mussed, lips swollen from kisses…

Yeah, he would've been wrong.

He reached out a hand and traced it over the curve of her hip. "Hi, baby," he murmured, his voice roughened from sleep. "Ready for another round?"

She grinned at him naughtily. "I am sad to say that I have to turn that offer down. Unfortunately, we need to get going."

His hand had already captured a brilliant blonde curl, letting it wrap around his finger. "Go where?" he asked lazily, not at all convinced that they needed to go anywhere, except maybe to Sexy Time Land again. He was pretty sure that was a good idea.

"You need to drive me to Georgia's house so I can change into something more appropriate for a street dance, and then we need to go to the street dance."

His mind was still playing catch-up – focused as he was on the to-die-for body in front of him, it was hard to think with any body part north of the belt line – so she prompted him. "Sugar and Jaxson got married today? You're one of the groomsmen? So yeah, we should probably attend the dance, considering. Plus, food from the Muffin Man! I try not to eat too many carbs but I'll make an exception for this dance." She slapped him on his naked ass. "C'mon, handsome, let's go."

He sat up with a huge stretch and mumbled, "You think I'm handsome?" around a jaw-cracking yawn.

She stopped, her dress halfway pulled up her thigh.

Mmmm…thigh…

Maybe he could just talk her into staying here and he could play the game of seeing how many kisses it took for him to go from her knee to her hip—

"Have you looked in the mirror lately?" she asked him, yanking him out of his daydream.

"No. Why? Is my hair sticking up or something?" He swiped at his head, trying to push his unruly curls into submission. His hair had a tendency of sticking in any direction but the right one roughly 84.1% of the time. People loved to ooh and aah over his hair, but that's because they weren't the ones trying to style it.

She shook her head with a laugh as she pulled the dress up over her delicious body, covering up her curves. Before he could protest, she said, "You are literally the sexiest guy I've ever seen in my life, bar none. Your hair, your eyes, your Superman curl over your forehead, your abs, your ass, your—"

"Superman curl?" he said, interrupting her flow of compliments. He hated to do that – he had no idea she'd been checking out his ass, for one, and any compliments that she wanted to dish out, he was pretty damn sure he wanted to hear – but he couldn't let that one go. He had *no* idea what she was talking about.

"Superman? Clark Kent? You get this curl over your forehead that is just adorable."

"Adorable?" he echoed. He could stand to be compared to Superman, of course, but being called adorable made him sound like he was seven years old.

"Yes, adorable. And kissable. And very, very lovable." She walked over and leaned down to lay one on him.

Hmmmm…

As the spit swapping and tongue dueling commenced, Levi decided that maybe being adorable wasn't so bad after all.

～

THEY STARTED WALKING towards the street dance from Georgia's house; Levi was pretty sure that the police would have the streets blocked off, making traffic a nightmare. Walking, even in the fading late afternoon heat, was definitely the better plan.

He snuck a look at Tennessee as they walked, hand in hand. Strappy sandals, short shorts, a thin t-shirt that said *Princess in Training,* and her blonde hair cascading down over her shoulders...she looked exactly the same as she had that day in the grocery store, when he'd overheard her conspiring with Georgia.

Except not only had she changed, willing to leave her parents and stand on her own two feet, not to mention learning how to weld — who could forget that?! — but his perception of her had changed, too. He'd been so sure that she was a spoiled rotten brat without a care in the world. He'd thought she was heartbroken over Moose breaking up with her. He'd thought she loved nothing as much as she loved playing the piano.

Despite years of hanging out together, her with Moose, him with Georgia, he hadn't really known her. He hadn't known her at all. He'd secretly been in love with her, but he was starting to realize now that he'd been in love with her façade.

But now that he was beginning to know the *real* her...

There were depths he hadn't known existed.

"What are you thinking about?" she asked softly, looking up at him through the fan of her eyelashes.

"That you're a surprise to me," he responded honestly, "even after all these years. We've known each other practically since birth, or at least known *of* each other, and still, I didn't know a damn thing about you."

She laughed lightly, the laughter tinkling out into the warm, still summer air. "Moose said the same thing to me, actually, months ago when he broke up with me." She shrugged and then lapsed back into silence, obviously not feeling the need to add anything else to the conversation.

So typical...

"I understand being private," Levi started to say as they neared the street dance, and then stopped. The country music was pounding and shouts of laughter were ringing out – they weren't going to have any privacy in roughly 3.7 seconds if they kept walking, so impulsively, he pulled her into the shaded doorway of the hardware store instead. Surprised, she stared up at him, her large blue-green eyes as mesmerizing as ever. He wanted answers, yeah, but he also wanted to just stare at her all day.

Some days, it was a tough decision.

"I understand being private," he said again, "but Tenny, you take it to a whole new level. Why? Why do you hide who you are from the world?"

She pulled her hand out of his and began to rub her arms as if she were cold. He just waited patiently for her to talk, knowing that getting her to say *something* to him was half the battle.

"My parents…you probably think of them as overbearing, meddling, smothering, invested in seeing me succeed…right?"

He nodded, not sure where she was going with this but willing to give her all the time in the world to get there.

"Well, they are all of that, it's true. But…" She worried her full, bottom lip with her straight white teeth, staring off into the distance as she tried to decide what to tell him. *The truth, Tennessee, just tell me the truth.* But he kept his trap shut. He didn't want to scare her off.

"But honestly," she said, pulling her gaze to look back up at him, "they don't give a damn about me. Not *me*. They care about how I make *them* look. They care about who I marry, how well I do in a competition, what clothes I wear, but only in terms of how it makes *them* appear. I'm the child version of a trophy wife. A trophy child? Yeah, one of those. Quite literally, actually. My parents have a room in the house with nothing *but* trophies and ribbons and sashes for me and Virginia. Oh, and my crown from being Miss Idaho, First Runner Up, of course." Her lips quirked into a ghost of a smirk and then flattened out into a straight line again.

"My thoughts, my feelings, my desires, what I want to do or say or where I want to go – none of that matters to them. It would be like asking your car if it really wants to go to the grocery store today. No, you just get in the car and drive to the grocery store. I am the means to an end; a way for my parents to get what they want out of life."

She was rubbing her arms harder now, faster, looking close to a breakdown. Her hands were becoming a blur against her skin.

"I've been told all my life that what I want does not matter. What I think, what I feel…none of it matters. There are only so many times that you can be told something like that before you start to hide shit from the world. Why tell you what I'm thinking if you're just going to tell me that it doesn't matter? It's easier to just hide it all. If I don't reveal my innermost thoughts to someone, then they can't hurt me by telling me that those thoughts don't matter; that *I* don't matter. So, I don't give them that chance to really twist the knife. Pretty soon, I'm not telling anyone any thoughts ever, because I've just shut myself down."

She shrugged nonchalantly, as if it was no big deal, but tears – fat, hot tears – began rolling down her cheeks, giving the game away. He pulled her against him and stroked her back, letting her get it all out. As he held her in his arms, he realized that this was the first time he'd seen Tennessee cry in all of the years he knew her.

No, that wasn't true. She'd cried while they were up camping and he'd been an ass to her. He'd almost forgotten that. But otherwise…he searched his memory and drew a blank. Tennessee Rowland was not a crier.

And after what she just told him, he understood why. If she cried, then she was exposing her soft underbelly to the world, just inviting them to stab her there. It was much better if she plastered a smile on her face and pretended that nothing hurt.

After what seemed like ages, she pulled back and snuffled, wiping the backs of her hands across her cheeks and looking up at him ruefully. "We're going to a party, you know. Now my makeup is all messed up."

She had just a small smudge in the corner of her eye, and Levi wetted his thumb and wiped it off. "There," he said softly, "good as new."

She stepped back, wiping at the front of her shorts nervously, her hands back to doing that dance that shouted to the world that she was nervous. "You always seem to do this," she said out of nowhere, shoving her hands into the back pockets of her shorts and rocking back on her heels. "I tell you things that I don't tell other people, and I'm not even sure why. I've wondered before if you're able to cast some sort of magic spell over me or something."

Levi let out a snort of laughter at that one. "Baby, if I was gonna cast a spell over you, it wouldn't be for you to tell me all of your secrets, although I'm honored that you have. No, I'd be turning you into my sex slave and we could—"

Her cheeks flushed a brilliant red and she smacked at his shoulder while she howled in protest.

"I cannot believe you just said that! You're such a guy sometimes."

"Well, if I were a girl, this would be a very different relationship between us." He winked at her. She rolled her eyes and looped her arm through his.

"Are you done prying things out of me that I have never told another soul in my entire life?" she asked rhetorically, already dragging him down towards the street dance.

"For now," he said, if only to keep her on her toes.

Yeah, he was "such a guy" pretty much all of the time. As they walked towards the crowd of people, laughter and shouts and country twang ringing out, the most beautiful woman he'd ever seen on his arm, he decided that wasn't such a bad thing after all.

Once they got to the party itself, the crowd swelled around them, people chatting with them both, shaking hands and hugging. It was pretty rambunctious, even for a party, and Levi quickly realized the reason for it – someone had set up a free beer table down at the end of the block. *Hmmm*...maybe he should head on down there and grab one.

But before he could figure out the best way to navigate through the crowd with Tenny in tow, he felt a hand clamp down on his shoulder. "How's it goin'?" Moose asked in his ear.

Holding on tight to Tenny's hand, Levi turned to look at his best friend cum brother. Looking at him, it washed over Levi yet again how painfully obvious it was that they were related. How he'd missed it all this time was beyond him, honestly. They were both stupidly tall, same dark curly hair, same jaw, same thick eyebrows…

Yeah, it was obvious, all right.

Sometimes, you only see what you want to see.

"Good, good," Levi said finally, clapping Moose on the shoulder with his free hand. He'd let go of Tennessee about the time he'd agree to only watch rom-coms for the rest of his life. "Is Georgia here with you?"

"Yeah, here somewhere," Moose said, craning his neck to look over the crowd. One of the bennies of being so tall – seeing above people's heads was as easy as simply looking around. "I think she went into the Muffin Man to get something to eat."

Just then, Adam Whitaker – the town's vet – caught Levi's eye. He had his arm around the thickening waist of Kylie VanLueven, looking pleased as punch. Levi was shocked. How long had they been dating? How could they have conceived a child together when Levi didn't even know they were dating?

Moose followed his gaze and read Levi's expression correctly. "Not his kid," he said, talking close to Levi's ear so not everyone in a 15-mile radius could overhear them. "She got knocked up and came back home. Went to work out at the clinic, and apparently, Adam ended up examining more than just the animals." He waggled his eyebrows mischievously.

Tenny leaned in close and smacked Moose on the arm. "You and Levi," she scolded him. "A bunch of guys."

Moose looked between Levi and her, a smirk playing around his lips. "What, did you think we were girls?" he asked teasingly.

Tennessee rolled her eyes. "Men. Why did I put up with you for so long?"

"My charm and good looks?" Moose supplied helpfully.

Levi bust up laughing. Moose looked at him, one eyebrow quirked. "Considering how much we look alike," he drawled, "I wouldn't laugh so hard at that statement."

Tennessee tugged Levi away before he could volley back a suitable retort. "Let's grab a beer," she shouted in his ear over the twang of *Red Solo Cup*. "We're both walking, right?"

But still, Levi flipped Moose the bird casually over his shoulder as they walked away. What else were best friends for?

CHAPTER 33

*G*EORGIA'S LANDLINE RANG AGAIN, but Tenny ignored it. The last three times, it'd come up on the caller ID as being her parents, so the chances were damn good that it was them again. Or, more specifically, her mother.

With a lack of other leads to follow, she must've finally realized that her darling daughter did, in fact, abscond with every piece of clothing in her old room. No doubt she wanted to grill Tennessee into submission, and into admitting that Virginia had helped her.

Nope, not gonna happen. Despite the fact that Virginia and Tennessee were the only children of Robert and Roberta Rowland, the significant age difference between them had always made Ginny seem more like the bratty kid from next door who followed her around and annoyed her constantly, rather than her sister. Asking Ginny to help with the

Great Clothing Theft of 2018 had brought the two of them closer together than they'd ever been before.

Tenny wasn't about to ruin that by ratting her out. No way, uh-uh.

Just then, her iPhone buzzed in her hand and she looked down at it with a grin on her face. Sure enough, it was Levi, sending her a text that simply said, "Miss you," with a sparkly heart. He was never going to win any writing contests with his texts, but they meant a lot to her because she knew he wasn't the 21st century version of Shakespeare. Words and writing didn't come easily to him, making each one he sent to her even more precious.

She sent back a kissy face and sighed happily as she switched over to the camera app to take yet more clothing pictures. A picture of the shirt as a whole, the tag showing the name brand and size, any neat details, then one with accessories to punch it up. Move the shirt off to the side, start again with the next one.

As she worked, she silently thanked Levi yet again for buying her the iPhone. After he got the job at WMI Fabrication, he'd brought the phone over as a surprise for her. She'd protested and told him that she should earn her own way in the world...even as she was eagerly logging into all of her social media accounts again. Being cut off from the world for the last couple of months...

Painful. Let's just put it that way.

What she hadn't realized was how much help the iPhone would be when it came to selling her stash of clothing. There were a couple of apps designed especially to sell high-end, used clothing, so that combined with the camera made the process a whole lot easier.

She looked at the mountain of clothes off to the side and let out a sigh. Maybe "easier" was stretching it. The evening gowns had been the worst. Too many memories wrapped up in each of them – this was the dress she wore during the Junior Miss competition. This was the dress she wore to her senior prom with Moose. This was the dress she wore to the national piano competition in Washington, D.C.

Yeah, "easier" was definitely stretching it. Some of the memories were good, some were awful, but all packed a punch. When she'd first conceived of doing this, it hadn't occurred to her how *emotional* it would be. She was saying goodbye to a part of her life, and even if that was a good thing, it was still overwhelming.

She glanced down at the phone in her hand and reopened the text thread with Levi, tracing her finger over the sparkling heart.

Maybe it was hard, but being the kind of person that Levi would want to have in his life? It made it all worth it. Maybe he didn't know every little detail of her past, but he did love her for her, and in her world, that was a first. She wasn't about to screw up this second chance on life.

She pulled another top out. Time to get to work.

CHAPTER 34

LEVI

THE SHOP DOOR OPENED with a loud jangle and Levi looked up from the weld he was working on, to see Rocky Garrett walking in.

No, not just walking in. Walking towards *him*.

Which meant he wasn't there to just order some metal or hire WMI to do some work for him.

Dammit.

He moved over as he pushed the welding helmet back on his head, flicking the welder off. Whatever his dad – *oh dear God, what a weird idea that is!* – wanted to talk to him about, Levi didn't want the distraction of worrying about burning the shop to the ground while they discussed it.

His dad came to a stop in front of him, his jaw set, looking like he was ready to do battle. *Shit.* Whatever Rocky had come in to discuss with him, Levi knew he didn't want to talk about it with every one of his coworkers able to overhear them.

Without saying a word to Rocky, Levi walked past him and towards the shop door. "Ben, I'm going to step outside with Mr. Garrett here for a moment," he told his boss. "Be right back."

He walked out without looking back and leaned up against the side of the building in the shade, waiting for his dad to follow. Seconds later, the shop door opened and Rocky came striding out, looking a little pissed to have been left behind like that.

Good.

Levi wasn't in the mood to be gracious, turned out.

He just cocked an eyebrow at Rocky and waited for him to say something.

After waiting for a moment for Levi to greet him, Rocky realized that he wasn't going to, and cleared his throat, looking even more unhappy than he had just seconds before.

Levi tried to suppress the smirk crossing his face, but failed. Mr. Rocky Garrett, one of the richest men in Long Valley County, was *not* used to being treated like this.

"I came over to see if you've given any thought to my offer," Rocky rumbled, his deep voice an exact replica of Levi's.

"You mean the one where you want me to screw over my best friend and half brother by stealing a dealership from him?" Levi said sarcastically. "*That* offer?"

"I told you before, you're not stealing from him!

You can't steal what ain't his. Deere made his choice and now he has to live with it. I'm giving you a second chance. Just change your last name and take over the dealership. Simple as that."

Levi was already shaking his head before Rocky had even finished speaking.

"Nope," he said, popping the P. "Anything else?" He started to push himself away from the wall where he'd been slumped insolently, a posture he'd adopted only because he knew it'd piss Rocky off. He hated it when people slouched.

Levi decided then and there to slouch anytime he knew Rocky was within eyesight.

"I don't get why you want to keep the name Scranton," Rocky said hurriedly, trying to get it out before Levi could walk away. "After all, Steve isn't your father, and he was a bastard of a man to you. Why keep that name?"

Levi paused, and then sank back against the building again.

Dammit. He hated that Rocky had a point, he really did.

Sensing progress, Rocky pushed forward. "I know that you and Tennessee are dating. Her parents had wanted her to marry Deere because he was supposed to take over the dealership from me. If you're really serious about her, think about what a boon it would be if you owned the dealership when you asked her father – and my best friend – for her hand in marriage. You can go to her dad as the former welder for the John Deere dealership, or you can go to her dad as the current owner of the John Deere dealership. Which one do you think will get you further down the road? Especially with the Garrett last name. He doesn't want a Scranton as a son-in-law, I can guarantee you that. But a Garrett…?"

He paused for a moment and let it sink in.

"Think about it," he said, and walked away, leaving Levi behind to stare after him.

CHAPTER 35

TENNESSEE

*W*ORKING TOGETHER, they pulled a long rusty piece of rebar out of the heap in front of them so she could inspect it closely. Once she decided that it was in good enough shape to purchase, she tossed it over to the "buy" pile.

Levi shook his head with a bemused smile. "Whatever happened to the Tennessee Rowland who took her curling iron and blow dryer camping with her, and didn't want to stick a worm with a hook?"

She wrinkled her nose at him. "I still don't want to stick a worm with a hook," she told him pertly. "I prefer my food to arrive already butchered and cleaned on my plate, thankyouverymuch."

"I'll get you to love fishin' soon enough," he promised her. "Once you realize how fun it is…"

She was busy digging through a pile of random steel pieces, trying to imagine how she'd use them in yard art, and decided to ignore that statement. Who was she to destroy his delusions?

"Oh, this one could be fun," she said, pulling out a triangular piece of steel. "Cat's ears – can't you see it now?"

Levi cocked an eyebrow at her. "No," he said bluntly, "but we've already gone over this. Creative ain't my middle name."

"And neither is proper English," she muttered under her breath, tossing the triangular piece into the "buy" pile.

"Are you making fun of me?" he gasped in horror, reaching out and tickling her. "Why's you makin' fun of me? I's just a poor Idaho boy."

She collapsed against him, tears of laughter streaming down her face. His hick accent was atrocious, to say the least, and freakin' hilarious because it didn't sound a damn thing like him.

"I was a product of the Idaho educational system, too, you know," she reminded him when she finally got her breath back, "and you don't catch me using *ain't*."

"There ain't a damn thing wrong with the word ain't," he said, moving the buy pile onto a flat-bed cart so they could push it up to the front. The scrap metal yard was the only one in a 50-mile radius and even though Levi kept muttering about their high prices, Tennessee figured she could make it back and then some after she'd turned this pile of steel into beautiful art. "Now, you's a ready to mosey on back to my shop so you's can start a workin' on welding all this here shit together?"

She laughed even harder. If anything, the hick accent was only getting more atrocious by the moment. "Smile big for me," she ordered him, once she could catch her breath.

"Why?" His accent was gone and he only looked baffled now.

"I'm just wanting to double check that you have all of your teeth."

He threw back his head and laughed, revealing his gorgeous white teeth in all of their magnificent glory. "All right, fine, I deserved that one," he admitted once he got his breath back.

They pushed the cart over to the purchase station and after she carefully counted out the cash she'd made from her latest sales, they pushed the cart over to his truck and began loading it up. Old Tennessee would have stood back and let Levi do all of the work, but new Tennessee was right there alongside him, pushing pieces into the bed of the truck. Granted, she chose the smaller pieces, but still…

One small step at a time, she was becoming more independent.

Once they were loaded up, they climbed into the truck and headed out of Franklin and back towards his shop. She settled in for the 30-minute drive, slipping her hand into his and snuggling down in her seat. She let out a big yawn, feeling her eyes tear up from the strength of the yawn. Maybe she'd close her eyes, just for a minute…

"Hey, I had something I wanted to talk to you about," Levi said seriously, and she sat straight up, her stomach instantly dropping to her toes. Whatever he was about to say, it wasn't good. Maybe it was the way he was drumming his fingers on the steering wheel. Maybe it was the way he'd tightened up his shoulders.

Whatever it was, she could tell he expected her to freak out.

"Yeah?" she said, trying to swallow her sudden nerves. "What's up?"

"Rocky came by WMI yesterday. He, uh…he wanted me to rethink my decision on taking over the dealership from him."

"No," she said, shaking her head before he even finished speaking. "No, no, no. Nothing that man does comes at face value. There is *always* a catch with him." The words were coming out faster now as she tried to say them before he could cut her off. He had to listen to her. She had to make him realize what a downright shitastic idea this was.

"This is the guy who was willing to force his own son to marry me, even though he knew Moose didn't love me, and I didn't love Moose. He's manipulative, Levi. I don't know why he and my dad care so much that the two families get united by marriage, except maybe a power thing? They want to be able to rule Long Valley? I've spent a lot of time thinking about this and I just don't get it. But whatever he said –

whatever he promised you – it won't be worth the price tag, I promise."

"You," Levi said softly. "I'm serious about you, Tenny, and I don't have a snowball's chance in hell of winning your father's approval if I go to him as the son of the town drunk. But if I change my name to Garrett and take over the dealership – your parents would give their blessing, I just know it."

"I don't want you stabbing your best friend in the back to get my parent's approval!" she shouted, feeling the heat rising up in her cheeks. This was absolutely ridiculous. He *had* to see that.

"But that's the best part!" Levi said imploringly. "I could hire Moose back at the dealership! He wouldn't have to work for Massey Ferguson any longer."

She bust out laughing, but it was a bitter laugh. There was no humor in it, or in her.

"Levi, I love you, but there are days when you're dumber than a fencepost," she said bluntly. "Do you really think that Moose would be okay to come back to the John Deere dealership and work for you, when it's actually supposed to be his? He's worked his whole life for that damn dealership and that damn man you two share as a father. It's okay to be just a salesman at Massey, because he was never supposed to be anything more than that. But at John Deere? He was supposed to own it. He can't come back and be just a salesman, even if he would be working for his best friend."

Silence.

He was staring through the front windshield as they passed the open fields between Franklin and Sawyer, thinking it over as they drove. She pulled her hand away from his and crossed her arms across her chest, instinctively trying to protect herself from him. From this fight they were quickly descending into.

Finally, he let out a long sigh. "You're right," he admitted softly. "I just…I wanted an excuse to be able to say yes. But Moose…he'd take it as a betrayal, and he'd be right to. I just want some sort of leverage when it comes to dealing with your parents."

She shook her head with a small laugh. "It's sweet of you to care so much about making my parents happy, but I promise you, *I* don't care. They're not worth a moment's worry."

"That's easy for you to say," he retorted bitterly. "It's easy when you have a family, to dismiss the value of that family. I'm pretty much an orphan, Tenny. My father isn't my father after all, and my biological father is an asshole who won't claim me publicly unless I screw over my best friend and brother. So yeah, it's easy for you to be dismissive of your family, but *I* don't take it that lightly."

"Levi," she said slowly and with great emphasis, "you are a certified jackass." He jerked as if she'd slapped him, but she barreled on. "That day that we went over to the Garrett house and you confronted Rocky, all you could focus on afterwards was you. You, you, you. In that moment, your best friend was hurting. His father had basically just spit in his face.

But what did you do? Focus on poor, poor pitiful Levi. You know what? I'm sick of the sob story. I'm sick of the pity party. Yeah, I have a family, and they suck donkey dick! In fact, Mr. Orphan, you do have a family. You've got a dickhead cheater who fathered you out of wedlock, and three half-siblings and a stepmom. There! Congratulations!" The sarcasm was rolling off her tongue now, fast and thick. "You have a family. Are all of your problems solved? No? Shocking!"

She fumbled for the door handle of the truck. "Slow down!" she yelled over her shoulder. "Let me out. Until you can figure out how to extract your head from your ass, you're on your own, bucko."

He slowed down, even as he said, "Let me drive you back to Georgia's house. It's still a ways from Sawyer. You don't want—" The truck rolled to a stop and she threw herself out of it, slamming the door behind her with all of her might.

"You used to think that money solved every problem," she shouted through the open window of the truck, staring up at Levi. He had this pleading look on his face, but she wasn't going to budge an inch. Not when he was being so stubbornly stupid. "And now, you think that family solves every problem. Well, I've had money and I've had family, and I'm here to tell you that my problems are *far* from solved. You, Levi, need to man up. Call me when you do, and we can talk then."

She turned on her heel and began marching down

the side of the highway, her arms swinging with self-righteous indignation. If her mother could see her right then, she'd be having a conniption fit. *My daughter is not a hobo to wander down the side of the road in public. What will people think?*

Tennessee marched faster. There was something very satisfying about telling off Levi and her mother in one move. A twofer!

"Tenny, please," Levi called out from the truck as he crept up beside her on the road. "It's a long ways to Sawyer, and it's hot out today. Just let me drive you back to Georgia's house. I...I promise not to talk the whole way if you don't want me to."

She slowed down just a bit.

Ugh.

She hated to admit it, but the back of her right heel was already aching and she could tell that she was probably going to have a blister there if she kept up this pace. There was also the fact that even though she'd become more active since she'd started blacksmithing, she wasn't exactly an athlete. No matter how pissed she was, hiking 10 miles just didn't appeal to her.

"All right, fine," she snarled, waiting for him to pull to a stop so she could climb back in.

She snapped her seat belt into place and then folded her arms over her torso. She really was going to give him the cold shoulder all the way back to town, though. He needed to learn that he couldn't just be a dick to everyone and they'd just continue to put up with it.

The silence in the truck was deafening, but Tenny continued to stare out the window, watching the fence posts as they rolled by. She wasn't gonna budge an inch.

CHAPTER 36

LEVI

*H*E LOOKED OVER AT TENNY with a knot in his stomach. She was right, of course. What was up with the Rowland girls always being right? It got downright obnoxious after a while.

Not content to just be right, she was clearly also going to make any apology as torturous as possible. At the moment, she was making a porcupine look awfully friendly.

He pushed down on the gas. The sooner he could take her to Georgia's house and show her that he meant it when he said he wouldn't talk to her on the way there, the sooner he could try to dig himself out of the hole he'd found himself in.

Finally, finally, the outskirts of Sawyer came into view. *Almost there, Levi. Just be a little patient.*

Painful, deafening silence throbbed in the cabin of the truck.

They rolled to a stop in front of Georgia's house.

Tennessee was already halfway out the door before he could say anything, but he plunged on anyway. "I drove you home without saying a word, right?" he called out. "Just like I promised. Please, just listen to me for a minute. If I don't change your mind, I'll let you go."

His heart shriveled and pulsed at those words, sending panic and pain through him. He couldn't lose her.

Please don't make me give you up.

Please.

She paused for the longest time, staring off into the distance, and then finally nodded her head. She heaved herself back up into the passenger seat and pulled the door closed behind her.

She didn't, however, buckle her seat belt. She'd always been a real stickler for doing that every time without fail, so for her to skip it this time...

Yeah, she was here, but he had better work hard to make her want to stay.

He pulled away from the curb and began to drive aimlessly through Sawyer, paying only enough attention to the road to keep from taking out a stop sign or a street corner.

"Do you know how Moose and I became such good friends?" he asked quietly. It was one of the most important days of his life, but that didn't mean she had a clue what had happened, or that anything had happened at all.

She shook her head.

"Third grade. Recess time. That was when all of the bullies came out to play. I was tall for my age – I had that going for me – but my clothes were always dirty and too small. This was before I figured out how to wash my clothes in the bathtub and lay them out to dry over the shower curtain. I was hungry – God, I was *always* hungry – and they knew it. They held out this bag of Dorito chips tauntingly. They were trying to see what I'd agree to do for a bag of Doritos. My stomach was gnawing my backbone and all I could think was that I'd do anything. Anything at all. I just wanted to eat *something*."

His voice broke and he swallowed hard. Taking a hard right, he began following a road up into the mountains, away from Sawyer. It was dangerous for him to be around people right now. He might hit someone and never see it coming.

"They were taunting me – calling me names. Playing keep-away with the chips. I was just a kid and…I was dumb enough to fall into their trap. Looking back, I should've just walked away with my head held high. If I didn't try to get the chips, then it wouldn't be any fun, you know? They'd give up and find someone else to torture. But I was hungry and I was a kid and I was dumb.

"And then there was Moose, wading into the group and knocking heads together. He hit a growth spurt before me, and he was the tallest kid in the class by a mile. He took them all by surprise, standing up to them like that. Of course, he got in trouble – sent to the principal's office for fighting. We both ended up there, side by side, matching black eyes, almost identical other than his clothes didn't look like shit and he didn't smell like shit. His parents actually bathed him every night.

"The principal called both Rocky and Steve. Rocky came to the school and picked Moose up; Steve told the principal where he could stick his phone and hung up on him. When I got home after school, Steve beat me for causing him problems."

His knuckles tightened on the steering wheel, turning white before his eyes. He'd left those days far behind him. He hoped that most people didn't remember that far back – back to the Levi who didn't bathe or brush his teeth and whose clothes had more holes in them than not. He'd thought about leaving Long Valley and starting over again somewhere where no one knew his history, but he hadn't wanted to leave Moose, and he hadn't felt like he could be disloyal to Rocky after he'd paid for his schooling to become a welder.

Oh, how times had changed...

"After that, Moose and I were inseparable. He took me home after school each day and his mom would make us an after-school snack. It quickly became the best part of my day, bar none. That food I ate at their house was quite often the only food I got that day, other than school lunch. I was a bottomless pit, and Linda was kind enough to never turn me down. Knowing what I know now...it must've been hell on her, having her husband's bastard child there every day, always wanting something to eat. But if it bothered her, she hid it well. I don't know if Rocky truly understands how lucky he is to have her. Most women would've thrown this back in his face and divorced his sorry ass."

He shrugged, trying to act as if none of it hurt. As if every child was forced to do laundry in the bathtub and collect empties to turn in at the recycling center for a little bit of cash to buy food with.

That was totally normal, right?

He let out a snort of laughter mixed with pain. Tennessee took his hand and he squeezed it tightly, hanging onto it for dear life.

"Looking back on it, I'm not really sure how I didn't end up starving to death, or in jail. By all rights, I should have. But Rocky and Linda…they saved me. I know he's a jackass of the first water, but he's done so damn much for me. It's all wrapped up together in my head. It's hard to hate him; not when there were times that he was the only reason I ate anything that day."

He pulled over onto the side of the road then, the tears blinding him as they slid, hot and painful and fat, down his cheeks, blurring the world in front of him and he was mortified that he was crying – he was a *man* and men didn't cry, for God's sakes – but still, the tears were coming.

"I'm not good enough for you, Tennessee," he whispered, his throat raw and constricted and tight.

"How many times have you flipped your underwear inside out so you could wear them another day? How many lawns have you mowed, the bar almost above your head, just so you had money to buy bread at the store?"

His voice caught and he couldn't talk and he swallowed hard and tried again. "Speaking of, I started mowing lawns for money, which worked really well until Steve figured out that I was making money. Suddenly, I owed him – I owed him almost everything I made as payment for putting a roof over my head, clothes on my back, food in my belly. So, I did what any kid in my shoes would do – I started lying to him about how much money I was making. That way, I still had enough leftover to buy food.

"Did you have to lie to your father, just so you had enough to eat?" He whispered the question and it hung, hauntingly, between them until she finally shook her head no.

"I'm not good enough for you. I never have been. I don't know what in the hell I was thinking. Talk about reaching above your station." He chuckled humorlessly. "Your dad would know better than to let someone like me marry his daughter. My only chance at happiness is if I stab my best friend in the back, and make my girlfriend so angry with me, she breaks up with me anyway. You're right – the price to pay when making a deal with the devil is too high. It's just that he never was the devil to me, and that makes it harder than anything else."

His voice was flat and dead and he wiped at his eyes with the backs of his hands and then threw his truck into gear. "I'll drive you home now. I'll leave the metal wherever you want. I won't bother you anymore."

And with that, he flipped a U and began heading back towards town. He might as well get this over with now. If he was going to be forced to rip out his own heart and stomp on it, he wanted to get it done before he lost all pride and begged her to still love him.

But he couldn't. He couldn't do that to her. He loved her too much to destroy her life like his had been destroyed.

CHAPTER 37

*D*ID YOU HAVE TO LIE *to your father, just so you had enough to eat?*

The words tumbled around and around in her mind, like a dryer set on high.

Just so you had enough to eat...

When she was in high school, she didn't eat because she'd wanted to stay thin, because she didn't want to − couldn't afford to − have an ounce of fat on her when she walked across the stage in a bikini.

But to not be able to eat because your father didn't think you were worth wasting money on?

That was a totally different world than the one she'd grown up in.

"My parents are poor," she blurted out before she could stop herself. The shame she felt at saying those words...it gave her just a tiny insight into what life must've been like for Levi his entire life.

"I'm sorry, *what?!*" Levi hollered, almost running

off the road in surprise. He jammed on the brakes and stared at her. He was shaking his head, as if trying to clear his ears. As if what she'd just said was so insanely off the rails, he had to be losing it.

She sent him a grimacing smile. "Poor as church mice," she said simply, and then started laughing hysterically. "I know, I know, it seems insane – when I first figured it out, I thought I'd lost my mind. The whole world shifted underneath my feet. There was just no way, right? But all these years, they've been basically grooming me so they could sell me off to the highest bidder."

She'd accidentally let that slip out once before, and she remembered how frantic she'd become when she'd realized what she'd done. She'd virtually thrown herself at Levi, seducing him, trying to sidetrack him because she didn't want him asking any questions.

She'd succeeded, of course. He'd forgotten about it completely…until now.

"Did you know this?! While it was happening, did you know?" Levi had pulled over onto the shoulder of the road and was staring at her wide-eyed, like she'd just announced she was an alien visiting from Venus.

"Not during…" She waved her hand around in the air to indicate her entire childhood. "I figured it out when I was moving out of my parent's house and into Georgia's. Mom started telling me that Dad had entered into talks with some farmer up in Washington. I was going to marry their son. Yeah…

dowries in the 21st century. Who knew?" she said sarcastically.

"Holy shit, holy shit, holy shit," Levi murmured. "Holy *shit*. This is like finding out that Santa Claus isn't real, times twenty. Your dad is the biggest farmer in the county. The chandelier in the foyer of your parent's mansion is dripping with *gold* for hell's sakes. How? How is it possible?"

"My grandpa," she said simply. "Everyone knows that when he died, my dad got it all, and my uncle got nothing. My grandpa…I loved him, I guess, but he was very old-fashioned in his thinking. The oldest son was supposed to get everything. The younger son was supposed to go figure out his own life and career. That's just the way it was. Well, my grandfather liked to play the stock market for fun, and he'd invested in some major companies early on. He made a fortune, or at least, it seemed like he had. It never occurred to me that my parents could spend it all and then some. I'm guessing my parents didn't think it'd ever run out, either. A farmer can live pretty nice, depending on the year and the crops he's growing and the price he's able to get at the market, but not enough to have gold chandeliers and a baby grand Steinway piano. So yeah, my parents were living high on the hog on my grandfather's estate…and then, it ran out."

She ran a hand through her hair, trying to decide what to divulge. She hadn't even told Georgia the truth. As far as Tennessee knew, her parents,

Tennessee, and Virginia were the only people in the world who knew everything.

But Levi had taken a chance on her. He'd told her the truth about his childhood.

She had to be brave and take a chance on him.

"Months ago, the power shut off at home. My mother was *pissed*. She called Idaho Power and ripped them a new one, demanding an apology for screwing up the payment like they had. When the employee came out to turn the power back on, she yelled at him, too. At the time, I didn't think much of it — mistakes happen plus my mother is a bitch equals yelling quite often — but when I finally put it all together, I realized that my parents hadn't paid the light bill. Robert and Roberta Rowland didn't have enough money to pay the freakin' light bill." She shook her head, still surprised after all this time.

Levi let out a shocked laugh, and Tenny looked at him, at a total loss.

"I know, right? Like…this just *can't* be true. And then I realized that my mom was always giving me new credit cards to use. She'd tell me that the new one had better points or some sort of incentive that made it worth it to switch. I didn't ask questions — I didn't really care. Whatever my mom wanted me to use, I would. As long as I didn't get declined at the cash register, what did it matter? And then I started the *shocking* habit of reading books on being frugal, and it all came tumbling down. I realized that my parents were moving credit card balances around, robbing

Peter to pay Paul. I have no idea how much my parents owe on that house, or on the farm. I'm guessing they took out loans against the equity a long time ago, but your guess is as good as mine. I was raised in the kind of family that it probably would've been more acceptable for me to ask about the shape of my dad's penis than it would've been for me to ask about the finances."

Levi let out a strangled laugh at that and Tenny shot him an unrepentant grin. "It's the eyes," she said blandly. "No one ever thinks that I have a naughty or inappropriate thought in my head when I bat my eyelashes at them."

"I used to think that I couldn't swear around you because you looked like an angel," Levi admitted, "and it just wasn't right to swear in front of angels."

"I promise, you wouldn't be the first one to use that metaphor," she assured him with a small laugh. "It's kinda nice on the one hand because no one ever suspects me of anything, but on the other hand, it can be exhausting to be perfect all the time. I'm not perfect, Levi. I'm not an angel. I'm a real human being with foibles and thoughts and opinions and parents who are ready and willing to sell me off to the highest bidder. To be perfectly honest, I'm surprised my parents haven't kidnapped me yet and stashed me away in the basement. No doubt they're hoping that I'll fail out in the real world on my own, and will willingly crawl back home. They're just delusional enough to believe that I might do that."

Levi put the truck into gear and pulled back onto the road. He took a right at the next intersection and began wandering the backroads towards Franklin. "Do you think Rocky knows?" he said into the silence of the cab.

"What – about my parents being poor?"

"Yeah," he said, tugging at his lower lip thoughtfully. "Do you think that's why he's pushing me so hard to change my last name and take over the dealership? Then I can marry you, Rocky can pay Robert the dowry, Robert gets enough money to keep afloat for a while, and Rocky gets to have his son taking over the family business. Everyone wins."

"Maybe?" Tennessee said doubtfully. "It's possible. I just...my parents have stupid amounts of pride. That theory would require them to admit to someone just how broke they are. They hid it from me for 26 years and even with me, I had to figure it out myself. Knowing my parents like I do, they would've done everything in their power to hide the truth from Rocky. They probably approached it like they would any business deal. The difference is, most business deals don't include the sale of your daughter." She let out a grim chuckle at that, and they collapsed back into silence again.

After a while, she looked at him seriously. "The reason I let the family secret out of the bag wasn't just to share malicious gossip, though. I told you because you need to know that you're not the only one coming from a poor background. It's true that I wasn't raised knowing I was poor; it's true that my parents have done everything possible to hide this reality from the world. But whether they want to admit it or not, it's true. My family having wealth or not having wealth… it doesn't matter. After all, I just told you that my parents are probably a hairbreadth away from bankruptcy. Do you love me less?"

"Of course not!" Levi exclaimed, obviously surprised by the stupidity of the question. "I don't love you because of how much money your parents have…" He trailed off and shot her a baleful glare. "I walked right into that one, didn't I?" he asked dryly.

"Pretty much!" she agreed with a cheerful laugh.

"But…but…" he sputtered, "my dad – Steve…he only cares about me if I bring him beers, and my biological dad wants me to be an asshole to the one person in this world who has always stood by my side."

"And my parents want to sell me off to the highest bidder," she countered swiftly. "C'mon, another one. This is fun."

His mouth opened and closed, but nothing came out but some sputterings. He looked like he'd just been poleaxed.

Tennessee wasn't about to let him off the hook so easily, though. It was like kicking someone while they were down, and she hated to do it, but he had to understand. He *needed* to understand.

"I've said it before and I'll say it again – you've got to pull your head out of your ass, Levi Scranton.

Yeah, you had a really shitastic childhood. Yeah, Steve is an asshole. Yeah, you're a literal bastard. But *everyone* has problems in their past. You like to believe that you're the only one who's struggling. I know I'm being blunt here, but that attitude has got to stop. Someone else having money doesn't mean their life is stress-free. Someone else having a family doesn't mean their life is perfect. Looking at the world like that…it isn't okay."

The silence in the cab was deafening again, as Levi thought through what she'd just said. He had that thousand-mile stare going on, and Tenny could only be grateful that they were on backcountry roads with very little traffic. She was fairly sure that he was paying just enough attention to his surroundings to keep from driving off the road, but not one more iota than that.

Finally, he blew his breath out tremulously as he nodded. "I get it," he said softly. "I didn't before – you're right. I was throwing myself a one-person pity party, complete with streamers and party poppers. It's…it'll take me a long time to really have it all sink in. Don't give up on me, Tenny. I promise I'll do my best to learn."

He leaned over the console and snagged her hand from her lap. She squeezed his work-roughened fingers tightly, and then brought them up to her lips to give them a kiss.

She'd told Levi that he had to stop expecting her to be perfect and now she realized, she needed to do the same in return. She couldn't judge him harshly for his mistakes, not when he was admitting to them and trying to change.

And anyway, he was still the only man who made her heart try to thump its way out of her chest. He was the only person she could truly tell everything to, and feel safe doing so. She trusted him like she'd never trusted anyone before.

She couldn't let that go now.

*L*EVI RAPPED LIGHTLY on the weather-beaten door and then pushed it open, the high-pitched screech of the un-oiled hinges ringing in his ears. "Dad, it's Levi," he called out, the words weird on his tongue. He wasn't his dad, but Steve didn't know he wasn't his dad, or maybe he did know and he'd just never told Levi, but either way, Levi had to call him Dad until he could tell him the truth.

Levi's head hurt.

The TV was blaring, the cats were swarming around his feet, the blinds were drawn, the same few lamps were on…the house smelled the same and looked the same as it ever did. Sure, maybe a few piles had been moved from one spot to the next over the years, but this was still the house he'd lived in the first 18 years of his life.

And with any luck at all, he'd never have to come here again.

It was the only thing that kept him moving forward.

He walked into the living room and Steve looked up and glared at him, the skin hanging off his face a little more than it had before. Was he losing weight? It was hard to tell.

"I don't see no Pabst in your hands, boy," Steve snarled out over the *Magnum PI* reruns. "What did I tell you about—"

"I've come over to tell you that I won't be coming over anymore," he said bluntly, cutting his fath–Steve off.

He's not your father. Never forget that.

"What?" Steve said, clearly confused as he stared up at Levi. "You came over here to tell me you ain't comin' over here no more?"

"Yes. And to tell you…" He took a deep breath. "That you're not my father."

There. I said it. I finally told the man the truth.

He took a deep breath, feeling like he'd just had a 100-lb pack taken off his back.

"No shit, Sherlock," Steve said sarcastically. "I got eyes in my head. I can see you don't look a damn thing like me. Too tall, too dark, too much hair…I always figured that you was the bastard of that tractor guy. Your mother was carrying on with him right about the time she announced she was pregnant."

"You…you knew?" Levi gasped. A small part of

him had thought that maybe he had; that it was within the realm of possibilities, anyway, but he hadn't actually believed it, if only because… "Then why did you keep me?" Levi asked, stunned. "When Mom ran off, why didn't you just turn me over to Child Protective Services or something?"

It couldn't be because Steve had a fatherly bone in his body. That wasn't possible. There had to be something in it for him. That's just the way Steve operated.

Steve shrugged, his thin shoulders pulling away from the stained fabric of the recliner for just a moment, and then molding right back into place, as if he'd never moved.

Steve will die in that chair.

Levi had never been so sure of something in all his life, as he was of that fact. Steve'd be found in that chair days, weeks, or maybe even months after he'd died.

"I kept ya 'cause I figured it'd be helpful to have someone around to help take care of things 'round here. Nip out to the store and pick up a case of beer, wash clothes, or whatever. I figured once you got larger, I could hire you out. People could pay to rent ya. You were bound to be a giant, considering how tall that bitch and her lover was, so I figured you'd get big fast and I wouldn't have to take care of ya for too long. Soon, you'd be takin' care of me."

It explained so much about Levi's childhood. Everything, in fact. When he'd started mowing lawns for money, Steve had been pissed — started going off about how he'd been coddling Levi for too long. It hadn't made much sense to him at the time, but now looking back…

Steve hadn't realized that he was tall enough to be able to mow lawns, until Levi just started doing it. No doubt he'd been kicking himself for waiting to press Levi into manual labor.

Steve was talking. "What?" Levi asked, realizing that he hadn't heard a word of what the man had been saying to him.

"I says, how'd ya figure it out? You never guessed growin' up, so why do ya know now?"

"DNA test," Levi said simply. "They can check to see where you're from. I took it, and didn't have a drop of Scandinavian blood in me. I knew something was wrong just from that. Then I got another email saying that I was related to Florence Garrett. That's how I found out that Rocky Garrett's my dad."

"I knew it!" Steve crowed. "That cheatin' piece o' shit bitch. I knew she was sleeping with her boss. She tried to tell me she wasn't, but you can't fool Steve Scranton, no how, no way." He thumped his fist triumphantly against his chest.

The triumph quickly faded and he looked up at Levi, confused and more than a little afraid. "Why're ya here, boy?" He shrank back into the recliner. "You here to beat on me? You can't, you know. Why, I took care o' you all those years, even though you was no blood of mine. You gotta give me the respect I deserve!"

Levi shook his head in bemusement. As a child and especially as a teenager, he'd fantasized quite often about beating Steve into a bloody pulp. If he could just show him one time what it was like to be on the receiving end of it, maybe Steve would stop dishing it out so much.

But ever since he'd found out that Steve wasn't really his father, it hadn't even crossed his mind to come over here and beat him up. He'd long ago let that fantasy go.

"Just here to tell you I won't be comin' back." And with that, he turned on his heel and headed towards the door.

"That's it?" Steve crowed. "Even now, you ain't acting like a man. I thought I'd raised you tougher than this. No matter how much I beat you, you never were willin' to do what needed to be done. You're sure no son o' mine."

"Just 'cause I'm not willing to beat up a frail old man about to die from cirrhosis doesn't mean that I'm not a man," Levi tossed over his shoulder and then he was escaping from the house and the smell and the darkness and the man who'd spent so much of his life making Levi's a living hell.

Steve was shouting something at him but the light breeze carried the words away, almost as if to tell Levi that he didn't need to know what was being said. It didn't matter anymore, the world was telling him.

You're free. You're free of Steve Scranton and you never have to go back again.

He climbed into his truck and folded his arms across the top of the steering wheel, dropping his forehead and letting the tears flow. For the second time in as many days, he let the water leaking from his eyes wash away the hatred and anger and fear and desperation in his soul. He'd always hated crying – if nothing else, Steve had managed to beat the belief into him that *real* men didn't cry – but the last couple of days, it seemed like he'd done nothing but that.

And felt better because of it.

As the flow of tears began to subside and he put his truck into gear to pull away, he decided that even if he didn't stab his brother in the back, he would make his father – his *real* father – happy in one respect: He was going to do the paperwork to change his last name to Garrett. Wash away every last trace of his connection to the bitter, hate-filled man inside of the most piece-of-shit house in Sawyer.

Levi Garrett.

It had a nice ring to it.

CHAPTER 39

TENNESSEE

SHE KNOCKED LIGHTLY on the front door of her family's home and then pushed it open. "Mom? Dad? Virginia? Anyone home?"

So. Many. Nerves.

Being back here in her parent's grand foyer…it was like she'd never left.

If Levi can talk to his family, I can talk to mine.

"Who's ther–Tennessee!" her mother exclaimed, coming out of the drawing room. She rushed over to Tenny's side and hugged her delicately, giving her air kisses on either cheek. "I'm so glad you came home!" She pulled back and looked around the foyer. "Where are your bags? Should I ask Virginia to fetch them for you? She's up in her room, doing God knows what."

The vague hint of disapproval in her mother's voice at the mention of Virginia was just as obvious as ever. Ginny could never make her parents happy, no matter how straight she sat in her chair or how many hours she practiced her cello or how many A's she brought home on her report card.

Because, you see, she wasn't Tennessee.

There were days where Tennessee wanted to take her parents by the shoulders and shake them like rag dolls.

"I don't have my bags here, Mom. I just stopped by to talk to you and Dad."

"Oh." The brilliant light in her mother's eyes began to fade. No matter how manipulative her parents were, there was a small part of Roberta Rowland who genuinely loved Tennessee.

Or, at least, Tenny liked to think so. Maybe her mother was just hoping that Tenny was here to move back home so she could hurry up and auction her off to the farmer up in Washington.

Huh.

Some days, being a pessimist sure was depressing.

"Is Dad home or is he out in the fields?" Tennessee asked, trying to steer the conversation away from the idea of her moving back home. She'd timed her visit to coincide with lunchtime, but it was possible that today of all days, her father was actually going to break tradition and not come in from the fields for his noon meal.

Her mother looked over at the monstrously oversized grandfather clock ticking away. "He should be here any minute now. Let me inform Cook that we have another place setting for lunch."

She hurried away, leaving Tennessee alone in the

imposing foyer. Rather than stare at all of the ostentatious trappings of the life her parents could not afford, she decided to head upstairs and say hi to Virginia without having her parents as an audience.

She rapped her knuckles twice on the door and then let herself into her sister's room. It was a typical teenager's room, except instead of rock bands and Hollywood stars decorating the walls, Ginny had posters of Yo-Yo Ma and Ana Rucner plastered everywhere. One was the greatest cello player in the world; one was an up-and-coming female cellist that Virginia was going to be "just like" someday.

At the sound of the door opening, Ginny looked up from her laptop, her face lighting up with surprise.

"Tennessee!" she hollered, throwing herself off the bed and at her older sister with delight. Tenny gave her a quick hug, surprised by the strength of her sister's hug. After the Great Clothing Theft of 2018, Ginny had sure become a lot more…clingy than she used to be.

"Are you here just to visit or to move back home?" Ginny asked as she pulled back, her eyes shining with excitement.

"Just to visit, sorry." The brightness dimmed just a bit in Ginny's eyes, and Tennessee plunged on, feeling like a jerk for breaking two people's hearts in as many minutes. "How are things going here?"

Ginny rolled her eyes dramatically. "The uzh," she said sarcastically, "with an extra dosing of interrogation just for shits and giggles."

"Ginny!" Tennessee scolded, and then burst out laughing. "You don't say that around Mom, right?"

Ginny just cocked an eyebrow at her as if to say, "How stupid do I look," and then continued on. "Mom's just sure you're the one who stole the clothes, and she's equally as sure that I helped. Sometimes, I think Mom should've become a private detective or an interrogator for the Russian mafia instead of a farmer's wife. But, I haven't spilled the beans, I promise!"

"Thank you," Tennessee said, squeezing her sister tightly against her chest. "I didn't mean to get you into trouble, but I couldn't have done it without you, so yeah…thank you. Are Mom and Dad treating you any better now that I'm not around?"

It had always been her secret hope that once she was out of the house, her parents would start paying more attention to their younger daughter, and actually start treating her well.

It was worth a shot, right?

Virginia rolled her eyes. "Now without you to hover over, Mom's just more focused than ever on me, and especially on all of the ways that I'm failing her as a daughter. News flash: I am the world's worst daughter. I'm telling you in case you didn't know."

Tenny let out a belly laugh and hugged her sister impulsively. "Well, worst daughter in the world, you're the best sister in the world in my book. Are you ready to go downstairs and indulge in the world's most awkward lunch?"

"When you sell it like that…" Ginny muttered sarcastically, and they started down the stairs together.

Was Ginny always this fun? Tennessee tried to remember back, but was drawing a blank. Her sister had always just been there, on the sidelines, quiet, trying to please their parents, begging for a scrap of attention from her older sister who was always busy with piano rehearsals and friends and beauty pageants. She felt a stab of guilt at how much she'd neglected Ginny. She hadn't been much of a sister to her.

I need to start hanging out with her more.

Boy, wouldn't that drive their parents crazy, if Tennessee was willing to hang out with Virginia but not move back home. It might be worth it just for the entertainment value.

Tennessee and Virginia entered into the formal dining room where Cook was laying out the dishes down the middle of the table, which was already set for four, just like it'd been for years.

Déjà vu all over again.

They slid into their seats and waited quietly for Mom and Dad to show up. It was okay for Tenny and Ginny to wait for their parents; it wasn't okay for their parents to wait for Tenny and Ginny.

There were rules that just shouldn't be broken.

Dad came into the dining room and straight over to Tennessee, hugging and kissing her on the cheek. "So glad you came back home," he said effusively.

"Well, I'm just here for lunch, and to tell you guys about the man that I am dating."

Mom, who was entering in behind Dad, let out a little squeak. It was hard to tell whether it was a squeak of surprise or a squeak of terror, but Tennessee was going to guess terror.

Dad, on the other hand, paused for just a moment, and then kept walking, standing behind Mom's chair so he could pull it out for her. Once she was seated, Dad sat in his seat at the head of the table. He pulled the roast beef over and began slicing it up and then dishing it out.

"What's this boy's name?" her dad finally asked, as if a good 15 minutes hadn't passed since Tennessee had first mentioned Levi.

"Levi Scranton," Tennessee said quietly.

"Scranton?!" her dad thundered, his calm façade instantly smashed to pieces. "You mean that man who's busy drinking himself into an early grave? I will *not* have my daughter dating the son of the town drunk!"

Tennessee held up her hands placatingly. "Levi's biological father is actually Rocky. Rocky Garrett. Rocky and Levi's mom, Jennifer, had an affair and Levi was the result. Levi and Deere are half-brothers."

Her dad was staring at her, mouth agape. He was quite literally stunned into silence. To be honest, Tennessee never thought that she'd see the day and was enjoying it a little too much.

"Is...is Rocky going to claim him publicly?" he

finally got out, just as Virginia was crowing, "I knew it. I *knew* it! I was talking to Zara one day and I told her that Levi and Moo...ummm, Deere looked a heck of a lot alike not to be related. She told me I was crazy."

"Rocky cheated on Linda, Rocky cheated on Linda," Mom kept repeating to herself, as if saying it multiple times made it real.

Tennessee wasn't sure who to address first, so after doing a mental coin toss in her head, she turned to her father and said calmly, "Rocky wants to legally claim Levi and give him the dealership. He—"

"Perfect!" her dad broke in, thrilled to pieces with the news. "When will it become official?"

"It won't," Tennessee said flatly.

Her mom finally stopped mumbling to herself and instead just stared wide-eyed at Tennessee. "He could take over the dealership and he's *refusing* to?! What... what..." She stuttered to a stop and then lapsed into silence, the news too much for her.

Tenny had visions of pulling out smelling salts and waving them around.

"Levi believes that Deere has worked for that dealership his whole life, and that he deserves to have it. He is not going to take it from his best friend who, it turns out, is also his half-brother. And he shouldn't. It isn't—"

"Tennessee," her father said condescendingly, "the business is Rocky's to do with as he likes. If he wants to give it to Levi, he can. Deere isn't owed anything at all."

"That's where you're wrong," Tennessee said bluntly, squirming inside as she said it. She couldn't believe she just had the guts to flat-out tell her father that he was wrong. That was...not a thing that happened.

Ever.

Which probably explained why his face was turning such a deep red.

"Deere has worked his entire life for that dealership," she hurried on before her father could explode, "and for his father, all with the understanding that he'd take it over 'someday.' Rocky basically used Deere as slave labor for years on end, and then decides to yank it all away because Deere refused to make him and I miserable for the rest of our lives? Rocky may stick with his decision to screw Deere over and not give him the dealership as he was promised his whole life, but Levi isn't going to play a part in it, and he shouldn't."

"Fine," her mother spat out, sounding as if it was anything but fine, "but you cannot marry a...a *welder*. We forbid it."

"Levi hasn't proposed to me," Tennessee said calmly. "Also, I'm not asking for your permission to marry or to date him. I'm simply informing you that I'm already dating him. He has chosen to take on the 'Garrett' last name since Rocky has been more of a father to him in some ways than Steve ever was, and has started the paperwork for that. But that is separate from the dealership."

"What happened to our sweet, darling daughter?" her mother asked rhetorically. "The one who wouldn't dream of talking to us the way you have today?"

"She grew up and found her backbone," Tennessee volleyed back. She pushed back from the table and stood up. "Speaking of…" she mumbled under her breath, and then, looking her mother and father right in the eye, she said bluntly, "I hate playing the piano. Hate it with a passion. Feel free to pull the Steinway out into the front yard and set fire to it."

She headed towards the front door, listening to her mother shriek behind her, "Tennessee Marie Rowland, you will come back here this instant! Did you steal the clothes?"

The sudden change in topic threw Tenny off her stride for a moment, but she recovered and kept heading for the door and out into the bright sunshine of the summer's day.

Freedom. This was what it felt like. Intoxicating, amazing…Tennessee was never going to let it go again.

She slid into Georgia's car – she'd borrowed it for today's task – and began winding her way down Mansion Way, back towards town.

She'd never felt as good as she did in that very moment. She'd found her backbone. She was no longer a mooch.

Life didn't get much better than that.

CHAPTER 40

LEVI

*T*HE CLINKING of the silverware and murmur of low voices were the only sounds in the posh restaurant. Candlelight flickered in the dim lighting, little sparks of light glinting out when the flames caught the silverware just right.

Levi felt like he was being buried alive. *What am I doing in this place? I don't belong here.* He'd picked the nicest restaurant in Franklin in hopes of impressing Tennessee. *See? I'm not such a hick after all. I know the difference between a salad fork and a dinner fork and a dessert fork.*

He didn't, of course, but he was awfully good at following Tenny's lead and picking up the right silverware at the right time.

He reached up to tug at the borrowed tie and then stopped himself. It wasn't actually choking off his airway; it only seemed like it was.

Tennessee caught the movement and the corners

of her mouth quirked up a little. "I know you don't believe me, but you look handsome in that tie," she told him seriously.

And that was the reason he'd been willing to wear it. He'd do anything for Tennessee, including wear a ridiculous tie and eat at a ridiculous restaurant and spend a ridiculous amount of money on overpriced food.

She flashed him a smile and he grinned back.

Yeah, fine, he'd wear the tie if she wanted him to.

"So are things still going okay at work?" Tennessee asked after taking an appropriately tiny bite of food.

Levi cut the bite of food he was about to eat in half. No wonder it took rich people so long to eat their dinner. They were only putting three calories into their mouths with every bite.

"Real good," Levi said with a surprised note in his voice. "I hadn't worked anywhere but the dealership for years, so I'm kinda liking the change anyway. I'm not just welding up tractors anymore. Makes me use my noggin' in a way that I hadn't had to in years."

The topic drifted on and they talked about what it was like to have a sister (weird) to having two brothers (although his relationship with Rhys was more in the theoretical stage at this point – Moose's younger brother was still in Japan in the Navy and wouldn't be able to come stateside for at least another year) to getting used to the name Levi Garrett.

"Has Steve contacted you at all?" Tenny asked

quietly, the candlelight catching the blonde in her hair and making her look like an angel, with a halo glowing around her head.

Maybe Levi was in over his head and he shouldn't be looking at Tennessee the way he was, but still…

He couldn't help himself. God help him, he was in love with Tennessee Rowland and it was a permanent affliction.

He shook his head. "No. He won't. I know it seems harsh – because it is harsh – but I was never more than a delivery device for beer and money for beer. He's not capable of love. I'm not proud of my mother's choice to have an affair with a married man but looking at Steve…it's not hard to see why she was starved for affection."

Tenny nodded her head thoughtfully. "He must've put up a front at some point, enough for her to be willing to marry him, but it seems like that disappeared pretty quickly."

Disappeared pretty quickly. That's what would happen to his and Tenny's relationship if he didn't man up and take the next step.

"I took you here tonight 'cause I wanted to ask you to move in with me," he blurted out, with all of the finesse of a bull in a china shop.

"Oh," Tenny said, her full lips making a perfect circle. Before he could work himself into a full-blown panic at the lack of enthusiasm on her face, she broke out into a huge grin. "Yes!" she whisper-shouted. She looked around the upscale restaurant as if waiting for a waiter to come along and hush her, and then leaned back towards Levi. "Yes, please," she said a little quieter, but with just as much feeling.

He reached out and squeezed her hand across the table, wanting to pick her up and twirl her around and around in circles to celebrate but restraining himself.

Barely.

"I'm full," Tennessee said out of nowhere. Levi cocked an eyebrow at her — her plate was only half empty — but she continued, "Want to go back to *our* place to celebrate?"

Suddenly, Levi found he too was stuffed to the brim and ready to head home.

Funny how that worked.

THEY BURST through the front door, hands flying as Levi tried to pull down on the hidden zipper tucked into the side of Tennessee's dress while she simultaneously tried to loosen his tie.

"Bweck!" he gasped when the tie accidentally went the other direction and truly did start cutting off his air supply. His hands dropped from Tennessee's side and he began scrabbling at his neck, tugging at it until it loosened and he could breathe again.

"So sorry!" she cried, looking up at him, horrified. "I didn't mean to—"

"I know," he said with a laugh. "Erotic asphyxiation doesn't seem like your cup of tea."

"Erotic asphy...are you being serious?" She was staring up at him in bewilderment. "That's a thing?"

"Don't ask," he said, laughing. "Now, back to what we were doing…"

But she wiggled out of his arms and headed down the hallway to the bedroom, leaving him to hurry along behind her. "I'll just draw these blinds real quick," she said casually as she began pulling on the strings to drop them down into place.

"Don't!" Levi said, pulling her back from the window. "I want to see your body this time. It's so damn gorgeous." He began nibbling on her neck and she laughed with delight, but he could also feel the tension in her.

"It'll only take a second," she promised him, pulling away and towards the window. "Let me just—"

"Why do you never want me to see your body?" Levi asked bluntly. She tensed and he tensed and she turned and stared at him and he stared back, levelly. Not blinking an eyelash. "Every time we've made love. Every. Single. Time. You never want the blinds open or the lights on."

"Well," she said, clearly stalling for time, "I just… what if the neighbor looks in or something?"

"You can't see in this window from the outside. Between the fence and how high that window is, unless my neighbor is renting a hot air balloon, we're fine."

She shrugged nonchalantly, but her hands...they were fluttering around, picking at the half-undone zipper on her dress, at her necklace, at her bracelet, at the ring on her finger.

"Don't ever become a poker player," Levi drawled. "You've got a tell that someone could see from space."

Her mouth dropped open in surprise. "But people always say that they can't read me; that I'm a closed book."

"Oh, it took me a while, but then once you see it, you can't unsee it. Your hands – when you're nervous, you fidget. I used to think that it meant you're lying, but it's just nerves. Today, though? Right now? It's lying. Tenny, I asked you to move in with me tonight. I'm serious as a heart attack about you. I've never loved another woman as much as I love you, and if we break up tonight, I never will again. You are it for me. There's no one else. But I can't stand liars. I've been lied to all my life about who I am, and I'm done. Done with lies, done with secrets. You either tell me why you're obsessed with my bedroom blinds, or you walk out that front door and you never come back. Them's your choices."

She stared at him defiantly for a moment, her fingers twisting a ring around and around, the yellow diamond flashing in the muted light when she turned it to just the right spot, but he didn't flinch. He didn't move. He didn't breathe. He just stared at her, and he waited.

Waited for her to finally tell him the truth.

.

.

She blinked.

He almost let out a war whoop at the tiny movement, but didn't. He wasn't about to move a muscle until she actually told him what the hell was going on in that crazy mind of hers.

Her hands went to her side and she tugged the zipper the rest of the way down, undid the clasp at the base of her neck, and then let the evening gown fall into a circle at her feet. For a moment, Levi forgot what they'd been talking about and just drank in the sight of her. Strappy high heels that most women would be clumsy in, but Tennessee wore as effortlessly as tennis shoes, led up to slim calves the color of golden honey, to the flare of her narrow hips where the lacy straps of royal purple underwear rested, up her flat abs, then the perfect breasts, held up by pieces of lace no bigger than a fly's ass, and up to her face. Her beautiful, supermodel face.

"I don't get it," he finally said, when he could speak again. "What am I supposed to be seeing, other than the most gorgeous woman to ever walk this earth?"

She turned her wrist upwards and held out her arm, letting the silver bangle slide freely on her arm.

"You're wearing a bracelet?" he asked, completely

bewildered, and then he saw it. Well, them, to be more exact. Line after perfect line, on the soft underbelly of her upper arm, almost in her armpit but not quite. White, straight, even lines. "What kind of surgery would cause—" He broke off.

The world tilted and then spun around.

"You did that," he whispered in a strangled voice. "You tried to kill yourself."

She shook her head adamantly. "No, never. I was trying to feel alive. I wanted to—"

"How could you?" he whispered, the shock of it like a punch to the gut. "How could you? You had everything – beauty and talent and money…was it the money? Did you do this when you found out your parents were poor after all?"

His mind spun at the idea. Did she really hate being poor so much that she'd rather die than live in poverty? Maybe she was the spoiled, self-centered brat he'd always thought she was. Maybe the "new" Tennessee was a façade and the old Tennessee was the real one. Maybe—

"No!" she practically shouted. "I stopped a long time ago. Well, a while ago," she amended, waving her hands in the air, trying to wipe the past away. "I didn't do it because of my parent's spending habits. What kind of person do you think I am?"

"I don't know what kind of person I think you are," he said slowly, shaking his head, trying to understand the world he'd just been dumped into. *My girlfriend is suicidal. How can I love someone if they're just waiting for the right moment to end it all?* "It turns out, I don't know you at all. I guess…I guess I never really knew you."

Her face went white at that, and then she shut down. Like watching a store shutter up at closing time, her face went blank, smoothing into impenetrable features. Calm, unflappable, unmarred by worry or frustration or anger, the old Tennessee was back.

It was creepy, that. He'd forgotten what Tennessee looked like when she was blocking out the world. It'd been so long since she'd turned her public face on him. She had been letting him in. She had let him see the true Tennessee Marie Rowland.

Except, she hadn't. She'd still been lying, even when he finally thought she was being truthful.

Just someone else in his life hiding the truth from him.

She was tugging her dress back into place, the graceful, sheer sleeves covering the scars.

Sleeves.

He had never seen her without sleeves. No matter the temperature outside, she wore short sleeve t-shirts, never tank tops. Her evening gowns all had some sort of sleeve on them, and with the cuts tucked away on the bottom side of her arm…no wonder she'd been able to hide them.

"How did you do the bikini?" he blurted out.

She stared at him, her fingers paused over her

phone. The phone he'd given her so he could hear her voice whenever he wanted.

Just so she could lie to me.

"The swimsuit portion of the pageants," he clarified. "How did you hide the scars then?"

"Makeup, and standing right. Not hard to do, if you're careful." Her voice was even and calm, as if they were discussing how hot it was supposed to get outside that day. She tapped the screen and then brought the phone up to her cheek. "Hey, Georgia," she said, no emotion in her voice. She was a life-sized doll. "Could you come pick me up at Levi's house?" Quick pause. "See you then."

She slipped her phone into her purse and then paused. She pulled it back out and placed it on the dresser.

"Have a good life, Levi," she said quietly, looking him in the eye as she spoke. "I hope you get what you want out of it."

She walked out of his bedroom and down the short hallway and into the living room, her heels clicking on the floor quietly, and then the front door closed behind her and Levi couldn't breathe or think but only feel.

Feel like shit.

CHAPTER 41

TENNESSEE

"I'M NOT HUNGRY," Tennessee said dully. Which was the truth. She wasn't. She wasn't trying to kill herself through starvation or cutting herself or anything else. She didn't want to die.

She just wasn't sure she still wanted to live.

And that was a totally different thing.

"Thank you for the offer, though, Uncle Carl. And for letting me use your garage. It's really sweet." She leaned up on her tiptoes and pressed a kiss to her uncle's cheek.

He blushed and muttered something before heading back inside the house, leaving her Georgia to stare at the pile of metal on the workbench.

After the Great Breakup of 2018, Uncle Carl and Aunt Shirley had offered to let her use half of the garage to work in. She'd taken them up on their offer because she had to keep working on welding and building up her business.

Or at least, she had to try. Or at least, she had to *pretend* to try.

"Are you wanting to work for a while," Georgia asked delicately, "or do you want to call it a day?" She hurried on, obviously not wanting to pressure Tennessee too much, "I mean, I'm good with either one. I just need to know and I can make it happen. Totally flexi—"

"I'm okay, Georgia. Truly, I am," Tennessee broke in before her normally unflappable cousin could babble on another ten minutes about absolutely nothing at all. "Just a little tired, is all." She sent her hovering cousin a convincing smile.

Georgia didn't look convinced.

Dammit.

"The funny thing is," Georgia said slowly, "you're exactly the same as you've always been: Polite, friendly on a surface level, beautiful, poised. You are the Tennessee I grew up with, and I had no idea you could be anything else. Not until you and Levi started dating. Then you became this new person who laughed freely and made jokes and didn't wear this front every moment of every day, and...I discovered that I had this kickass cousin all this time that I never knew existed. I'd always known that I had a beautiful and talented cousin, but I never knew that I had a funny and free and gregarious cousin. And now that I know she's in there somewhere, I can't help but miss her."

Tennessee's chest hurt, a stabbing pain that radiated through her. It was so strong, so overwhelming, she wondered for a moment if it truly was possible to die of a broken heart.

"I was open and free with Levi," she whispered. "Then in the end, I told him the truth because he forced me to, and...you know that saying that the truth will set you free? I never realized that they meant free from your relationships; free from ever loving someone again. I *wanted* to love; I didn't want to be set free from it..."

She trailed off, staring at the metal pile in front of her, overwhelmed by it all. With Levi by her side, she was invincible. She could stand up to her parents, she could weld metal, she could steal her own clothes and sell them to earn money to start a business, she could...

She could show him the scars of her life, hidden from the world who would judge her harshly if they knew about them.

And then he could reject her for revealing that truth to him.

"It can't be that terrible, right?" Georgia said quietly, breaking into her thoughts. "I mean, you're Tennessee Rowland. You've probably never so much as jaywalked in your life. I just don't understand... what caused him to react like that?"

Tennessee sent her talented and smart and hard-working and driven cousin a sad smile. "I told him the truth."

*L*EVI STOOD BACK, wiping his hands on an oil rag. His truck was now good to go for another 3000 miles. He felt good. Accomplished.

He saw a flash of movement at the open garage door and looked up to see Georgia standing there, biting her lower lip, looking like she was debating whether to come in or not.

The good feeling disappeared as quickly as it'd come. She was there to talk about Tennessee. He didn't want to talk about her. He wanted to stay right where he was, cocooned and safe away from the Rowland girls and the pain that seemed to follow behind them wherever they went. First Georgia broke his heart, then Tennessee. All he'd need to do now was wait for Virginia to graduate from high school and then ask her out. She could make it the holy trifecta.

She read the look on his face correctly, and instead of backing slowly towards her car like any sane person would, she plunged in. "We need to talk," she said, her tone brooking no argument. He opened up his mouth to argue anyway, and she held up a sheaf of papers, cutting him off. "Actually, we're not going to talk. I'm just going to give this to you, you're going to read them, and then you're going to pull your head out of your ass."

Before he could protest her highhanded ordering of him around, she shoved the papers into his hands. "Read them all. Then go talk to Tenny. You ought to know that she's exactly the same as she's always been, which is terrifying the ever-lovin' hell out of me. She changed so much since you two started dating. And now…she's back to hiding behind her impenetrable wall. You've damaged her in ways that I don't think anyone else – not her parents, not Moose, not me – had the ability to do, because she let you in. You at least owe her the time it takes to read this."

And then she was marching out of the garage, head held high, sure as always that she was doing the right thing.

Levi wanted to throw the papers at her retreating back. He was so utterly sick of being bossed around by the Rowland girls, he could spit. Tennessee had screwed up big time, not him. How could he date and fall in love and trust someone who was sick enough in the head to want to kill themselves? And not just once. Again and again, she'd tried. That wasn't his fault.

She'd made that choice and now she had to live with it.

Pissed as hell, he began shuffling randomly through the papers Georgia had ordered him to read.

Ordered, like he was a child. What were they going to say – that it was okay for people to try to kill themselves? That it was a phase?

The shuffling slowed. The word *cutting* kept popping up. He pulled an article out at random and began to read.

And then he sank into the passenger seat of his truck, and kept reading.

CHAPTER 43

TENNESSEE

*T*ENNY LOOKED at the opening bid for a pair of knee-high Jimmy Choo boots with a happy sigh. She'd make enough from this to finally pay for that high-end welder she'd been eyeballing. Uncle Carl had a welder that he affectionately called "That Piece of Shit," and after having used it for a week now, she was starting to see why.

Too bad I couldn't wear these boots for Levi just one time. The things they did to my ass…

She ground down on her back teeth, pissed at herself. Why did she let him in like that? He didn't deserve a place in her thoughts. She shouldn't be thinking about him at all. Never again. She could just block him out, like he deserved.

Despite her very sure thoughts, all grown up and correct and just what she should be thinking, she felt the bloom of pain spread through her anyway. It just hurt so damn bad. If she could just cut a little; move the pain into her arm instead of in her heart, she could let it all go. She wouldn't ache so much. She just needed a little bit of relief…

She yanked her hand away from the shoebox she kept tucked underneath her bed, a small knife buried beneath some scarves she couldn't bear to get rid of, and jumped to her feet. Ever since she'd become serious about not cutting anymore, she'd done research online about what to do when the urge seemed overwhelming, and the answer was unanimous: Find some way to distract yourself.

Listen to music. Talk to a friend. Dance. Pet a puppy. Anything that would cheer her up.

Tenny leaned over and clicked on the YouTube tab on her laptop, and then clicked play on the music video she kept cued up day and night, just in case.

The happy tune came pouring out of the speakers – *Chumbawamba* by Tubthumping.

We'll be singin'
When we're winnin'
We'll be singin'
I get knocked down, but I get up again
You're never gonna keep me down
I get knocked down, but I—
"*Tennessee!*"

She spun on her heel to find Levi standing in her bedroom doorway. "Oh!" she yelped, and spun back around to turn the music off. She smacked frantically at the keyboard until the song blessedly turned off, and then slowly turned back towards him, as embarrassed as could be. Maybe she could dive past him and out the door and—

But he wasn't standing there. It was a cloud of yellow roses standing there instead.

"Levi?" she said, blinking, trying to get her mind to catch up with reality. He lowered the bouquet of roses so she could see his face.

"Hi," he said softly.

In that moment, Tenny was pretty sure that even her toes were turning red.

CHAPTER 44

LEVI

*H*E'D BEEN SO NERVOUS, pulling up to Georgia's house. Was Tenny going to throw him out on his ear? Was she going to slam the door in his face?

The one thing he didn't expect was for her to be dancing around her room, singing *Chumbawamba* at the top of her lungs.

"I didn't know you were into alternative rock," he said into the painful silence of the room.

She shrugged. "Not usually, but that song makes me happy. When I want to cheer up, I turn it on and turn it loud." Her face, which had been awash with panic and surprise, began to shut down again. The surprise was gone and she was back to hiding from the world. "Can I help you?" she asked politely, as if they were strangers meeting on the street for the first time.

He held the roses out. "I bought them for you," he

said, as if that wasn't patently obvious by the fact that he was giving them to her.

But she didn't say, "Well, I'm glad to know that you didn't steal them from Carla at Happy Petals!" and she didn't laugh and her face didn't light up.

"Thank you so much," she murmured politely, taking the roses from him and giving them a cursory glance. "They're beautiful. Carla does a great job of bringing in the freshest flowers."

Monotone. Pleasant. No emotion to be found. If he hadn't just caught her dancing around her room, singing at the top of her lungs, he would've guessed that she'd been replaced by a robot while he wasn't looking.

Maybe robots can sing and dance now…

She was staring politely at him, a small smile planted firmly on her lips, simply waiting for him to tell her why he was there and then go on his way.

His eyes dropped to her hands, hoping and praying that they'd give her true thoughts away, but she was holding the roses loosely in her hands, no fluttering or twisting of her fingers.

He looked back up to her cool blue-green eyes, looking at him like she would a stranger on the street, waiting for him to speak. "Georgia came to my house," he blurted out.

Tennessee blinked. Twice.

The slightest crack in her façade, and then it was gone again. She was back to looking at him cooly, every lash and muscle in place. Waiting for him to speak.

"She gave me a bunch of articles. Told me to read them, and then pull my head out of my ass. Your cousin…" He blew out a laugh and ran his fingers through his hair. "I really think her middle name should've been Blunt instead of Ruth."

The corner of Tennessee's mouth quirked up in acknowledgment of his joke, but the smile didn't reach her eyes. They were still pinned on him, huge and gorgeous and somehow intimidating as hell in that moment.

"The articles were all on cutting," he continued on, watching for a reaction – *any* reaction – as he spoke. "Why it is that people cut, and what they're trying to accomplish. They're not…you're not trying to kill yourself when you do it."

A bitter laugh spilled out of her at that. "*I* told you that. I told you that I didn't want to die; that I wanted to feel *alive*. But, I'm glad that an article on the topic finally pounded the truth into your brain. Go ahead. What else did you learn?"

He'd been wanting a response out of her, but now that he got one…he wasn't so sure he wanted it after all. Sarcastic Tennessee wasn't a pretty sight.

He didn't know what else to do, though, other than to keep talking and hope that he managed to break through her defenses somehow.

Tentatively, he kept going. "That more girls than boys tend to cut, although there's a small subset of boys who do it, too. That cutting gives you a way to control the world when you don't have control otherwise. That people often believe that cutters are trying to kill themselves and freak out over it, even when that's not what is happening, and this freak-out doesn't help and usually makes things worse."

"These sound like mighty fine – and accurate – articles," Tennessee drawled.

"As usual, your cousin was right to give them to me, and order me to read them. Not, of course, that I appreciated it at the time, but I get what she was trying to do now. If you ever feel like sharing some of your tact with her, though, I don't think you'd go amiss."

Tennessee let out a small laugh at that. "I'll keep that in mind while we're sharing personality traits over dinner one night," she said dryly.

Levi shot her a huge grin – she'd made a joke! – and as if she knew exactly what he was thinking, she shut back down again.

She was pissed, and she was gonna make him pay for it.

Groveling was all that was left, so grovel he did. She was worth it – whatever it took.

"I screwed up, Tenny. Big time. You'd been trying so hard to hide those scars from me for such a long time; I should've taken a step back and realized that if it was that big, then maybe I needed to be more delicate in my approach to the topic. Instead, I just thrashed through it like a bull in a china shop, smashing your heart along the way."

"It isn't that I think that cutting is good," she said softly, interrupting him. He gladly shut up and waited to hear what she had to say. "I quit cutting shortly after I moved out of my parent's house. It's like drugs or alcohol – it's addictive. You have to cut deeper and more often, the longer you do it. One of the best ways to quit is to listen to loud music, and sing your heart out. It helps sidetrack you and get you to stop thinking about whatever it was that was making you contemplate cutting."

They both looked at her laptop, then back at each other.

"I'm not going to lie and pretend that that wasn't *exactly* what I was doing when you showed up," she said baldly. "Like I said, it's an addiction. I don't just decide to stop one day and never have the urge again. It doesn't work like that. Despite my reputation," she gave him a wry smile, "I am not, in fact, a robot."

He waited for a moment, wanting her to be able to finish saying whatever it was that she wanted to say, but when she appeared to be done, he said, "Everything I read – there was always a reason for doing this. Something going on in a person's background to make them feel like this was their only option. Uhhh…" His face flushed a brilliant red and he felt his heart constrict in his chest, but he had to say it because he had to give her a chance to tell him the truth, no matter how hard it was. "Your father –

was there…" He broke off, unable to say the words out loud.

"Oh no," Tenny said quickly, shaking her head adamantly. "My father can be a dick, absolutely, but there was never anything inappropriate there." Levi felt a rush of relief at her words; knowing that she hadn't been through that made him feel a whole lot better. "It was…" She trailed off and looked around the room for a moment. "Why don't we sit down? It feels weird to stand here like we're business associates." She gave him another wry smile.

They sat down on the bed together, and Levi instantly felt his dick spring to attention. Tennessee, even fully clothed and talking about cutting, was still so beautiful, it made his teeth ache. Add a bed into the equation…

He forced himself to concentrate.

Once Tenny was snuggled up against the headboard, hugging a pillow defensively against her chest, she started talking. And soon, Levi forgot all about having sex and the state of excitement of his dick, and just *listened*.

"Perfect. Ask anyone. That was the word used most often to describe me. I had the perfect body and perfect teeth and perfect hair and perfect nails and perfect skin. I never said the wrong thing or laughed too loud and I could play the piano…perfectly." She laughed sarcastically. "I know that this is virtually the definition of #FirstWorldProblems, but do you know how *exhausting* it is to be perfect All. The. Time? I couldn't just throw my hair up in a ponytail and run to the store in sweatpants like everyone else. Yeah, I enjoyed doing my hair and makeup and shopping and whatever, but even I wanted to be lazy sometimes. That was never, ever an option.

"But more than being required to be perfect all the time, it was the fact that I had no control over my own life. Didn't want to play the piano? Too bad. Didn't want to enter into a beauty pageant? Too bad. Didn't want to marry Moose? Too bad. Didn't want to eat caviar? Too bad. Big and small, every decision was made for me. Cutting was the one thing I could control. It was *my* choice. No one could tell me no. No one could take it away from me. It was my little secret. My dirty little secret."

She shoved her hands into her hair, looking distraught. It hit Levi then how little he'd seen her look anything but happy or, at least, serene. An upset Tennessee – he'd seen it a couple of times.

But not very often.

"Because of you and Georgia, I've finally started to stand up for myself a little bit. I mean, my God – *welding*. You don't get much more lowbrow than that." She let out a little chuckle. "Oh, and stealing my own clothes, and checking out books from the library, and reading books on how to be frugal, and then there was the time where I actually dared to move out of my parent's house at age 26, and refused to marry Moose...

"I'm pretty sure my parents think that I'm out of

control. Tennessee has really lost it now! Except, you know what's funny? The more control I've taken back from my parents, the less often that I want to cut. Strange how that works." She laughed lightly.

"So if you don't want to cut very often," Levi said slowly, hoping that he was doing this right – that he was asking the right questions, "then what triggered you today?"

She stared at him for a moment, silent, nothing showing on her face, and yet he knew – he *knew* – that she was debating what to tell him. He was sure it'd be some version of the truth, but how much she revealed…she was weighing his soul and trying to decide if he was worthy of her trust.

"You," she whispered.

He felt like he'd been punched in the gut.

She shrugged and smiled as if it was no big deal, but it was. Her unflappable demeanor was flapped, and she was in pain, whether she'd admit to it or not.

"I missed you. I missed the person I was around you. Fearless. Brave. Believed I could take on the world, and most especially that I could take on my parents. I stood up to them for you. And then you decided that I wasn't worth loving anymore. How could you do that?" she whispered, her voice breaking. "How could you do that?!" But this time she was yelling and she swung her pillow and caught him full in the chest with it. The surprise of it knocked him over on the bed and she whacked him again with the pillow. "I stood up for you. I told my parents how wonderful you were. I chose you over everything else in my life – all of the stability and money, I chose *you*. And then you just threw me away." She hit him again with the pillow, and then yanked it up against her chest, sobbing into it, curling up into herself, wrapping herself up into a ball to protect herself from him.

Levi froze, not sure of what to do. He wanted to reach out and stroke her back and hold her while she cried, but she'd just finished telling him how angry she was with him. Maybe she didn't want him to touch her. In her shoes, he probably wouldn't want that either.

So he just sat there, frozen, waiting for the tears to subside and for her to tell him what she wanted him to do. Whatever she wanted, he'd do it. Anything at all.

The tears just kept coming, though, and her body was shaking and he couldn't believe how awful he felt. He just wanted her to be happy. How had he screwed up so badly?

He reached out and patted her shoulder awkwardly. To his surprise, she didn't turn around and deck him, or slap him, or even hit him upside the head with her pillow/Kleenex. Instead, she rolled towards him on the bed, buried her face in his lap, and really let loose.

He paused for a moment. Was this better than before? She seemed to be crying even more, so he'd be hard pressed to qualify it as better, but on the other hand, she was snuggled up against him now, so...

He took a chance and started stroking his fingers through her hair. "Shhh..." he murmured. "It's okay...it's gonna be all right." He ran his fingers through her hair, rubbed her between the shoulders, stroked his hand down her arm...and she cuddled ever closer to him. She almost seemed to want to climb inside his skin. He'd never had anyone want to be as close to him as she seemed to desire in that moment.

Finally, the waterworks died down, and she pulled back with a laughing grimace. "I can't believe...I don't think I've ever cried that hard in my life. Sorry you had to see that."

He shook his head. "More than any person in my life, Tenny, I love you. Holding you while you cry... it's the least I can do. Especially since I was the one who caused those tears. I know you don't have much of a reason to trust me or believe me right now, but I promise to always hold you whenever you need it, and to be the cause of your tears as little as possible."

She laughed a little at that. "So realistic. At least, you know better than to promise to never cause me to cry like that again."

He let out a surprised laugh of his own. "If there was a way to guarantee that sort of thing, I'd be all over it. But I'm pretty sure I'm going to screw up again."

"And I will, too," she said firmly, staring him straight in the eye.

She'd smudged her makeup all over her face, and he reached out a thumb to wipe the black smudges away. She didn't blink, though, or turn away. She simply stared at him until he dropped his hands and stared back, giving her forthcoming words the weight she wanted them to have.

"Levi Garrett, I want you to know right now and never forget it: I am *not* perfect. I do *not* want to be put up on a pedestal where every small mistake is something to beat me about the head with. I've spent my entire life trying to live up to this ideal and it slowly drove me to the point where cutting myself seemed like the only option I had left. I'm not going back there ever again. I have to be able to make mistakes."

Levi shook his head at the irony of it all. "I've had the opposite problem all my life – no one expected anything out of me. I was just the son of the town drunk. I wasn't going to go anywhere. I wasn't going to succeed. I'm not sure which is worse."

She took his hand and threaded her fingers through his. "It's funny, isn't it," she said softly, "how different you and I are. And yet, you complete me. You're the yin to my yang."

He picked up their hands and pressed a kiss to the back of her hand. "Before I overreacted and screwed everything up, I had a present for you." Reluctantly, he pulled his hand out of hers so he could dig down into his Wranglers. He pulled out a bright pink key with tiny embedded rhinestones in the top. "Tennessee Marie Rowland, will you move in with me?"

She plucked the key out of his fingers and stared at it with wonder in her eyes. "Oh Levi," she breathed, "it's so perfect. So absolutely perfect."

As they kissed, Levi's only thought was that no matter what Tennessee believed, 'perfect' really was the best way to describe the life he'd been blessed with.

~

AUTHOR'S NOTE

Hi, amazeballs reader! I'm so thrilled that you made it to the end of *Fire and Love* – I'm guessing you finished the novel because you loved it. *crossing fingers* At least, I hope you didn't force yourself to read it all the way to the end while secretly putting pins into voodoo dolls named Erin Wright the whole time!

Fire and Love was definitely an unusual love story because of the background of both Levi and Tennessee. As different as they are on the surface, though, they really do complete each other, or as Tenny puts it, he's the yin to her yang. 😊

But along with the love that I tried to portray between the two of them, I also thought it was important to touch on the difficult topic of cutting. It's a controversial topic (as any self-harm is) so I thought I'd take a moment to tell y'all – now that you're done with the book – why it is that I made this such a prevalent part of *Fire and Love*.

About a year or so ago, I found out that my beautiful and talented and incredibly intelligent niece was cutting as a way of dealing with the things that were happening in her life that she felt she didn't have control over. I was shocked – I had no idea that she would do something like this to herself, and of course, I immediately thought that she was trying to kill herself. It wasn't until I started to research cutting that I found out how prevalent cutting was among teenage girls, and that my reaction to it is far from atypical. In fact, that is the most common reaction that cutters get – a freakout over the idea that the cutter is trying to commit suicide.

As one cutter put it online, if they were trying to kill themselves, they'd be dead. In fact, they're trying quite actively *not* to kill themselves. Cutters know where to cut, and how deep to cut, and they make sure to never use rusty or unclean blades. Many cutters sterilize the blades before using them, to make sure that they don't get an infection from the cut.

These are not the actions of someone who has a death wish.

As Tenny says, cutting is an addiction, just like drugs or alcohol or anything else that gives you a "high" and a way of dealing with pain. Someone who starts out by cutting has a much higher statistical probability of continuing onto other high-risk activities (drugs, alcohol, unsafe sex, etc) than someone who does not cut.

And just like with every other destructive behavior

you can indulge in, there is also social pressure to cut. It can be the "cool thing" to do within a group of girls. (As Levi discovers in the book, statistically, cutters are *much* more likely to be girls, although there are some boy cutters out there).

If you find that someone you care about is cutting, the most important step you can take is to find out *why*. The mere fact that they are cutting isn't nearly as important as you initially might think it is; stopping them from doing it by taking away all of their blades, for example, will just mean that they will start dripping hot wax onto their skin, or inhaling paint thinner, or other self-destructive behavior.

The problem isn't the cutting; the problem is whatever is causing the girl to think that she needs to cut.

That's the problem that needs to be solved. The cutting will resolve itself naturally after that.

The other big reveal in this book – that Levi isn't Steve's son after all – came as inspiration from an article I was reading on the topic of DNA tests. Since DNA tests have become so easy and prevalent, there has been case after case after case of people finding out that their parents (usually the father) isn't who they thought they were.

In one extreme case, two older ladies (I want to say they were in their 70s or 80s, but I can't find the article now) found out that they'd been accidentally switched at birth. One was a redhead in a family without another redhead in sight, and the other one was the only non-athletic child in the family. She could never figure out why it was that she was absolutely awful at sports when everyone else in her family played them professionally. Because of DNA tests, they eventually figured out that they'd been swapped at birth and that their family wasn't actually their family.

Of course, I found this *fascinating* and immediately decided that it was going to end up in one of my books. (I often make the joke that I am not actually creative at all; rather, I'm just good at re-appropriating other people's stories, lol). If you find this sort of thing as interesting as I do, you should do a Google search for stories on the topic. You'll spend the rest of the day reading hilarious / awful / jaw-dropping / horrendous / heartwarming stories about the truth revealed by DNA tests.

You're welcome.

Last but not least, I wanted to say that any author worth a bucket of warm spit will take the time to do research so they can write accurate books. As always, I have Handsome Hubby to thank for all of his help in researching *Fire and Love*. I had to learn how to fish so I could write the scene down at the lake accurately, and – would you believe it – I even learned how to weld so I could write that scene also. If you go back and reread that first welding scene, it's virtually a straight recounting of how my first welding lesson went. My first weld was absolute chicken scratch, but by the third round, I'd improved immensely and my husband was in awe of how quickly I was picking it up. How cool is that?!

The one part that *isn't* true in my own life is when Levi says that he "ain't creative." In my case, my husband is *absolutely* creative. In fact, here are some shots of the yard art that he welded together, using old shovel heads:

And here's a close-up of just the head:

My husband can out-weld, out-blacksmith, out-sew, out-cook, and out-fish any other person I've ever met. Sadly, my creative talents seem to lie solely on the written page. 😛 This just means that my hubs is the yin to my yang, too. Love you always, Reagan. 🩶

While I'm thanking people, I also want to give a huge **thank you** to all of my fans for making my career possible. I literally couldn't do it without you. Every book that you buy, every social media post that you share, every newsletter that you read, helps me succeed as an author. I have the best (most amazeballs!) fans in the world, and I hope y'all know that.

The last book in the Firefighters of Long Valley series (*Burned by Love*) focuses on Troy, the quietest Sawyer City firefighter in the bunch. They always say that the quietest ones are the most interesting, and I think that you'll agree when you read Troy's story – it truly doesn't get much more interesting than him. 😊 I can't tell you more than that (and ruin the storyline!) but believe me when I say that you'll never see it coming. Definitely keep reading for the excerpt from *Burned*.

Thanks again for all of your support – love and hugs to you all,

~Erin

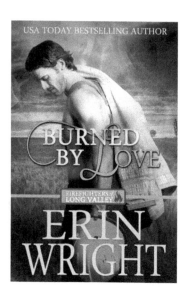

BURNED BY LOVE

He's a man of few words...

Troy Horvath doesn't need much outta life. His fellow firefighters, a good beer, and...well, one date with the most gorgeous woman in town couldn't hurt, right?

Penny is beautiful, sassy, and everything he *doesn't* need.

But she's exactly who he wants.

He knows from the get-go she isn't planning on staying in Sawyer. She just isn't a small-town girl. With those heels and her striking red lipstick, she's a firecracker, and destined for so much more.

But maybe, just maybe, he can make all of her

big-city dreams come true – if only she'll give him a chance...

She may've friend-zoned him...

And now Penny's realizing that may've been a mistake. Troy is hot. Like, firefighter-calendar hot.

She swore when she came back to Sawyer to care for her mother, it would only be temporary. So... maybe a relationship with Troy could be temporary, too?

Except deep down, Penny knows Troy wants so much more, and there's a chance she does, too.

He's hiding something, though – something big.

Can she be the one to finally get him to open up?

And if she does, will their relationship survive the truth?

Read on for a taste of *Burned*...

TROY

MAY, 2018

*T*roy Horvath had always been the quiet one of the bunch, and to be honest, he liked that about himself.

The way he saw it, it allowed him to sit back and take in the world, without being required to yack the ear off whoever was closest to him at the moment.

The way his aunt and uncle saw it, on the other hand, was that it allowed him to let the world pass him on by without even sparing him a second glance.

Actually, take that back – it made his *aunt* think it allowed the world to pass him on by without a second glance. His uncle had never said a word about the fact that Troy wasn't on the chatty side, at least not within earshot of Troy.

But then again, Aunt Horvath was (not

surprisingly) a woman, and as far as Troy could tell, all women ever wanted to do was talk about their feelings, dreams, and desires, preferably all at the same time, and if a man didn't feel the same way, well then, there was something wrong with him.

Sparky was the only female Troy knew that didn't fall into the must-always-be-talking trap. She was content to just *be*, and didn't need him willing to discuss politics, religion, or the price of bananas down at the Shop 'N Go. Being the perfect female, all she wanted was for someone to pet her (preferably 24/7/365 if it could be arranged) and feed her doggy treats. He'd just adopted her a few days before, but they'd already formed a bond between them that was unbreakable. She trusted him with all her heart and soul, and after all she'd been through, that meant a hell of a lot.

As if she could read his thoughts, Sparky stood up and stretched, her back arching as her mouth opened wide, showing off all her pearly white canine teeth, and then she snuggled up against his legs, looking up at him with her soulful brown eyes. She was unabashedly begging for some pettings, and of course, Troy was happy to oblige. It wasn't hard to love on a dog that'd been through so much, but had somehow come out the other side sweet as pie. Her eyes closed in pleasure as her silky white tail began stirring up clouds of dust from the dirty cement floor.

He coughed a little from the dirt flinging through

the air, but otherwise ignored it. He was used to working in dusty environments – his uncle's mill had dust floating through the air so thick, he could practically swim through it – so the dirty fire station floor didn't even rate a second glance.

No, what Troy was focused on was the Dance of Desire happening right in front of his eyes.

He was at the monthly training session for the Sawyer Fire Department, and all of the volunteers (and the paid fire chief, Jaxson Anderson) were gathered at the station to learn better firefighting techniques or safety procedures or whatever else their brave leader wanted to teach them this time. Back when Troy's uncle was the fire chief, they didn't do *nearly* as much training as they did now, and it was certainly something that Troy could begrudgingly compliment Jaxson for improving since he took over back in January.

This training meeting was nothing like any other training meeting, though, because this time, a *female* was here.

In her typical, Georgia-Rowland-is-always-in-charge style, Georgia had voluntold the whole department that they were to be interviewed by a local reporter about the wildfire that had blazed through Long Valley over the last couple of days; a wildfire where Moose Garrett had saved her ass by breaking every rule in the book, and no doubt some that weren't written down, just for funsies.

Based on how Georgia and Moose were looking at each other right now, it seemed pretty damn clear to Troy that they'd done more than survive a wildfire together. Troy's hand stroked down over Sparky's silky fur as he watched the two pretend to be "just friends," even as the sparks that flew between them were so blindingly bright, he probably oughta go grab his sunglasses from his truck. Did Georgia and Moose think they were being sneaky, that no one was noticing that they were sending glances to each other that were bound to set the dry grass outside ablaze and start up a second wildfire? He knew that people in lust were oblivious, but surely not *that* oblivious, right?

Idly, he glanced away from the couple mooning over each other and checked his phone. This reporter guy was supposed to have arrived five minutes ago. How long were they gonna sit around and wait for him to show up before they moved on with their evening? It wasn't that Troy had anything he *needed* to go home and do – although it wouldn't hurt to do a load of laundry, and his kitchen could use a good scrubbing, none of that was pressing – but if given a choice between hanging out at the fire station and watching two lovebirds simper over each other, or being at home in just his boxers, watching a game with a beer in his hand…

Well, that choice was pretty obvious.

He tugged at the collar of his button-up shirt, wishing he hadn't bothered to change before coming to the meeting that night. Normally, getting dressed up in a collared shirt so he could go hang out with a bunch of guys in a greasy, dirty building for a couple of hours was *not* something he'd sign up for. But because of this reporter coming tonight – wherever the hell he was – Jaxson had put out the word for everyone to come dressed and cleaned up and ready for a photo shoot, just in case that was what the reporter wanted to do. Troy scrubbed at his clean-shaven jaw with a regretful sigh. He'd had a nice seven-day start on a beard going; now he'd have to start all over again.

Why Jaxson cared so much about what some dumbass reporter thought of them was beyond him. Uncle Horvath never would've stooped so low as to court the approval of the press. Chief Horvath focused on what needed to be done, and to hell with the rest of them. Jaxson seemed like a nice enough kid, but he sure had a lot to—

The air changed just then. The chatter of the men died away; even Georgia's giggle over whatever amazingly brilliant comment Moose had just made disappeared. Troy's head shot up as the crackle of electricity around him made the hairs on his neck stand straight up. Not a sound was heard in the cavernous fire station, other than the click of heels on pavement as the most gorgeous woman Troy had ever seen in his life came striding into the joint.

Holy

Shit

There were athletic, pretty women like Georgia Rowland. There were beauty queens like her cousin, Tennessee Rowland. There were cute, next-door-neighbor girls like Sugar Stonemyer down at the bakery, who Jaxson had started dating.

And then, there was this woman.

He rather felt like he'd been clobbered upside the head by a 2x4. Maybe a padded one, but there was *definitely* a 2x4 involved. As his gaze followed every slim curve of the woman's body – her long legs, her strappy high heels, her tight skirt, her styled blonde hair, her ruby red lips curved into a self-confident smile – he tried to make his brain work. There was something…

Something wrong here.

It was…something.

Oh yeah, why is this woman here?

Supermodels didn't tend to walk into a rural fire station on a Friday night just to hang out with a bunch of blue-collar guys and shoot the shit.

That just didn't happen.

The roar of surprise and lust in his ears finally died down enough for him to hear what she was saying. "Hi, I'm Penny Roth," she said as she shook hands with Levi Scranton, one of the guys on the force. "How long have you been a firefighter?"

He missed Levi's answer, too stunned to hear anything but the roar in his ears again. There was only one reason for this woman to be shaking hands with all the men and asking questions about being a firefighter.

But that meant...

His brain staggered to a stop. Seriously? This was the reporter? This paragon of beauty and legs and sparkling high heels was a reporter for the two weekly rags in the area?

Sparky whined and nudged Troy's hand, apparently not happy with the speed of his pettings. He looked down at her blankly for a moment, trying to remember what he was doing. Who he was. Where he was. Sparky whined again, and absentmindedly, he scratched her behind the ears, her tail resuming the rapid thumping of joy and pleasure at his touch.

His mind swam as he tried to put the pieces together – the reporter for the *Sawyer Times* and *Franklin Gazette* was a drop-dead gorgeous woman. No spare tire around the middle; no balding spot on the back of her head; actually, no male qualities whatsoever. She appeared to be as feminine as they came.

It wasn't that Troy didn't think that a woman could be a reporter; it'd just never crossed his mind that she would be. The stereotypical reporter that Troy had imagined...

Well, that image was nothing like the woman in front of him, that was for damn sure.

She'd reached Moose and was now shaking his hand, chatting easily with him as Georgia looked on and glowered possessively. Even as Troy was busy trying to accept the truth of what he was seeing in front of him, he also found his mouth quirking up a bit with humor at the territorial look on Georgia's face. What, exactly, had happened up at Eagle's Nest when Moose and Georgia had tried to stay safe from the wildfire raging around them? It sure looked like they'd practiced some mouth-to-mouth resuscitation on each other.

And then, Penny Roth was walking towards him, and his mind went blank.

How she'd noticed him over in the corner, sitting on the tailgate of the water truck, accustomed – and expecting – the world to walk right on by, he'd never know. He wasn't used to being noticed. In fact, he counted on it, so her laser-focused gaze on him as she walked over…he just didn't know what to think.

Or perhaps it was the aforementioned 2x4, padded or not. He'd been walloped but good, and he wasn't quite sure he was breathing.

"Hi, I'm Penny Roth," she said again, reaching her hand out to shake his. He was frozen on the tailgate of the water truck, Sparky leaning against his legs and trapping him there even though he should be rising to greet her but moving didn't seem possible just then, except for his hand – thank God he could move it – so he raised it up and shook hers, and when their palms touched…

It was like grasping a bolt of lightning. Her gaze flared, as bright and brilliant as her smile, as they locked eyes. "Troy Horvath," he got out, wanting to hang onto her hand for the next six months or so. Just until he got used to the feeling shooting up his arm. Then he could let go.

But not a moment before.

Somehow, though, she seemed to be immune to this overwhelming desire to keep their palms pressed together to feel the electricity arcing between them, and instead pulled her hand out of his, dropping to her knees in front of Sparky to love on her. "Aren't you a sweetie," she cooed to Sparky, letting his dog give her face a bath while Sparky's tail swept up a storm on the dusty cement floor.

Troy was in shock. Moose was in shock. Levi was in shock. Every person in the room just froze, watching this unfold in front of them.

Sparky didn't like anyone except Troy. Not even Moose and Georgia, who'd saved her from the wildfire just two days ago, were freely allowed to pet her. As best as they could figure, she'd been beat by some sadistic son-of-a-bitch and now chose who was allowed within ten feet of her very, *very* carefully.

She didn't give out face baths easily. Hell, Troy'd just gotten his first one from her this morning. And here she was, loving on Penny like they were the best of friends.

His heart twisted a little at the sight.

Of course, it was good to see Sparky love someone else other than Troy. He was happy that it was happening. He was just in shock, was all. Nothing more than that.

"So, you're the one who saved Georgia from the fire?" the reporter asked, looking up at Troy, her eyes intense as she studied him from her kneeling position on the dirty fire station floor. She didn't seem to notice that Sparky was shedding white and black hairs all over her skirt and blouse, just like she shed all over everything else she came in close contact with. Troy had given up on being dog-hair free about an hour or so after he'd adopted her; it just wasn't gonna happen. Was Penny gonna be pissed when she saw where Sparky's fur was ending up?

He opened up his mouth to warn her, but decided to answer her question instead. This'd be a good test to see how much she really liked dogs; if she freaked out about having some stray hairs left behind, well, that'd tell him all he needed to know. Unlike Jaxson, Troy didn't believe he had to bend over backwards to impress the press.

He balled up his fist where her hand had slid into his, pushing the buzzing electric feeling away.

"No, not me." Troy finally managed a reply to her question – embarrassingly slowly but he got there – and jerked his head towards Moose, who'd followed Penny over to the water truck, Georgia trailing along behind him. "He did."

"I thought the dog was found up in the fire," Penny said, her brow knotted with confusion. "How did she end up with you, then?"

"She likes me," Troy said simply, shrugging his shoulders. *Just like she likes you* were the unspoken words left hanging in the air. Sparky loving on someone else…Troy was pretty sure in that moment, he could've been knocked flat on his ass with a feather.

Sparky did another swipe across Penny's face with her long pink tongue and Penny laughed. "How long have you been a firefighter?" she asked, continuing to pet Sparky as she looked up at him, ignoring the whole supposed reason for her being there – i.e., Moose and Georgia and the wildfire that'd burned hundreds of acres before nature had intervened and had kept the valley from going up in flames. Troy'd gone out on that call, of course, but by time they'd begun their work, nature had already taken pity on them and had reversed course.

You win some, you lose some, and sometimes, you're just damn lucky. Georgia had been the one to name Sparky; perhaps she should've named her Lucky instead.

Troy forced himself to focus on Penny's question. If he kept answering her ten minutes after she asked him something, she was gonna start to think he was slow in the head.

"All my life, it feels like," he admitted. "My uncle used to be the head firefighter," he was choosing his words carefully, as carefully as he ever had, landmines waiting for him at every turn as he did his best to hopscotch across them. "So I began young. But he retired, and Jaxson—" he felt his tongue wanting to seize up but he got the name out without making an ass of himself, "—took over in January."

Out of the corner of his eye, he saw Moose and Georgia move away, and he wasn't sure if he wanted to thank them for it, or yell at them to come back. He wasn't supposed to be the one talking to the reporter; they were. They were the ones who saved the dog. They were the ones who lived through a wildfire all by themselves up in the wilds of Idaho. Troy'd had as much to do with all of that as he'd had helping Santa Claus deliver presents this last Christmas. But telling Penny to go talk to someone else, to go pin someone else down with her sparkling eyes, intent on drawing answers out of them…

He gulped.

"Your uncle was the fire chief, but after he retired, they didn't choose you to be the next one?" she asked, the surprise clear in her voice.

He laughed a little at that. "It isn't a hereditary position," he said carefully, choosing each word before speaking it. He shrugged. "Plus, I didn't apply. I didn't want the job."

He heard Moose and Jaxson say something to the guys, and then everyone laughed. He hadn't heard what they'd said, but he was sure – absolutely sure – that they'd been discussing the two of them. He felt the tips of his ears go red. He wanted to shoot them a glare and tell them to back off, but pretending deafness seemed like a much safer plan.

Less talking was involved, anyway, which always made it a safer plan.

"What job do you have that is better than fire chief?" Penny asked, finally standing and swiping at the hair and dirt all over her clothes. She didn't seem pissed that she was filthy; she was just straightening herself out. Her curled blonde hair swung as she worked to clean up, and his mind paused on the idea of touching it. Would a curl wrap around his finger?

He forced himself to concentrate on her question.

Huh. What was her question again?

Job. She wants to know where you work, you dumbass.

"The Horvath Mill. The new one outside of town," he clarified. Sadly, the old one had burned to a crisp this past January after the mayor's son had thrown a cigarette butt into a pile of old rags and set the place on fire. Damn teenagers. That building was part of his family's heritage, and his heart still hurt at the idea of it burning like it did, leaving a shell of blackened bricks behind.

"Horvath, eh?" She slid onto the tailgate next to him, seemingly oblivious to the dirt and grime encrusted there. She was settling into place before Troy could stop her, so again, he snapped his mouth shut. The damage was done now, and hell, her elbow was brushing up against his. He could no more warn her to move than he could chop off that elbow. "Is the mill owned by your uncle, the former fire chief? Or by someone else in your family?"

Damn, she was quick on the draw. Family

relations and who owned what and who was related to who was a constant struggle to keep straight in a small town, but Miss Penny Roth was apparently up to the task.

"Uncle," he said simply. It was the Horvath family mill, and as soon as Aunt Horvath could convince her husband to retire fully, it would be Troy's. None of their three kids wanted it, and since Troy'd been working there for most of his adult life, it just made sense for him to take it over.

And most importantly, it was what he was supposed to do. He always did what he was supposed to do.

"Do your parents live in town, too?" she asked as Sparky laid her head on Penny's lap and began begging for some attention. Troy sent his not-so-loyal dog a dark look of his own. It was good to see her feel comfortable enough that she would allow other people to touch her, of course, but did she have to go *that* far? Penny began absentmindedly stroking Sparky's head, scratching right behind her ears just like the spotted setter loved, and sure enough, Sparky's tail started flying again, dirt and hair going every which way.

"No, they live in Boise. I've lived here with my aunt and uncle since freshman year, though." He tried to quickly come up with a question to ask her so he could just listen to her talk and he could be free to retreat into blessed, comfortable silence, but she beat him to the punch.

"Have you fought a lot of fires, then, since your uncle was the fire chief? Is it an old hat to you by now?" Her eyes were pinned on him, a mysterious dark blue color that matched her shirt. He'd never seen quite that shade before, and wondered for a moment if she was wearing colored lenses.

He laughed uncomfortably. "Firefighting is never an old hat to anyone. Complacency is a good way to get yourself killed. But I have fought a lot of fires – both house and wildfires." He was surprised by how many words were rolling off his tongue effortlessly, as if speaking easily to a beautiful woman – or anyone at all – was something that he did all the time. Did she know how strange this was for him?

Looking at her – beautiful, smart, outgoing – he was pretty sure she had absolutely no concept of what it was like to be trapped inside a body that didn't always cooperate.

"You guys are all volunteers, right?" she asked, bringing him back to the present. He nodded, and she continued, "I've always wondered if it was hard to find people to volunteer to risk their lives. Why are you willing to do this if you're not even going to get paid?"

"Volunteer doesn't mean unpaid," he hurried to tell her. "We get paid every time we respond to a fire. We just don't get paid otherwise. It is hard to find volunteers, though. People are busy with their own lives." He shrugged. It was understandable, really. He'd been raised to focus on the fire department and making sure that every fire was responded to no matter what, but he wasn't like everyone else, and that was okay. They didn't need a hundred guys to respond to every call-out; just enough guys to make sure the people of Long Valley were safe.

Anything beyond that was a bonus.

"Is fire chief also a volunteer position?" she asked.

He flinched. Without meaning to, she'd hit right on that sore spot with a hammer.

Looking at her, really trying to gauge who she was, Troy hesitated. Penny was part of the press. The press could say whatever they wanted; could twist his words and make him out to be a jealous jackass or a real gentleman. It was all in how she wrote it.

Could he trust her enough to talk about how virtually the entire town had been up in arms over Jaxson being made a full-time employee from day one, when Uncle Horvath had been a simple volunteer like everyone else? Last month, after Jaxson had saved Gage and Sugar from the Muffin Man bakery fire, the town had settled down a whole lot, seemingly forgiving Jaxson for being an upstart kid from the big city, there to raise their taxes and tell them how it was done in a *real* town, but for Troy, it still smarted a little.

Finally, he settled on telling Penny the truth, but nothing more. Personal feelings didn't matter anyway and certainly weren't newsworthy.

"He's a full-time employee," he said simply.

Penny raised one eyebrow in response to that,

silently asking him to tell her the rest of the story, but Troy sidestepped the unspoken request. "Are you from Franklin?" he asked instead. He was damn sure she wasn't from Sawyer – if he'd ever laid eyes on her before, he would've remembered it.

Forgetting Penny Roth just wasn't something that happened.

"Born and raised," she said with a disgruntled sigh. Sparky let out a blissful sigh of her own as she snuggled deeper into Penny's lap, looking like a poster child for relaxation. With her eyes closed, the dog missed the second dark look Troy sent her way. Did she *have* to appear so at home so quickly? "I graduated in 2006," Penny continued, oblivious to the looks Troy was sending his traitorous dog. "You?"

"2000. Been here ever since. You?"

"Left town on graduation night." She shot him a laughing look. "Yup, I was one of *those* kids – attended graduation with my car packed to the brim with my stuff. I couldn't get out of here fast enough. Got my bachelor's in graphic design from a university down in San Diego. I—" She caught the surprised look on his face, and grimaced. "Being a reporter is just a temporary gig." She waved her hand dismissively. "I'm going to be leaving Long Valley soon, thank God, and heading back to civilization. No more living in a town where the most exciting thing that happens all year is the quilt auction, or when Mr. Cowell's cows get out and block the road into town."

Troy forced a polite smile onto his face, even as his

heart sank. Of *course* Penny the Reporter wasn't planning on staying in the area. What part of the elegant, gorgeous woman sitting next to him looked like it belonged in rural, mountainous Idaho? Not those sparkling high heels. Not the frilly blouse. And certainly not her bright red lipstick. There wasn't a damn inch of her that fit in here, which would probably explain his overwhelming gut reaction to her. Of course he'd react that way. She was like no one else in the whole of Long Valley.

But now he knew she was leaving, and that meant she was untouchable. He'd be better off letting her walk away, no matter what the burning sensation in his palm where they'd touched was urging him to do.

He pushed off the end of the water truck. "Ready to go interview?" he asked, jerking his head towards the group of firefighters who appeared to be training on safety equipment. Georgia was still there, sitting off to the side at a decrepit desk covered with yellowed forms, patiently waiting around for Penny to ask her questions.

Penny pushed herself off the tailgate of the water truck also, a tight smile on her face, both of them ignoring the very humanlike groan from a disappointed Sparky. "Absolutely! I better get my job done, right?"

As they walked towards the knot of firefighters, Troy told himself that she wasn't the only one there who had a job to do. His whole purpose in life was to take over the Horvath Mill, nothing more, nothing less.

Dating the local reporter who was on her way out the door just wasn't in the cards, no matter how many 2x4's were involved.

Burned by Love, *the 4th book in the Firefighters of Long Valley series, can be found on your favorite storefront!*

THE STORY DOESN'T END...

You've met a few people and have fallen in love...

You're probably wondering when and where you can meet everyone else. Here's the list of books, current and to-be-released, in the Long Valley world:

Accounting for Love – The bank's threatening to foreclose on Stetson's farm...and the auditor on the case is damn hot. Jennifer doesn't mind a tough job, but handsome Stetson is trouble. And then came the night she had to spend on the farm. Can she find a way for him to save his farm? And if she can't, will he ever forgive her?

Blizzard of Love – Luke never expects to end up

spending Christmas at the Miller farm. Everyone knows he hates Christmas. But Bonnie *adores* Christmas, so when her best friend invites her to the Miller farm, she jumps at the chance. When a blizzard hits, sparks fly. Can the magic of mistletoe tear down the barriers between them?

~

Arrested by Love − When Wyatt Miller ended up in the Long Valley County Jail over Christmas, he never expected to receive the greatest gift of all: Love and forgiveness...from his jailer.

~

Returning for Love − If Declan could turn back time, the rugged cowboy would do things differently. For one, he would've never let go of Iris Blue McLain. Fifteen long and lonely years, and the ache in his heart is as painful as ever. When he sees her again, he can't deny his feelings any longer, and vows to win the only woman he's ever loved.

~

Christmas of Love − This December, Ivy wishes she could just skip all the festivities. Parties? No thanks. Getting together with family? Not even. Mistletoe? Let's not go there. But everything changes when she meets a rugged cowboy with a slow, sexy smile. Austin's kiss melts her heart, but can two people with painful secrets have a chance at happily ever after?

~

Overdue for Love – When Dawson left Arizona nine years ago, he never expected to see Chloe again. Until he runs into her at a diner in Sawyer, Idaho, and finds that she has a memento of their last meeting in tow...

~

Bundle of Love – Dr. Adam Whitaker, vet extraordinaire, has spent the last nine years helplessly in love with Chloe, and deserves his own happily ever after. Except, what if the love of his life comes with one condition...a baby?

~

Lessons in Love – Elijah hasn't exactly made stellar choices in life, but the one thing he's never regretted? His daughter, even if his ex-wife is doing all she can to keep them apart. In the midst of their custody battle, something unexpected happens: He begins to fall in love. Everyone knows your daughter's elementary school teacher is off-limits, but someone forgot to tell Elijah's heart...

≈

Baked with Love – When Gage took over his grandparent's bakery three years ago, love was the last thing on his mind. Despite the best efforts of his wanna-be-matchmaker sister, Emma, he was content to keep his nose to the grindstone, work his ass off, and make the bakery the success he knew it could be.

That all changed the day the neighbor from hell bought the shop next to his and began remodeling, destroying Gage's well-ordered life in the process. It really was too bad she was so damn gorgeous... [COMING APRIL 2019]

≈

Bloom of Love – Carla has always been a romantic; after all, she couldn't run the flower shop in town, Happy Petals, if she didn't believe in true love, right? But she also happens to be single, and she'd just about given up on love for herself when Christian comes into her life. For one brief, shining moment, she thinks she might be able to have her own happily ever after. But nothing worth having comes easily... [COMING SEPTEMBER 2019]

≈

Banking on Love – Tripp has a real talent for everything he touches: His job at the local credit union, the weights down at the gym, and the panties of women everywhere.

He's quite happy to continue honing these skills… right up until he meets his match: Amelia. She's the classroom aide for a 5th grade teacher; she hates treadmills on principle; and she hasn't had a guy catch a glimpse of her panties in years.

On paper, there's absolutely nothing about the two of them that should work.

It's a damn good thing Tripp's never paid attention to "shoulds"… [COMING MARCH 2020]

~ Firefighters of Long Valley ~

Flames of Love – Jaxson's not interested in love, or the perils that come with it. His priority is caring for his two small boys, and being fire chief of Sawyer. Everything changes the day he catches sight of Sugar, the pretty girl with the fragile smile. He wants her all to himself, and preferably in his bed – a no-strings arrangement that won't break what's left of his heart. But love's as unpredictable as fire…

Inferno of Love – Georgia has spent a lot of years – roughly 26 of them – pretending Moose wasn't the finest man in town. For the record, she barely notices how his slow, sultry smile makes her knees weak, and always ignores the close fit of his faded jeans. But when she gets trapped in the flames of a wildfire out in the hills of Long Valley, Moose appears amidst the smoke, ready to walk through fire. For her...

Fire and Love – Levi has wanted Tenny for forever. Too bad the town's beauty queen is *waaay* out of his league.

While she grew up with money, he grew up dirt poor. While she's a daddy's girl, his father's a mean drunk with a vicious back-hand.

Levi should just forget about the high-class blonde, but she has a secret that changes everything. When the ghosts of the past return, he must choose between love...or betrayal.

Burned by Love – Nephew of the former fire chief of Sawyer, Troy was happy when no one looked his way to take over after his uncle retired. Troy appreciates his solitude, and just being a part of the background makes it easy to guard his secrets.

But secrets have a way of forcing themselves to the surface, no matter how hard one tries to hide them...

~ Music of Long Valley ~

Strummin' Up Love – Zane was on top of the world...

until a car wreck took his wife's life and left his son badly crippled. Late one night, he makes the rash decision that if he's going to hide out somewhere and lick his wounds, it might as well be in Idaho. But when Nurse Louise comes strolling into his life, there to help his son recuperate, Zane quickly realizes his son isn't the only one who needs her healing touch... [COMING JULY 2019]

Melody of Love – Georgette Nash's father hadn't exactly been an involved parent. In fact, just when the three Nash children needed him most – the night their mother walked out and never came back – was the night he disappeared into himself and never reemerged. So when Georgette met the father of one of her students and realized what a dedicated and devoted father actually looked like, it was hard for her to keep her distance. Who wouldn't love a handsome and caring man?

But sometimes, life isn't as simple as it seems, and secrets lurk just beneath the surface, ready to snatch any hint of happiness away... [COMING MAY 2020]

~ SERVICEMEN OF LONG VALLEY ~

Thankful for Love – Gunner Nash left town the day after high school graduation, and hasn't looked back since.

He and his twin sister, Georgette, were happy living anywhere but Sawyer. But he's finished his stint in the Navy, and is now drifting, looking for a purpose in life, or at least a roof over his head. His older brother, Luke, offers him a place to stay until he can get back on his feet.

He never expects to find love in the process... [COMING NOVEMBER 2019]

Commanded to Love – Nicholas had grown up knowing that he wanted nothing more than to join the Marine Corps. It was his calling, his passion, and his duty. But after only one tour in the Marines, he came back to Sawyer, drifting and dispirited. It wasn't until he ran into his high school sweetheart that he realized maybe his life had a purpose after all; it just wasn't the one he'd dreamed of all those years ago... [COMING AUGUST 2020]

~ FIREFIGHTERS OF LONG VALLEY ~

Flames of Love

Inferno of Love

Fire and Love

Burned by Love

~ MUSIC OF LONG VALLEY ~

Strummin' Up Love (July 2019)

Melody of Love (May 2020)

Rock 'n Love (March 2021)

Rhapsody of Love (February 2022)

~ SERVICEMEN OF LONG VALLEY ~

Thankful for Love (November 2019)

Commanded to Love (August 2020)

Salute to Love (June 2021)

Harbored by Love (November 2021)

Target of Love (July 2022)

ABOUT ERIN WRIGHT

USA TODAY BESTSELLING AUTHOR ERIN WRIGHT has worked every job under the sun, including library director, barista, teacher, website designer, and ranch hand helping brand cattle, before settling into the career she's always dreamed about: Author.

She still loves coffee, doesn't love the smell of cow flesh burning, and has embarked on the adventure of a lifetime, traveling the country full-time in an RV. (No one has died yet in the confined 250-square-foot space – which she considers a real win – but let's be real, next week isn't looking so good…)

Find her updates on ErinWright.net, where you can sign up for her newsletter along with the requisite pictures of Jasmine the Writing Cat, her kitty cat muse and snuggle buddy extraordinaire.

Wanna get in touch?
www.erinwright.net
erin@erinwright.net

Or reach out to Erin on your favorite social media platform:

facebook.com/AuthorErinWright

twitter.com/erinwrightlv

pinterest.com/erinwrightbooks

goodreads.com/erinwright

bookbub.com/profile/erin-wright

instagram.com/authorerinwright